A P̶R̶I̶V̶A̶T̶E̶...

Also available from Headline Liaison

The Journal by James Allen
Love Letters by James Allen
The Diary by James Allen
Out of Control by Rebecca Ambrose
Aphrodisia by Rebecca Ambrose
Voluptuous Voyage by Lacey Carlisle
Vermilion Gates by Lucinda Chester
The Paradise Garden by Aurelia Clifford
Hearts on Fire by Tom Crewe & Amber Wells
Sleepless Nights by Tom Crewe & Amber Wells
Dangerous Desires by J J Duke
Seven Days by J J Duke
A Scent of Danger by Sarah Hope-Walker
Private Lessons by Cheryl Mildenhall
Intimate Strangers by Cheryl Mildenhall
Dance of Desire by Cheryl Mildenhall

A Private Affair

Carol Anderson

HEADLINE
Liaison

Copyright © 1995 Carol Anderson

The right of Carol Anderson to be identified as the Author of
the Work has been asserted by her in accordance with
the Copyright, Designs and Patents Act 1988.

First published in 1995 by
HEADLINE BOOK PUBLISHING

A HEADLINE LIAISON paperback

10 9 8 7 6 5 4 3 2 1

All characters in this publication are fictitious and any resemblance
to real persons, living or dead, is purely coincidental.

ISBN 0 7472 5211 4

Typeset by Avon Dataset Ltd, Bidford-on-Avon, B50 4JH

Printed and bound in Great Britain by
Cox & Wyman Ltd, Reading, Berks

HEADLINE BOOK PUBLISHING
A division of Hodder Headline PLC
338 Euston Road
London NW1 3BH

A Private
Affair

Chapter 1

23rd February 1923

Charles Garrison pulled Annie closer, his expression closed and tight. The girl whimpered but she didn't resist him as he laid her down across his desk. In the moonlight, her feral eyes were reduced to bright pin-pricks; her hot compliant body a silvery translucent shadow.

He moved closer, unbuttoning his fly, relishing the sense of excitement her unquestioning obedience gave him. Against the dark polished wood, Annie looked like an ancient erotic sacrifice. He smiled and pushed her legs apart roughly with his knee.

The girl moaned deliciously as his fingers found the moist contours of her sex. He guided his cock to nestle between the inner lips, rewarded instantly by the tantalising sensations of her body's heat and wetness tightening around him. She moaned again as he slid deeper.

'Be quiet,' he hissed between gritted teeth. 'She'll hear us.' Leaning over her, he breathed in the heady scent of her body, watching her bright anxious eyes as she surrendered to him.

Her breasts brushed against his coat. He shivered, imagining the sensation of her firm dark nipples against his chest. He liked her to be naked when they made love; it added to his sense of power and her air of vulnerability. As he pressed her down harder against the cold wood, he could feel her trembling. Charles Garrison smiled wolfishly and closed his lips around her nipple.

A large car drew up to the front door of Garrison Lodge. Helen glanced out of the window. Overhead a razor-grey sky promised snow later.

'Charles, the car's here, darling.' She could hear Charles muttering to himself from his study. 'I said—' she began a little louder, trying to control the frustration in her voice.

He appeared around the door, tying his muffler tight and tucking it into his coat, 'I heard you, Helen. Are Max and Liddy in the motor?'

Helen peered out into the gloom. It was impossible to see inside the car in the dark, 'I'm not sure, darling.'

Charles snorted, looking at Helen crossly. 'You really should come with us; it's a family tradition. First fair of the year, you know. The Garrison family always puts in an appearance. It's important.'

Helen sighed theatrically, 'It looks like snow.'

Charles picked up his gloves from the sideboard. 'Another tradition, it always snows for the mart.' As he spoke the doorbell rang, and he turned and hurried back through the hall door, calling loudly to their maid. 'Don't worry, Annie, I'll get it myself.'

2

Helen moved closer to the log fire and folded herself into one of the leather armchairs. From the hall came the sound of raucous laughter and raised voices. Charles peered back around the panelled door. 'It's Max, and Liddy is with him. They thought they'd just pop in for a swift one before we leave—'

Helen sighed; by the sound of it they'd already had enough. Not going with them to the fair had seemed such a little thing but she knew that Charles was annoyed with her. She was constantly dogged by the feeling that he disapproved of everything she did.

Seconds later, Charles' elder brother, Max Garrison, and his wife, Liddy, staggered into the room. Helen flinched as Max lurched across the floor and slumped into the chair opposite her.

When he spoke his voice was too loud. 'What's this then, Helen? Charlie says you aren't coming to the mart. We can't have that, can we, Liddy?'

Liddy, who was already helping herself to a drink from the sideboard, shook her head. 'Oh no, we really can't have that,' she slurred. 'You have to come. It's a family tradition.'

Helen sighed and admitted defeat. God alone knew what sort of state Charles would arrive home in if she didn't go with them. She nodded. 'All right then, I'll just go upstairs and get changed.'

Max cheered and leant forward to slap her on the knee. 'Bravo, there's a good girl,' he said, breathing whisky fumes into her face. Helen shuddered and hurried upstairs.

In her bedroom she glanced into the mirror,

twenty-eight, a bright intelligent woman who, she thought sadly, had probably made the worst mistake of her life marrying into the Garrison family. She opened the wardrobe to find her warm winter suit.

She'd met Charles in London just after the war. He'd seemed such a decent chap then, desperately handsome in his uniform. She sighed heavily. What she hadn't bargained for was Charles' sense of obligation to his family, particularly to Max, his elder brother. Max had always struck her as a spoilt, arrogant man. He seemed to think his little brother far too dull, far too ordinary for anything other than running the estate. Tenancy of Garrison Lodge was their consolation prize. Helen was sure Max and Liddy, who lived in the main Hall, despised them both.

On the bed, which was tucked tight, lay her nightdress and Charles' pyjamas; both were folded with military precision. She thought sadly that it spoke volumes about their marriage and Charles' restrained unhappy love-making. He wouldn't even look her in the eye after they had made love, as if he were ashamed of his own desire. His perfunctory touch left her body aching for fulfilment as he rolled off her, almost apologetically. She picked up her hat and moved towards the door.

Sometimes it was hard to recognise Charles as the bright young officer who had courted her.

'Come on, woman, what's taking you so long? Young Charlie says he'll drive us,' Max's voice snapped up from the bottom of the stairs, breaking her train of thought.

4

* * *

As they drove through the bleak Norfolk fenland the first flakes of snow fell. Max insisted they drink a toast to the goosedown feathers as they blew and stuck onto the windscreen.

Helen took a small sip from Max's hip flask and spluttered unhappily as the Scotch bit into her throat. From the back seat, Max and Liddy burst into peels of laughter.

Helen took out her compact to powder her nose. Behind, caught in the shimmering reflection, Helen could make out Max's muscular body pressing closer to Liddy. His voice had dropped to a low intimate murmur. Helen stared into the mirror, unable to take her eyes off their reflection. Max's hand, silvery in the darkness, slid inside Liddy's coat, fumbling beneath it, pushing the fabric aside. Helen stifled a gasp as she realised that Liddy's breasts were naked. Max snuggled lower, pulling her blouse open as his mouth pressed to Liddy's dark puckered nipples. From behind Helen, Liddy let out a soft throaty moan. Helen shivered and watched as Max's hand snaked lower. Liddy lifted herself to let him touch her. His moonlit fingers dragged at the thick material of her skirt, revealing her stocking tops and beyond ...

Helen snapped her compact closed and swallowed hard. Behind her, Liddy whimpered. Helen stared ahead, trying to keep her mind on the twisting ribbon of country road. Beside her, Charles hummed flatly, tapping out a rhythm on the steering wheel.

* * *

When they reached the fairground, Charles helped her from the car. His expression was still tight and discontent. 'It'll be all right,' he said quietly, taking her arm. 'We won't stay very long. Liddy hates the cold.'

Helen shook her head, 'So do I, Charles. Why didn't you just say we weren't coming?'

As she spoke she thought about Liddy's soft, suppressed moans from behind her shoulder, the whispered words of love that Charles had been unaware of. She blushed and pulled her coat tighter around her.

Charles looked even more uncomfortable, 'It's tradition, we always come—' he stammered.

Helen sighed and, taking his arm, they walked across the muddy field to the lights of the fairground. Behind them Max and Liddy staggered, holding each other up and laughing maniacally. Glancing back over her shoulder, Helen shivered as she saw them kiss, a long sensuous kiss, alight with desire.

'Roll-a up, roll-a up! Try your strength, sir. Ring the bell and win a prize for the lovely lady . . .' Barkers bellowed out their cries. Their sing-song voices braided with the sound of the steam organ as it piped out bright marching tunes.

In spite of her reservations, Helen began to relax. The atmosphere amongst the crowd was alive with excitement and good humour. Charles bought them both a hot baked potato and, as they walked arm in arm around the bright gaudy stalls, they quickly lost Max and Liddy in the crowd. Above them, the snow fluttered down in huge feathery flakes, melting as it landed on the lights around the booths.

Charles leant closer and kissed Helen lightly on the cheek, 'I'm glad you changed your mind. Shall I win you a coconut?'

Helen laughed, feeling happier now that his mood had improved. 'I'd like to see you try,' she teased.

Charles snorted and, rising to the challenge, picked up a wooden ball from the barrel at his feet. Glancing at her, he sent it whipping down the stall. It struck the coconut full tilt and let out a noise like a pistol shot. The coconut didn't so much as twitch.

Charles looked indignantly at the stall-owner.

'They're weighted at the bottom,' said a deep voice behind Helen.

She glanced over her shoulder straight into the dark wild eyes of a man standing no more than a breath away from her. She gasped and stepped back.

The man grinned easily as Charles took up another wooden ball. 'Give it your best shot, sir.'

Charles touched his cap in salute to him and grinned, 'I intend to, my fine fellow, I intend to.' He wound up a shot that exploded into the canvas at the back of the stall as it ricocheted off the coconut. 'Damn me,' Charles snorted and slipped off his jacket before dipping again into the barrel of balls.

The man behind Helen moved a little closer. Helen shivered.

'Don't hurry away from me, ma'am. I just came to see if you're Captain Garrison's missus.'

Helen shook her head. 'No, I'm married to Charles.' She nodded toward her husband as he let off another corking shot. 'Why do you want to know?'

The man took a puff on his cigarette. His unshaven face was striking and somehow deeply disturbing. Helen swallowed hard, astounded that she found herself thinking of the rough man as desirable.

His eyes glinted like jet in the lamplight. 'He's getting himself into a bit of bother over in the gambling tent. But, if you're not his lady—' The man shrugged and turned away.

'Wait,' said Helen quickly, catching hold of his arm. 'I'm his sister-in-law. What kind of trouble?'

'Playing dice with some of the fairground lads. They'll gut him if he can't pay up.'

Helen shivered. 'But he will.'

The man's dark eyes flashed with mischief. 'He won't when he finds his wallet's been lifted, ma'am, and the lads around here play rough.'

Helen turned to Charles and then back to her informant but he had vanished into the crowd.

'Charles?' She called as he was about to let another ball go. Her voice distracted him and the ball dropped harmlessly beneath the cups at the back of the stall.

'Oh Helen,' Charles groaned crossly, 'I nearly had one that time.'

'It's Max, he's in some sort of trouble.'

Charles grimaced, 'I wouldn't have thought so. Liddy is with him.'

Helen sighed heavily. Liddy was most likely to be at the heart of the trouble, not preventing it.

'Where is he?'

'Over in the gambling tent.'

'We'd better go and take a look,' Charles said, picking up his jacket. He took her arm and they pushed their way through the crowd.

Outside the gambling booth, a tight circle of punters had gathered, peering eagerly into the gloom. Helen and Charles eased their way through the press to the front. Inside, Max was huddled over a table, rolling dice. The roll came up double one. Max's opponent, a surly-looking, thickset man, spat on the floor. 'You lose again, sir. Now, will you pay up or go again? Double or quits.'

Charles slipped into the tent with Helen close behind him. 'My brother will settle up and we'll be off now,' he said, in a strong even voice.

Max looked up drunkenly and lifted his hand in salute. 'Why, little brother. There you are! Liddy has gone back to the car, doesn't feel too good. Just one more roll and I'll be with you.'

Charles picked up the dice from the table. 'I don't think so, old man.' Charles glanced across at Max's opponent. 'How much does my brother owe you?'

The thickset man grinned, 'Fifty guineas.'

Charles blanched. 'Fifty guineas,' he stuttered, 'that's impossible.'

Max swung unsteadily towards Charles. 'No, no. He's right. Pay the man, Charlie.' He patted his jacket pocket. 'I've got my wallet in here somewhere, if you can count out the money for me.' Uneasily he patted again and then began frantically to empty the contents of his pockets onto his lap. He looked desperately from face to face. 'My wallet seems to have gone,' he stammered.

Around the table, the men began to make small dark noises of dissatisfaction.

Charles laid the dice back on the table. 'You have my word that we will bring the money back here first thing tomorrow,' he said evenly. He reached for his pocket book, 'I'll leave you a marker . . .'

The burly man at the table glowered. 'What do you think I am? Bloody daft?'

Helen pressed closer to Charles, sensing the danger. 'We will pay you, I promise,' she said evenly.

The dice-player spat onto the floor. 'No show, missus, I want me money now.'

As he spoke, Helen saw the glint of a knife in his hand and had no doubt in her mind that he knew exactly how to use it. Almost as she thought it, the heavy man made a grab across the gaming table and caught hold of Max by his lapels. The glittering knife blade slid up easily until it nestled tightly against Max's exposed throat. Charles went to leap forward but Helen held his arm tightly.

'So, how are you going to pay me?' the man hissed at Max. He glanced across at Helen. 'How about I take your nice little woman instead, eh? What do you think, lads? Is it fair exchange?' Around them the crowd made lewd noises and gestures.

Helen felt her colour rising and fought to maintain her composure.

Max, his eyes bright with terror, glanced across at Helen. The blade pressed tighter against his throat. On his top lip beads of sweat formed. He shuddered as the man pressed the knife into his flesh.

'What do you say then, mister?' hissed the man, malevolently. 'How are you planning to settle yer debt?'

Charles leapt forward furiously only to be grabbed by members of the crowd.

'All right,' Max whispered, his voice trembling with fear. 'Take her, I'll bring you your money in the morning and then you let her go.'

The dice-player laughed obscenely. Helen felt her colour drain.

Struggling to fight free from his captors, Charles screamed furiously, 'No! For God's sake, man, that's my wife you're talking about.'

From the shadows, the man Helen had seen earlier stepped forward. 'I'll take this wager off you, mate,' he said softly to Max, throwing a heavy leather pouch onto the dice table.

The dice-player picked up the purse and weighed it speculatively in his hand. 'There's not fifty guineas in here,' he snapped.

The dark man nodded, 'Right enough, there's twenty-five there and another twenty-five I have hidden safe. I'll play you double or nothing for the woman and the money. You win, you get them both. At least you stand a chance to get some of your winnings. You'll get nothing from them two.' He nodded towards Charles and Max. 'And if I win, I'll take them both.'

As they spoke Max, released by his opponent, slid drunkenly to the floor. Charles, white-faced and desperate, struggled to free himself. Only Helen stood calmly amongst the mêlée. She felt removed, almost as if she were dreaming.

The dice-player mulled the possibility over in his head and nodded, 'Right enough, but leave the purse on the table where I can see it.'

The dark man glanced across at her, eyes glittering, jewel-like and hard. She could see something in his expression that made her shiver. 'Do you agree to the wager, ma'am?' he said softly, his voice barely above a purr.

She looked him straight in the eye and nodded. 'Yes,' she said slowly, 'I agree.'

Charles bayed in pain, 'No, by heavens, Helen. Do you know what you've just said?'

Helen, her eyes not leaving the dark man's face, nodded again.

'One thing,' said the dark man, as the dice-player picked up the dice cup. 'We play with clean dice.'

The dice-player snorted and then laughed, 'Fair dues, man,' and took another pair from his waistcoat pocket.

The dark man took them from him and weighed them carefully in his hand before nodding. 'Fair enough, seven to take it?'

The dice-player smiled toothlessly, 'Aye, seven for the pot.' As he spoke he looked across at Helen. 'Takes it all,' he murmured and dropped the dice into the cup.

Helen looked away as the burly dice-player took his throw, trying hard not to catch Charles' eye. She heard the restlessness in the crowd as the first die clattered and then hit the baize. The crowd, to a man, whispered their disappointment. There was the sound of hollow knocking as the dice dropped into the cup again, the rattle, and suddenly the whole tent seemed to erupt into a frenzy.

'Seven,' roared a sea of voices in jubilation.

Glancing back at the table she saw the dark man scoop up the purse and then look up at her.

Slowly, he extended his hand. Charles screamed in protest as Helen stepped forward. She turned and looked Charles straight in the eye. 'It was your brother who made this bargain,' she said softly.

'No,' snarled Charles, 'I'll not have this. Will someone go and fetch the constable. Now!'

The dark man stopped in his tracks, his hand still extended. Quietly he said, 'Has anyone a scrap of paper?'

From behind the gaming table, one of the fairground men produced a handbill and the dark man pulled a stub of a pencil from his jacket. He turned and, pressing onto the baize table, began to write in a laboured round hand. As he wrote he read the words aloud, 'I,' he looked up at Helen, 'what's your name?'

Helen bit her lip and said softly, 'Helen Garrison.'

The man bent back over the table. 'I, Helen Garrison have gone with Jack Hartman of my own accord, and am under no duress.' He paused and handed her the pencil and paper. Dizzily Helen leant forward and signed her name.

Charles was almost in tears. 'For God's sake, man,' he pleaded. 'Come to the hall tomorrow, I'll pay you double what my brother owes you, but, in the name of mercy, let my wife go.'

Jack Hartman didn't even look at Charles, instead

he held up the paper to the light and looked at Helen. 'Is what you've signed a true account, Mrs Garrison?'

Helen nodded, 'Yes,' she whispered, not daring to look at Charles.

Jack Hartman folded the paper into his pocket. 'Then all you witness, here and now, that Mrs Garrison is going with me of her own free will?'

There was a murmur of assent from the crowd. Jack walked around the table and took Helen's hand. 'Best we be off then, lady,' he said, glancing back at Charles, who was still being held tight and Max, who was slumped in a drunken heap on the mud and grass floor.

Jack led Helen out through the crowd which opened before them. As they passed through the main throng around the gambling tent, Jack glanced down at her feet and grinned. 'Good job you've sensible boots on, lady; we'll have to run for it.'

Helen hesitated, 'Run?'

'Aye, how long do you think those men will hold back that husband of yours, once we've gone? They'll be keen for the hounds to follow the hare. They're out for sport tonight. Come on—' He broke into a fierce trot, his fingers still linked with hers. Instinctively she ran with him. They hurried between the groups of fairgoers, Jack setting a sharp pace.

Once out of the crowd they headed across the icy field towards a dark line of trees.

'Where are we going?' gasped Helen between snatched breaths.

'The river,' called Jack back over his shoulder. 'My boat is moored down there.' He nodded towards the low trees. 'Hurry, they'll be after us any minute.'

Behind them, above the low throb of the crowd noise, Helen could hear voices raised in indignation and anger. Jack raised the pace and dragged Helen down amongst a tangled web of bushes.

Through the gloom, Helen could make out the low shape of a punt on the grey water below. She glanced at Jack. The moonlight was reflected in his dark eyes. She felt him tug on her sleeve and, stooping, they pressed through the dense muddle of stems and wet bare stalks.

Letting go of her, Jack Hartman pulled in the mooring line and eased the punt closer. He clambered in. Turning back towards the bank, he offered Helen his hand. She stood for a second and listened to the noises from the fairground. Above all the other voices she could hear Charles, his voice shrill and angry.

Jack didn't move. 'You have the choice, lady,' he said softly. 'You may go back now if you choose and no more will come of it.'

She heard Charles again, his voice almost sounded like a whine. She glanced back at Jack. 'If I come with you, it will bring you trouble,' she said evenly.

'Aye, that it will,' said Jack. 'But no more than I've had afore. Will you come with me, Helen Garrison, or will you stay?'

Helen leant forward and took his hand firmly. 'I'll come with you,' she said. 'But don't say I didn't warn you.'

In the gloom she heard Jack Hartman laugh and stepped over into the punt. 'There's a rug in there, lady,'

said Jack. 'Cover yourself up and try to keep warm.'
Helen nodded and felt around to find the blanket. It
was damp and as she pulled it up around her she could
smell dogs and the scent of the river.

'They'll come after us,' she said as Jack pushed away
from the bank.

'Aye, but they'll have a job to find us out on the river,'
he said flatly, straining against the long pole. The punt
lurched sideways and then began to move evenly into
the broad stream. Helen glanced up at the snow, still
falling, and now hanging like lace among the dark trees.

Across the field, Charles Garrison was struggling to
haul Max back to the car. Inside, Liddy was lying
sprawled across the back seat. Charles was close to
tears as he propped his brother up against the sleek
wet side of the car. He opened the door. Almost to
himself he murmured, 'What in God's name possessed
her to go off with him?'

Max snorted drunkenly, 'Perhaps she's fed up with
being married to a boring little bastard like you,
Charlie.'

Charles drew back his fist and hit his elder brother
as hard as he could. Max's lips exploded like a ripe
apple and he careered back into the car, crashing onto
the unconscious Liddy. Charles slammed the door shut,
shaking his hand to drive the pain of the punch away
and then hurried back across the damp field.

When Jack and Helen had travelled a little way
downstream, Jack laid down the punt pole and

clambered to the front of the boat. It swayed unsteadily. Helen let out a little shriek of panic. In the darkness she heard Jack laugh. A second or two later she saw the bright flash of a match and the river ahead was suddenly illuminated by a circle of lamplight.

'Won't they see you?' she said quietly.

Jack, a black shadow against the grey sky, turned towards her. 'They will most probably not realise we're on the river. I need to see where I'm going.' He stepped past her and back up onto the back of the boat.

Helen's thoughts were jumbled and hazy, as if she were on the edge of sleep. The gentle dip and slush as Jack pushed the punt through the water lulled her, whilst ahead the light gave the impression that they were sailing into a long dark tunnel. Helen said, almost to herself, 'I feel like Persephone going into the underworld.'

From behind her Jack chuckled, 'Well, there aren't any pomegranates where we're going.'

She swung round in surprise, 'You know the story?'

Jack snorted, 'It's very dangerous to assume that education is wholly restricted to the upper classes, ma'am.'

Helen slipped lower into the punt, trying to get away from the biting wind. Silence reigned except for the dark dip of the pole in the water and the shadowy sounds of the river at night.

In a showman's caravan parked close by the fair, Charles was trying to explain the situation to the local constable, a plump middle-aged man with a dramatic handlebar moustache. Standing by the caravan stove was the owner of the gambling booth, warming his hands.

'My wife has been kidnapped,' Charles said unsteadily.

The policeman looked grave, 'That's a very serious charge, Mr Garrison.'

The showman snorted, 'She weren't kidnapped. She went off of her own accord.'

Charles shot him a furious glance. 'She did not,' he snapped.

The policeman looked from face to face. He knew the Garrison family well and, though he had little time for the arrogant older boy, he'd always thought Charles was a decent enough sort of fellow.

The showman moved closer. 'She signed a piece of paper to say she was not being pushed into anything.' He glanced around the caravan, 'This has got nothing to do with the fair, you know. It's a local matter.'

The policeman made a note in his notebook and then glanced back at the pale tense face of Charles Garrison. 'It's very dark to start a search now, Mr Garrison,' he began gently.

Charles slammed his fist down onto the table. 'Hang it all, man. How would you feel if it was your wife who'd gone off with some bloody tinker for the night, eh? Would you say it was too dark then?'

The policeman coughed uneasily. 'Best if we go down to the station I think, Mr Garrison. The duty sergeant will sort it out.' He looked back at the fairground man. 'Would you come along as well? The more information we have the better.'

The stall-holder shrugged and then nodded. 'It's all the same to me,' he said shortly. 'But make sure your sergeant understands it's got nothing to do with them on the fair. This is a private matter between him,' he pointed towards Charles, 'and that other bloke. Our lads had nothing to do with it.'

In the bleak winter landscape the stream had broadened into a river. Helen gazed out from beneath the blanket, astounded that sleep called her so strongly. 'Are we nearly there?' she said.

Behind her, Jack broke his stroke, as if her voice had startled him. 'Where I live is a long way from here but we'll hole up for the night at a place I use nearby. First thing tomorrow I'll take you up to Ferrybridge, you'll be able to ring your husband from there.'

Helen said nothing, aware of a dark but tangible pulse that crackled between them. She wanted to say something but couldn't quite catch hold of the words. Ahead of them was a dark angular silhouette against the bleak winter sky.

'We're almost there now,' he said. 'Up there, on the bank.'

Helen peered at the shadowy outline, 'What is it?'

'An old pump house. Stay low, we're going in under the sluice gates.'

As he spoke, she could see a dark cavernous mouth coming alongside them and couldn't suppress a gasp as Jack steered the boat under a crumbling arch of stonework. Inside, it was pitch black except for the light from the little lamp which picked out tortured shapes of broken machinery and hanging chains. From all around came the sounds of water dripping. Jack pulled the boat to one side and clambered out of the punt, dragging the rope with him.

'Come up,' he said firmly. 'Climb to the top and I'll sort out the punt. Have a care, it's slippery.'

Without protest, Helen leaned towards the sound of his voice and in the dark found his strong warm hand. She pulled herself up and found, with his guidance, the rungs of a creaking ladder.

So close, in the intimacy of the darkness, she could smell Jack's musky body and feel his heat. She shivered and then climbed up the crumbling rungs while, below, Jack secured the boat and slipped the lamp from its fastenings.

'Stay still,' he said. 'Not another step until I'm up there with you.'

As he climbed up alongside her, she could see why. The ladder she had climbed was bolted to a narrow platform with rusty iron rings set into its pitted surface. More unnerving, it was barely more than a yard or so square, a tiny island surrounded by oily black water.

He grinned at her in the lamplight. The glow contorted his dark features into a maniacal mask. For the first time, Helen felt genuinely afraid. As Jack moved towards her, she flinched and drew back.

He laughed, 'You've nothing to fear, lady,' he said, and leant across behind her to pull up a narrow plank bridge. In the lamp's jaundiced light she could see there was a door behind them, separated from the platform by an expanse of water. Jack laid the planks down and then stepped across, pressing the heavy door open on the other side.

He turned back to her, arm extended.

'Let's go inside and get ourselves warm,' he said softly and, without hesitation, she stepped out onto the planks. She walked slowly into the dark room, whilst Jack hauled the boards up behind them as if taking up a drawbridge.

In Ferrybridge police station, Charles Garrison sat in the sergeant's office, huddled miserably over a mug of tea. Behind his desk the sergeant listened, wide-eyed, to the story of Helen Garrison's abduction described by the constable. He stopped the account now and then to listen to the comments of Charles and the fairground man.

Finally, with a sharp look at his constable, he asked the stall-owner to leave and moved closer to Charles. 'If I was you, sir,' he said in a low, conspiratorial voice, 'I'd be very tempted to keep my mouth shut about all this.'

Charles looked up, stunned. 'What?' he blustered furiously, 'but what about my wife?'

The older man shrugged, 'Do you want it made common knowledge around the village that your wife spent the night with some tinker? I mean what would folk make of it? They like nothing better than a tad of gossip, you know that. If you say nothing and she comes back tomorrow then you save face and your wife's reputation is intact.' He hesitated, seeing the anger and disbelief in Charles Garrison's face. 'Not that I'm saying anything will be amiss, sir, if you get my drift. But you know what people around here are like. I'd keep it a private affair, myself.' He let the implication hang in the air between them.

Charles' face cleared as comprehension dawned. 'That bastard,' he hissed. 'If he lays one finger on her . . .' His voice faded away and then he glanced up at the sergeant, 'If this gets out, she'll never be able to hold her head up again. The family will be a laughing stock.'

The sergeant nodded, 'Right enough, sir. Common sense would say, as long as she comes home tomorrow, it's perhaps a case of least said, soonest mended. As I said, a private affair.'

Charles thought about Helen. A sharp picture of her face filled his mind. She was by nature cautious, almost prissy in her habits. He shook his head firmly, 'I'm sure she will be all right, officer. She's a very sensible woman. I'm certain she'll be home tomorrow.' His words rang with a confidence he did not feel.

The sergeant slipped back behind his desk, 'Aye, I'm sure you're right, sir. In fact, I wouldn't be surprised if, when you get home, she's back already. And if we get out a search party everyone will know, won't they, sir?'

Charles nodded uneasily, knowing that in some way he was betraying Helen by not searching for her but he did take the sergeant's point. If news got out that his wife had gone off with some raggedy man for the night, the family would be a joke. After all, the Garrison family had its reputation to uphold.

He thanked the sergeant, promising to ring with any

news of Helen. He made his way through the snow
back to the car. In the back seat, Max and Liddy were
still sound asleep under a tangle of rugs and coats. He
glanced at his pocket watch. Perhaps the sergeant was
right, perhaps Helen was already back at home. And if
not, if she didn't come home the next day— He paused.
What would he do then? There would be no choice but
to ask the sergeant to form a search party. He shuddered at the idea and slipped into the driver's seat, his
mind racing.

Inside the cottage that adjoined the old pump house,
Jack Hartman lit a roaring fire. The room beyond the
door had once been a kitchen. It was small and quite
clean with whitewashed walls and a sound wooden
floor. Helen crept closer to the fire, suddenly aware of
how cold and wet she felt. She looked at Jack, crouched
over the flames.

'Do you often come here?' she said.

He glanced at her. 'Once in a while. I use it as a
stopping off place on my way through to Ely or Kings
Lynn.' He pulled a large sack out from the hearth side.
'I left some food and stuff here on my way through to
the fair this morning. Are you hungry?'

Helen nodded, realising that she was ravenous.

Jack pulled a pot from the sack and hung it on a
hook over the fire. 'You look as if you're wet as well.
Don't worry, it'll soon warm up in here.'

Helen looked down at her legs. They were so cold
that she hadn't realised her boots and the bottom of
her skirt were soaking.

'It's from the bottom of the punt,' he said. 'Wait on.'

He stretched himself and then disappeared into the shadows beyond the arc of the lamp. A few seconds later he came back with a great bundle of sacking and a roll of blankets. Seeing the question in her eyes, he said, 'I'd planned to sleep here tonight.'

Helen nodded dumbly, unspoken words hanging in the air between them. She looked up as he threw the sacking mattress down in front of the fire. His eyes were dark glittering pools. He glanced across at her and she wondered if he would read the expectation in her face.

'Take off your clothes,' he said steadily.

She shivered and bent to unlace her boots.

'No,' he said slowly, 'start with your coat and blouse. I want to see what it is I've won.'

Inside, her stomach leapt with a subtle mixture of fear and desire. 'It's so cold,' she mumbled.

Jack squatted beside her, his face alight with expectation. 'I'll soon warm you, lady,' he whispered in a low voice, and sat back on his haunches to watch her.

She shuddered and then slipped the first button undone on her coat. Her fingers fumbled uneasily, not just from the cold but a strange sense of elation. Finally the buttons gave and she slipped the coat off her shoulders. Jack threw more wood onto the fire, sending out a great crescendo of sparks. He looked back at her. 'And the rest.'

She slipped her suit jacket off to reveal a thin silk blouse beneath. Against the sheer fabric her nipples pressed through her camisole top, erect from the

24

excitement and the cold. Between her legs she felt a shadowy flutter of arousal as his eyes moved across her. She undid the necktie of the blouse, sliding the tiny buttons open with her fingers. It slipped noiselessly over her shoulders, leaving only her camisole top.

He leant forward and cupped one breast through the delicate lace. She shuddered at his caress as his fingers lifted to the shoestring straps and pulled them down, uncovering her small rounded breasts. He sat back and let out a low groan of appreciation. 'I'd have fought to the death rather than have any other man take you from me,' he said softly. 'Let me see the rest.'

She stood up, her back cold, her front hot from the fire. She slid her hands into the waistband of her skirt and pushed it down over the curve of her hips. Jack knelt up on his heels and caught hold of her around the waist, pulling her to him.

Her whole body quivered at his caress. His face was pressed against her belly. She writhed away but his grip was insistent. He pressed his lips to her navel, his tongue lapping at the sensitive skin.

Slowly his head dropped and he nuzzled against the dark swell of her sex, breathing in her scent. 'By God, you smell wonderful,' he murmured. His fingers moved over her legs, the roughness of his hands catching against her stockings.

Helen shuddered, his caresses and desire lighting a thousand tiny lamps in her mind. He kneaded the heavy swell of her buttocks, caressing the curves through the sheer fabric of her drawers. With glittering eyes he looked up at her. 'Take these off too,' he said coolly, tugging at the elastic. 'For tonight, Helen Garrison, you are mine.'

She stepped away, realising that his dominance excited her. Slowly she slipped off her knickers with her stockings. She felt the bite of the cold nipping at her and shivered as goose bumps lifted on her arms.

His eyes were hypnotic. He lifted a hand. 'Come lay with me by the fire, woman,' he ordered. She dropped to her knees and moved closer, leaning against his thickset body, drinking in the sensation of his closeness. He slid his arms round her, holding her tightly. His unshaven face pressed into the soft curve of her neck. 'Lie down, my woman,' he said softly. 'We have all night.'

Wordlessly she lay down beside him on the sacking mattress and closed her eyes, barely daring to breathe, waiting for his caress. She shivered as his fingers stroked across her, touching her breasts, stroking along the sensitive curve of her armpit. She whimpered, her senses alight.

'You're a brave and beautiful woman, Helen Garrison,' he said evenly.

Her eyes closed, she could hear him fumbling and straining as he slipped off his clothes. She dare not look at him; instead she lay still, her breathing shallow and ragged, until she felt the heat of his body next to hers. An instant later, he folded a heavy blanket down over them both, trapping the heat between them. She felt his breath on her cheek and turned towards him. Her lips opened in anticipation of his kiss. He pressed his mouth to hers. His lips were insistent and fierce, as if he would drain the life from her. His tongue pressed home between her lips and she let out an excited gasp as his hands moved to her breasts, his fingers kneading at her sensitive flesh.

His kisses were hot and needy. He ran his tongue around her lips and then down over her chin, nibbling at her ears, stroking her into a frenzy. The touch of his tongue awoke great spirals of pleasure in her. His lips closed around her nipples, sucking them in, milking her dry.

Her whole body quivered and she knew that she was wet, feeling the first traces of her juices trickle onto the sensitive skin around her sex. His fingers moved lower and he rolled on top of her. As she felt the weight of him above her, she gasped.

His knee slid down between her thighs, pressing them apart. She let out a shrill cry, silenced by his kisses, while between her legs she could feel the hard arc of his cock brushing against her. Its angry presence, pressing so close to the engorged lips of her sex, made her whimper.

She opened her eyes as she felt him move forward, his cock pressing her open in its path. Above her, his shadowy face was framed by a tangle of dark hair, his eyes were those of a wild cat and his lips set in a tight line. She felt a wild mixture of anticipation and fear as he moved closer still, sliding into her. The silky folds of her body opened eagerly to take him in. She shuddered and then gasped when he grabbed her hands and pulled them back above her head. As he did so, he slid full length into her moist waiting sex and she squealed as he filled her.

His belly and broad chest rubbed against her as he started to move. The dark hair on his body stroked her, teased her, while below she felt his hips grinding, seeking out a place that would pleasure them both. She lifted herself up to him, encouraging him, driving him deeper.

He grinned down at her and she shivered, drinking in his animal longing, relishing the musky masculine smell of his strong body. She tilted her hips to allow him deeper. As she moved, his body brushed deliciously against the tight bud of her clitoris. It was a sensation she had only dreamed existed during the frustrating nights with Charles. The swirling circles of pleasure made her afraid; it felt as if she was losing every vestige of control.

'Oh my God,' she hissed, trying to wriggle away from the excitement he was lighting in her belly; the fear making her fight the sensation. She whimpered, unable to escape from the insistent heady rhythm his body was setting in hers. His head dipped to kiss her breasts.

'Don't fight it,' he murmured in an undertone, 'come with me, lady, come with me.'

His gentle husky invitation was all the encouragement she needed. She let the sensation engulf her, too compelling to resist. Ensnared, she matched him stroke for stroke, rolling under him in an effort to keep fierce hold of the heat that threatened to burn her from the core outwards. It felt as if she were losing herself completely in the act of passion. As the madness and pure animal instinct took her to the very edge, she wrenched against the hold he had on her wrists. Twisting and bucking, his body drove her higher and higher until she believed she would die on the damp straw mattress by the fire.

Just as she was convinced there would never be an end to the journeying, great flames of pleasure roared up through her belly, lighting sparks behind her eyes. She screamed out as she felt herself falling through space, taking her mind and her body to a place she had never known existed.

Deep inside, as if her whole being was centred around her sex, she felt the rippling contractions of her orgasm sucking eagerly at Jack's cock. Above her, she heard him gasp as he finally lost control, driving raggedly into her. His thrusts were instinctive, all-consuming. She lifted her hips again and was rewarded by a dark guttural moan, low in his throat, and then a cry of pure animal satisfaction as his climax roared through them both.

At Garrison Lodge, Charles poured himself a stiff Scotch. He'd dropped Max and Liddy off at the Hall and now stood staring out of the open curtains to the snow beyond. He was angry with Helen for causing so much trouble, forgetting that it was his brother who had agreed to give the fairground dice-player his wife to settle his gambling debt. He took a bitter mouthful.

It was most likely, he decided, that the chap had taken her back to his cottage to let her stay the night with his wife and children, just making his point so he didn't lose face or, more likely, he'd taken Helen into town and dropped her off at a hotel.

Charles tightened his grip on the whisky tumbler and imagined Helen's face. He was immediately convinced in his own mind that, because she had been feeling put upon, not wanting to go to the damned fair in the first place, she'd decided to spite him by not ringing.

Within those few minutes, between pouring the first drink and finishing it, Charles smoothly transferred all guilt from himself and Max onto Helen. Instead of being worried about her, he was now furious.

He poured himself another drink and, while doing so, forgot about the knife at his brother's throat, his own inadequacies and the dark threat of the fairground dice-player. Helen, he decided angrily, was doing this purely to spite him and to put a taint on his family. She really needed to be taught a lesson, which was why he wouldn't search for her. Her ridiculous behaviour deserved to be punished.

Downing the Scotch in one long swallow he hurled the empty glass into the hearth and hurried up to bed.

On the landing he glanced back down to the hall. Dimly lit, it had been furnished with things Max had been kind enough to let them have from Garrison Hall. Helen had never liked Max, never seen how kind he was to them both.

Charles switched off the lights and hoped, bitterly, that his wife was sitting in some frozen little cottage out on the Fens somewhere and was realising exactly what a fool she had been.

As he reached his bedroom door he hesitated for a few seconds and then turned towards the back stairs. Perhaps Annie might still be awake. If she wasn't, she soon would be.

Helen lay sleepily in the circle of Jack Hartman's arms. Beside them the fire glowed warmly, whilst above it the black pot steamed, billowing delicious meaty smells into the air. Jack raised himself up onto one elbow, tucking the blanket around them. His eyes shone in the firelight.

'Hungry?' he said, leaning closer to press his lips to her forehead.

She nodded and snuggled up against him, one finger idly tracing the tight puckered circle around his nipple. 'Yes,' she said softly, 'but it will keep for a while, won't it?'

Jack Hartman grinned and slipped down beside her. 'Aye, it will, lady,' he whispered.

She reached out and pulled him down towards her.

Chapter 2

Liddy's Party

Helen was woken by the sound of something scraping. She sat up quickly, confused and disorientated. Squatting by the hearth, Jack Hartman was scraping mud from the soles of her boots. Helen blushed furiously, realising that beneath the blanket she was completely naked and that her body still ached from his caresses. He had taken her to places she never knew existed with Charles. She thought about Jack's lips, his fingers and the mesmerising hypnotic image of his cock. Nothing had prepared her for the pleasure she now knew she could share with a man. Embarrassed by her own thoughts, she pulled the blankets up around her. As she lifted them, she could smell the lingering musk of his raw body heat mingling with hers.

Jack looked across at her, his face dark and closed. 'There's tea,' he said flatly.

She shuddered. 'What's the matter? Are you angry with me?'

Jack shrugged. 'It's really of no consequence what I feel, is it?' He lifted up her boots, 'I've cleaned them up for you. No need for you to carry all that clay and mud around.'

Helen nodded dumbly.

Jack sat back on his haunches. 'These boots of yours made me think. They're made of the finest leather, lined with kid, with a little fur cuff at the top – look at the workmanship.' As he spoke he turned them over in his strong hands. 'I couldn't buy a pair of boots like this. They'd not let a man like me in the cobbler's shop that made them – and the price?' He whistled, holding them out to look at. 'What price were these boots?'

Helen leant across and snatched them from him, dragging the blankets around her as she clambered up off the mattress. 'They've cost me everything,' she said furiously. 'For two pins, I'd hurl the damned things into the fire.'

Jack looked astounded. 'I don't understand,' he spluttered. Helen snorted and started to collect her clothes together. Oblivious of her nakedness she pulled them on carelessly. Jack passed her a mug of tea, which she took, her eyes glassy and full of tears as she finally pulled the short leather boots over her stockings.

'Will you take me to Ferrybridge soon?' she said without emotion. Jack nodded and Helen stooped to tie her laces. 'These boots belonged to Lydia, my sister-in-law. She gave them to me because they pinched her toes.' Helen peered down at the boots. 'My husband said I should be very grateful that Liddy thinks of me.' She glanced angrily at Jack. 'You've jumped to too many conclusions about me, Jack Hartman,' she said, picking up her coat and slipping it on. 'Will you take me back to Ferrybridge now?'

Jack nodded, 'Aye, if you're ready.'

Helen smiled bitterly, taking a swig of the dark tea. 'I'm not sure I'll ever be ready to go back,' she said softly and turned towards the door. 'So perhaps it's best we go now, before I change my mind.'

Jack pulled on his jacket and followed her.

Outside on the river the new day's air was crisp and clear. As far as the eye could see the landscape was covered in virgin snow.

Once clear of the pump house, Helen hunched silently beneath the rough blankets in the punt and closed her eyes. She tried not to think about what might await her back at the Lodge.

Jack pushed away from the derelict building and guided the little boat out into the centre of the stream. Within sight was the stark iron bridge that spanned the river at Ferrybridge and the silhouette of the houses and shops that made up the little Fenland town. Helen shuddered and let the silence of the river enclose her.

Stepping from the punt under the shelter of the bridge's arch, Helen walked wordlessly up towards the road, too afraid to speak and too unhappy to look back.

At the door of The Hansard she finally turned. Jack Hartman was already just a distant indistinct shape, guiding his little craft through the sluggish water. Helen shivered, suppressing the urge to call out to him and beg him to take her away with him. Instead she sadly watched his progress until he disappeared from view around a bend in the meandering river.

Pulling her coat tight round her, Helen stepped inside the hotel, feeling as if she had lost more than she could possibly bear. The reception desk was deserted. She glanced into the mirror above the hearth, her dark-rimmed eyes betrayed only unhappiness. She sighed and rang the bell. When a girl finally appeared, Helen asked her to bring her a pot of tea and call her a taxi.

'Why in God's name didn't you ring me?' Charles snapped as Helen slipped off her coat in the hall of Garrison Lodge. He was standing in the door of the sitting-room, his handsome features dark and stormy. 'It's a matter of common decency . . .'

Helen turned around, her expression incredulous, 'What?'

'What did he do last night? Drop you off at The Hansard over at Ferrybridge?'

Helen looked away, thinking about the low roof of the pump-house kitchen, the warm inviting glow of the fire and the shadows of the flames dancing on the ceiling above them. She swallowed hard before she turned back to face her husband. 'No, I didn't stay at The Hansard,' she said stiffly, hoping her face would not betray her.

Charles stuffed his hands miserably into his jacket pockets. 'Good job I took the sergeant's advice then, under the circumstances. I must give him a ring this morning and let him know you've arrived back safely.'

'What advice was that, Charles?'

'He suggested we didn't send out a search party for you last night. He said it would be better to see what happened today. I mean, how would it have looked if one of our tenants had found you holed up in front of some tinker's hearth? Couldn't have that, could we now?' As he spoke he laughed a small dry humourless laugh.

'No, of course not,' said Helen, without emotion. His attitude astounded her. She slipped off her winter boots, trying to stay calm. Inside, a white hot plume of anger burned furiously. 'I think I'm going to have a bath now. If you'll excuse me.'

Charles nodded, 'Can't say as I blame you. I'll get Annie to bring you up some carbolic soap. It'll help shift the smell.'

Helen looked back coldly over her shoulder and then hurried upstairs.

In the bathroom she drew a deep tub full of hot water, knowing their maid Annie, against Charles' orders, would have sense enough to keep the fires in so that the back boiler would heat the water to almost boiling. Gallons of swirling frothy water gushed into the cast-iron tub as Helen undressed.

She rubbed a circle of mist from the bathroom mirror and gazed at her reflection. From the outside she looked exactly the same, except for the hint of tiredness darkening the skin beneath her eyes. It almost surprised her. She rubbed her eyes and looked again and then smiled. Perhaps it was just as well the outside hadn't changed – at least her face would not betray her.

She hesitated for an instant beside the bath, regretting that she had to wash away the tantalising smell of Jack Hartman's body. She glanced down into the hot clear water and then smiled. Stepping in, she let the water take her. There would be other times, she was sure of it.

When Helen finally came back downstairs Charles was in the sitting-room with an accounts ledger on his lap. Beside him, on a low table, the daily papers were folded and pristine, awaiting his attention. He glanced up as she came in.

'It's really thrown me out of kilter, all this fuss over that damned tinker,' he said, laying the accounts book aside. 'I had planned to pop over to Home Farm this morning and see Harry Wallis.'

Helen looked up at the ornate clock above the fireplace, another unwanted treasure from the Hall, out of place on their simple mantle shelf. 'It's not eleven yet, Charles, there's still plenty of time for you to go over there.'

Charles nodded, 'Perhaps you're right. By the way, you haven't forgotten Liddy's dinner party tonight, have you? She's counting on you to pop up there and help her organise everything.'

Helen sighed, 'She ought to arrange those things herself, Charles. She's the lady of the manor, isn't she? Landed gentry and all that?'

Charles looked horrified, 'Helen, what on earth possessed you to say that? It's extremely ill-mannered. Liddy and Max depend on us and don't forget—'

Helen spun round, suddenly unable to control her fury. 'That they're very good to us? Oh, for God's sake, Charles, without us the estate would fall to pieces. I arrange all Liddy's domestic affairs, you run the farms.

And have you forgotten your drunken brother pledged me as a betting wager last night?'

Charles' face flushed scarlet. 'For goodness' sake, Helen, calm down. Max has always said I have a special talent for managing the estate. After all, it's in our best interests to ensure the income is good. And Liddy? I'm surprised you can be so damned ungrateful. She's not used to having to deal with the practicalities of life, she's delicate. You'd do well to take a leaf out of her book.' He paused and then said, very slowly, 'And, as for Max's unfortunate brush with that chap at the fair last night, you really didn't have to go with him—' His voice sounded tight, as if he were holding himself under control.

Helen was speechless. No, she thought darkly, but you have no idea how glad I am that I did. She stared levelly at Charles and then sighed; it was pointless to argue. 'Charles, Liddy isn't delicate. She is a lazy, self-indulgent drunkard and so is your brother. They use us both because we're foolish enough to let them. I'm sure they both laugh at us for being so gullible.'

Charles, still red-faced, got to his feet. 'I don't want to hear another word about this, Helen, and I think,' he said very slowly, his voice crisp and controlled, 'that I will take a drive out to Home Farm. I suggest perhaps you have a little lie-down before you go over to see Liddy. You're obviously still overwrought.'

With an overwhelming sense of defeat, Helen nodded. 'Yes, Charles,' she said softly. 'I may well do that.' And she turned back slowly towards the fireplace. The heavy gold-rimmed clock struck the hour while, behind her, Helen heard Charles quietly close the sitting-room door.

Upstairs she slipped off her dress and slid between the sheets. For an instant they seemed immeasurably smooth and luxurious compared to the rough abrasive blankets that had covered her and Jack as they had rolled and kissed, locked together in each other's arms by the kitchen hearth. She shivered, thinking about the way he had held her body against his and the great soaring flames he had ignited in her belly. She could still imagine the feeling of his lips on her breasts and his cock pressed up deep inside her. She closed her eyes and let sleep claim her, her dreams tumbling with images of Jack's glittering eyes and his rough hands on her breasts.

Liddy was curled onto a *chaise longue,* cradling a gin and tonic when Helen finally trudged across to Garrison Hall in the early afternoon. The newly fallen snow lay thick and crisp across the park land around the huge mansion, softening its stark lines. Despite her discontent, Helen couldn't help but be impressed by the beauty of the old house. It seemed such a shame to her that everything couldn't be more balanced, more amicable between them all. If only Charles could understand.

'I was going to phone you,' Liddy said, by way of greeting. 'Charles said you'd be over first thing this morning.'

Helen grimaced. Obviously Max hadn't told Liddy about the events of the night before – assuming he could remember them himself. As if reading her mind, Liddy said, 'And Max has got the most awful split lip. He said he can't remember how the hell it happened.'

Helen wondered if perhaps the fairground men had decided to beat their wager out of him after all but said nothing. Grateful to be out of the chilly afternoon air she moved closer to the fire to warm herself.

Liddy smiled as Helen stooped over the coals and rubbed her hands. 'I see my boots fitted you,' she said lightly. 'I really must see if I've got anything else upstairs that will suit you. Max has promised me faithfully we'll go to Paris in the spring. Before we do, I'll hunt you out some things I'm done with. What luck we're the same size.'

Helen bit her lip and felt the bright coppery taste of blood bubble up in her mouth. 'What time are your guests arriving, Liddy?' she said with forced lightness.

Liddy took a long pull from her glass and then looked up at the clock, 'Teatime, I think. I've asked quite a few of them to stay overnight so everyone will have a chance to settle and bath before dinner. The others are arriving around seven-thirty.' She looked at her empty glass thoughtfully and then held it out towards Helen. 'Would you mind awfully, getting me another g-and-t as you're up, darling? I'm feeling so washed out today.'

As Helen poured the gin into the glass, Liddy stretched languidly. 'Is it true you used to be a nurse before you married Charles?'

Helen turned, 'Yes, I worked for the Red Cross during the war, why?'

Liddy pulled her delicate heart-shaped face into a little

grimace of pain. 'It's that I feel so tired and heady-achy all the time. I wondered if you might have any idea why.'

Helen passed Liddy the gin and tonic and shook her head. Liddy grabbed it greedily and took a long swig.

'No idea at all,' said Helen sarcastically; a tone that was totally lost on her sister-in-law.

Liddy's house guests began to arrive in the early evening. Helen excused herself before Max put in an appearance and hurried back to the Lodge to change for dinner. Despite the snow, all the guests, mostly old friends of Max's, seemed set to turn up. As Helen made her way along the avenue through the icy drifts she was passed by at least half-a-dozen elegant motor cars.

In their bedroom, Charles had already got his dinner jacket on and was struggling with his tie. Helen stepped over and, without a word, tied it into a neat bow.

Charles smiled at her, 'Thanks, old girl.' He paused. 'So sorry I blew my top at you this morning, hadn't really thought that you might be a little upset after last night.'

Helen smiled and nodded dumbly, opening her wardrobe to find her evening dress.

Charles pressed on, 'Have many of Liddy's guests arrived yet?'

Helen would have liked to get dressed in peace but instead said, 'Yes, it looks as if everyone is going to turn up. The drive is full of cars.'

Charles nodded, 'Good show. What are you going to wear tonight?'

Helen lifted a dress from the wardrobe. It was made from delicate blue silk, with narrow shoe-string straps and decorated with row upon row of silver bugle beads which ran up and down the bodice. The straight skirt was decorated in swirling random patterns of the same tiny glistening beads.

Charles' face clouded. 'I'm not really sure that it's very suitable—' he said icily.

Helen turned away from him and played her ace. 'Actually, Liddy gave it to me,' she said flatly. 'She bought it from London last time they went down there but it's a little small for her. She did say, if it had fitted she would have worn it tonight.'

From behind her she heard Charles muttering. Helen picked up two small boxes from the shelf beside her bed. 'She was very generous, she's given me the shoes, the bag and the hat she had made to match.'

'Right,' said Charles briskly, 'well, I'd better go and get the car round. I should put a good thick coat on with that dress if you're going to wear it.'

Helen washed quickly and slipped on Liddy's dress. She pulled the little beaded cloche hat on before turning to look into the mirror. Seeing her reflection, she laughed aloud. The transformation was quite astounding. She always wore comfortable, classical clothes, chosen for durability, not style, so she wasn't prepared for the startling metamorphosis from country wife to daring flapper. She leant closer. The dress might have been made for her. Falling to mid-calf in a straight tube, it was cunningly cut to allow the fabric to move with her, clinging to every curve, showing off her slim figure to good advantage.

Helen turned a little, watching the bugle beads twinkle in the lamp light. When Liddy had offered her the outfit, her first instinct had been to say no; now she was glad she'd changed her mind.

She teased a curl or two from under the beaded cloche and then glanced around the dressing-table. Somewhere, she was sure, she had some lipstick. Her train of thought was broken by Charles' reappearance. He looked her up and down, his expression quite unreadable.

'Are you sure you're going to be warm enough in that?' he said coldly.

Helen raised an eyebrow and was about to ask whether he would ask Liddy the same question, but thought better of it. If they disagreed now, Charles would be sullen all evening, so she nodded.

'I think so. The Hall is very warm, besides I'm going to wear my fur coat and boots to go up there in. I'll take my shoes and maybe,' she glanced back towards the wardrobe, 'I'll take that lovely shot-silk stole you bought me for a wedding present.'

Charles smiled, flattered by her choice, and helped her on with her winter coat.

As Helen picked up her bag, she turned to Charles, 'Did you tell Liddy I used to be a nurse?'

Charles looked uncomfortable. 'I may have mentioned it, why?'

Helen shook her head, 'No real reason. I was just curious who'd told her, that's all. Did you tell I'd taught as well?'

Charles shook his head. 'I'm not really sure now,' he said evasively and quickly turned away from her.

The magnificent entrance hall of the Garrison family home was alight with candles. Even though Helen had seen it at least a dozen times before, she was never anything other than overawed. The candlelight reflected and refracted in the huge mirrors and cut-glass chandeliers. In the vast fireplace a huge log fire crackled and flickered, casting dramatic shadows of its own onto the vaulted ceiling.

Liddy and Max were standing by the great sweeping staircase to welcome their guests while the footmen moved silently between the couples serving champagne cocktails. Liddy looked stunning in a silver sheath dress which fitted as if it were a second skin. Max, as close to sober as he ever got, looked dark and handsome in his dinner suit. The only blot on his refined elegant features was the dark, livid bruise around his mouth.

Charles handed their coats to the footman and took a drink from the tray, then guided Helen across towards his brother and his wife.

Liddy's eyes twinkled when she saw Helen in the new outfit. 'You look absolutely gorgeous,' she whispered, stepping close to brush her lips against Helen's cheek.

Helen smiled back. 'You too,' she said, for once feeling genuine gratitude towards her sister-in-law. The dress allowance Charles considered adequate would have never run to the outfit Liddy had given her.

The guests were a mixture of half familiar faces, Liddy and Max's usual crowd. Helen didn't know any of them well but had met them enough times to be able to exchange chit-chat and social pleasantries. She also knew, as the footmen made another round with their trays of cocktails, that Charles would suggest they left early. Max's drinking and hospitality were legendary and, though he had never said as much, Helen suspected that Charles disapproved of his elder brother's showy hospitality.

Beside her, a couple she had met at Christmas downed another glass and turned for a refill. By the time they were called through to dinner everyone was more than a little tipsy. Helen took her place at the table opposite Charles, who was busy talking to one of Max's cronies about the price of beef.

The dining-room was as impressive as the hall, with a huge walnut dining-table that easily accommodated their party of twenty-four and could be extended to take double that number.

The noise level had already gone up round the table. As the footmen and butler served the first course, a delicate buttery mushroom soup, Helen wondered why she had bothered to help arrange such a beautiful menu – the guests were far more interested in the wine. By the time dessert was served everyone, except for Helen, was drunk.

Across the table, Charles swayed unsteadily, taking wild stabs at the luxurious blackcurrant sorbet that Helen and Liddy's cook had devised. Unaware that

Helen was watching him, he leered drunkenly at the breasts of the woman on his left. Helen shivered and turned her attention to the sharp icy dessert.

Max enjoyed female company far too much to stand on the tradition of the gentlemen retiring for port and cigars whilst the ladies withdrew to the drawing-room to gossip. Instead, next door to the dining-room he had refurbished a large sitting-room for his guests' after-dinner amusement. The room was complete with a gramophone and cocktail cabinet and a collection of comfortable settees and armchairs for everyone to relax in, all arranged around a roaring fire.

Liddy, an enthusiastic dancer, immediately wound up the gramophone whilst coffee and liqueurs were served. Helen, cradling a brandy, went in search of Charles, who she had last seen on the arm of the woman who'd been sitting next to him at dinner. It was a relief to step into the stillness of the shadowy hallway and close the door on the raucous laughter and raised voices.

She wondered where Charles could have gone. He didn't normally leave without telling her. Surely he wouldn't have gone very far? She finally found him, alone, in the games room, clinging unsteadily to the side of the billiard table. He turned towards her when he heard the door open. 'I must have eaten too much,' he stuttered unhappily.

Helen sighed, 'Yes, darling. Do you feel ill?'

Charles nodded, 'A glass of wine too many I think. I feel absolutely dreadful.'

Helen nodded, 'Maybe we ought to go home.'

Charles staggered over to an armchair by the empty hearth. 'I don't want to spoil Max's dinner party by making a fuss,' he said miserably.

From the sitting-room across the hall came the sound of voices raised in raucous laughter. 'I really don't think they'll notice. Why don't you let me get one of the footmen to drive us home.'

Charles took hold of her hand, 'You don't have to come back if you want to stay. I really don't want to spoil your fun.'

Helen started to say it was all right when Charles continued, 'But I suppose now dinner is done with – that's the thing you were asked to organise, wasn't it? – you might as well come back with me. After all, these really aren't your sort of people, are they?'

Helen froze, 'What do you mean?'

Charles sniffed, 'You're always saying that you've got nothing to say to Max and Liddy's friends.' He leant forward miserably, clutching his stomach, 'It's really down to the matter of class, isn't it? I mean you haven't exactly got a lot in common with them, have you?'

Helen felt herself flush. Charles had never mentioned the fact that she wasn't landed gentry or from a wealthy background and, until then, she'd never considered whether it meant that much to him. She felt a little flutter of fury growing in her belly. Although her family had never been wealthy she'd had a good upbringing and education.

Charles stroked her arm proprietorially. 'You shouldn't be so upset when Liddy tries to help you, Helen. She's really only trying to help you feel at ease.

I know you're out of your depth sometimes, that's why I explained that you were a nurse and that you taught before the war. She thought it was all dreadfully worthy ... You know, you do look stunning in that dress, an absolute corker. You've been a real help to Liddy tonight. The food was glorious, you did very well.'

Helen leant across him and pulled the bell rope that would call a footman. 'Yes,' she said softly, 'not bad for a working girl, eh, Charlie? And a lot more convenient for Liddy than hiring a decent housekeeper.'

Charles looked up bemused, 'What did you say, Helen?'

Helen smiled, using the cool professional smile she had perfected on the hospital wards. 'I said, we'll get someone to take you home. I'll come home in a little while. After all, darling Liddy might need a hand to clear up.'

Charles nodded drunkenly. 'Oh, absolutely,' he murmured as a footman appeared at the door.

Helen helped the footman manhandle Charles into their car and then stood on the steps of the hall, watching the lights of the car as they tracked between the trees. The car made slow progress along the avenue that led down to the Lodge.

Helen swallowed hard, her bright angry tears threatening to spill over. They had been married barely a year. The previous winter Charles had taken her to Europe, showing her sights that he'd seen on a tour he'd taken in his twenties. It had seemed to her that they were perfectly matched: the handsome young army officer and his bright attractive nurse.

She shivered, suddenly feeling the bitter biting cold through her thin dress. He had been a totally different person then. They'd come back from their honeymoon in Europe and everything had been so perfect until they'd moved into the Lodge. And then . . .

Helen turned and hurried back inside. And then, she thought unhappily, slow, unimaginative Charles had realised that she would never be the same as the lovely Lydia – nor would she want to be. Lovely drunken Lydia with her blue blood and inability to do anything without a posse of hired help.

Helen slammed the heavy door shut, and went back to the games room. As she closed the door quietly it occurred to her that Charles was ashamed of her. She let the tears spill freely down her face. Snatching up the brandy she had been carrying when she discovered him, Helen downed it in one hot choking mouthful.

From across the hall came the echo of Max's robust drunken laughter. Helen sat down heavily in the armchair by the empty fireplace and wondered what she should do next. Jack Hartman's dark sensual face appeared inside her mind. He had given her pleasure that she never dreamt existed. If only . . . she stopped herself. 'If only' was too dangerous a game to play. She was Charles' wife, for better or worse.

From beyond the open curtains she could see the bleak snow covering the park land. She was just wondering whether perhaps it would be better if she did go back to the Lodge when the games room door opened.

One of the guests, a tall insipid-looking man called

Alex, peered around the door. On seeing her, he held up a hand in apology, 'I'm so sorry. I didn't know there was anyone in here.' He glanced back over his shoulder to an unseen companion. 'Sorry, darling, we'll have to look for another venue. Looks like the billiard table's spoken for.'

From behind the door a woman laughed uproariously, 'I always thought it was far too draughty in there anyway. Why not try the Chinese room?' As the woman spoke Alex stepped back through the open door and quietly closed it behind him.

Helen thought about what she had just heard. Usually she and Charles left Max's gatherings early and she had no idea how the guests spent their time after dinner. She got up and walked across to the door, opening it just a fraction.

Outside, from the door of the room where Liddy and her friends had been relaxing, couples were appearing hand in hand. Max stood, like master of ceremonies, watching them depart into the depths of the house. Clinging on his arm, pressing herself close to him, was the woman Charles had been drooling over at dinner. She leant forward and kissed Max, rubbing herself up against him. Max growled and cupped her chin in his hand. 'Just wait a minute,' he laughed. 'And don't kiss me so damned hard, my lip is killing me.'

Liddy appeared a second or two later, hand in hand with another of their dinner guests. Their closeness spoke volumes.

Helen held her breath as Liddy and her companion kissed and then hurried towards the staircase.

Max grinned lasciviously at the woman on his arm and pulled her towards him, his lips seeking out hers. 'Gently gently,' he hissed as she returned his kiss.

'Our turn now?' she murmured huskily.

Max nodded and caught hold of her hand, 'Damned right and I know the perfect spot. I want to get there before Liddy and that pervert Bracken beat us to it. Come on.'

When they had gone Helen stepped silently into the magnificent hall. All was quiet now except for the crackle of the logs in the grate.

If she doubted what her instincts told her a low throaty chuckle from the open door of the dining-room confirmed her suspicions. She crept closer and peeped inside. What she saw made her gasp.

Lying across the huge table was a statuesque blonde, her dress pushed up over her thighs. Standing between them, another guest, a fat man with a balding head, caressed her exposed sex with casual familiarity.

The woman laughed as the man undid his flies. 'Not so fast, you naughty boy,' she murmured huskily. 'You know what I want.'

The man grinned down at her and then leant forward to plant a kiss on the open lips of her quim.

The woman shivered. 'Better,' she whispered, 'much better.'

Helen felt her colour rise and rushed back across the hall to the cloakroom to rescue her coat, her senses reeling.

Outside, the night air was like a bitter knife, ripping

at her face. Helen dragged the coat up round her chin and stuffed the blue silk cloche into her pocket. Glancing out at the freezing snow drifts she was glad that she had had enough sense to bring her boots. She hurried down the broad flight of steps and away from the dark disturbing scene inside the Hall.

Between the trees, she could just make out the tiny glittering lights of the Lodge in the distance. Bending her head against the cutting wind, she started to walk briskly towards them.

The avenue was lined with tall trees. Once under their shelter she slowed her pace, letting the images she had seen at the Hall fill her mind. She still found it hard to believe what she had seen. She was concentrating so hard on the memory of Max's husky invitation to the woman on his arm and the erotic tableau in the dining-room, that she didn't see or hear a dark shape approaching her through the bushes.

Just as she rounded the bend that led into the long drive that would take her home, a man stepped out into her path. She let out a thin high-pitched scream of terror, stifled an instant later as Jack Hartman's face pressed close to hers. He grabbed her firmly, catching hold of her arms.

'What are you doing here?' she gasped in horror.

Jack grinned. 'I couldn't get you out of my mind,' he said quietly. 'So sad and silent when I dropped you off at Ferrybridge.'

He paused and she realised, as her eyes adjusted to the gloom, that he looked frozen.

'How did you know where I lived?' she asked.

'I've been here several times – beating for the Hall shoots, doing a little poaching in between times.' He grinned.

She hesitated and then said softly, 'So you knew who I was last night at the fair?'

Jack nodded, 'Aye, and that foolish man of yours and his drunken brother. Not that they'd remember me. Those sort never notice us.' His teeth chattered as he spoke.

She glanced at him. 'You look so cold—'

'I am. It's bitter out here tonight. Is there somewhere we can go to warm ourselves?' Despite the cold his voice was teasing and mischievous.

Helen hesitated. Vivid images of their night in the pump house bubbled up in her mind. She glanced towards the distant lights of the Lodge and then back towards the dark dramatic outline of the Hall set against the snow-grey night. 'Charles is home at the Lodge,' she said, trying not to think of the pain he had made her feel. 'And Max and his guests are –' she stumbled over the words ' – fully occupied,' she said after a second's pause. 'If we're quiet, we could probably find somewhere in the Hall where you could get warm.'

Jack caught hold of her again, his lips pressing against hers for an instant. 'I'd like the chance to warm you too, lady. I've thought of nothing but you since this morning,' he said huskily.

She shivered under his touch and then leant against him, surrendering to his kisses. His mouth pressed hard against hers, his tongue darting to seek admission between her lips. Even through his coat she could feel his desire. It would be so easy to give herself up to him amongst the dark shadowy trees. He pulled her closer, groaning softly.

She tore herself away, fighting for control. 'Not here, Jack,' she gasped breathlessly. 'We'll go this way,' she said quickly. Fearing her courage might fail her she took hold of his hand and turned back towards the Hall.

In silence they hurried through the snow. Even in the dark Helen could feel the insistent pulse of desire that throbbed between them. Her rational mind knew what she was contemplating could end in disaster but her body demanded the satisfaction she knew only Jack Hartman could give her.

Beneath the huge portico of the Hall, Helen mimed for Jack to be quiet and then opened the door. Inside, the huge hallway was deserted, candles guttering in the ornate candelabra, the log fire reduced to a low inviting glow.

Helen beckoned Jack inside. 'The servants will be in bed by now,' she whispered, 'but there are a lot of people in the house. Max and Liddy's guests. It might be better if we went down to the kitchens. It'll be warm enough there.'

She pointed towards the back of the hall where a door was set discreetly into the ornate panelling. On the other side of the room the double doors of the dining-room were still slightly ajar. Helen hesitated. The service door in there would lead them directly down into the Hall kitchens. She decided against going inside. She couldn't risk their being discovered if, as she suspected, the blonde woman and her companion were still engrossed in their erotic game.

Helen hurried across the open hallway with Jack in her wake. At the servants' door Jack paused and looked back into the magnificent entrance hall. He pulled the door to behind him, not quite closing it, in case they were heard.

Helen waited for him at the top of the landing on the other side. As he stepped through she glanced up into his dark glittering eyes. His face betrayed no fear, only the heady compelling flicker of his desire. She didn't resist when he pulled her to him, his hands catching her face to his, his lips eager to seek out her mouth.

'I want you so much,' he whispered.

'Not here,' she managed to gasp, as his hands dropped to the fastenings of her coat.

Max Garrison stepped unsteadily from the shadows of the corridor into the main hall, straightening his clothes. He wondered where Liddy could have got to. Surely that chap, Bracken, wasn't that engaging?

The huge room seemed deserted. Max snorted. His companion, the delightful Aretha Blackmore, hadn't turned out to be quite so much fun as he anticipated. She'd had rather too much claret. She'd ended up, after a very unsatisfactory bout of love-making amongst the verdant green plants in the heated veranda, passing out on one of the cane *chaise longues*.

He glanced around, wondering what chance he had of finding another partner or perhaps making up a threesome. The prospect cheered him up.

Unsure quite which way to go, he stood by the fire to warm himself and then noticed, on the marble floor tiles, dark pools of water – snowy footprints – that led from the front door towards the servants' quarters. He doubted that any of his companions had the stomach for an outdoor romp in this weather. The door to the servants' quarters was not quite closed which struck him as very peculiar.

Intrigued, Max followed the damp trail. The labyrinth of corridors below the Hall were gloomy and uninviting. Max had begun to wonder whether to leave it until the morning to discover if anything was amiss, when he heard a low throaty noise echoing along the empty corridors; a noise that intrigued him. Keeping to the shadows, he headed stealthily towards the kitchens.

Close to the main kitchen was a large room used to dry the household laundry and heated by pipes from the Hall's boilers. Max hesitated outside the door, hearing sounds of movement from within and soft low moaning. He wondered whether he should burst in and surprise them, for he felt certain it was two of his guests, adding a little excitement to their love-making by venturing below stairs. He rested his hand on the door knob and then changed his mind; it might be more interesting to see who the lovers were first. He wouldn't want to join in with Harry and George for a start. Grinning merrily, he looked around for another solution.

Beside the laundry room was a store room, connected by an internal door to the laundry, which – he seemed to remember – had a grating in it. He pushed open the store room door and crept inside, giving his eyes a little time to adjust to the gloom, before picking his way between the racks of shelves and boxes.

From the grating in the laundry room beyond came a soft golden glow and, far more inviting, the compelling sounds of a couple engrossed in the heights of passion.

Max pressed his face to the grating. Perfectly framed, opposite the little window, was a small dark woman, naked except for her shoes and stockings, which were held up with delightful silky garters. More exciting still was the dark bulk of her lover, kneeling between her open legs. The woman arched back against a stout wooden table, her hands pulling her lover's face towards the gaping lips of her sex. In response to her desperate demands, her lover parted them with his fingers, seeking out the engorged sensitive places before lapping at her with his tongue.

Max shivered with excitement, feeling the familiar press of an erection against the thin fabric of his evening trousers. The woman was really rather magnificent. Her small breasts were flushed with passion, her tight nipples puckered and dark. Max smiled; it would be a real pleasure to join them. Just as the thought formed in his mind, realisation dawned, and his mouth formed the woman's name, 'Helen.'

'My God,' he hissed, instantly denying the possibility. Surely she had already gone home with Charles? His eyes convinced him he was wrong.

Inside the laundry room, Helen moaned, stretching back in delight as her lover's fingers plunged inside her. She shivered and started to move rhythmically against him. Her expression was ecstatic.

Max found it impossible to drag his eyes from the scene unfolding before him. Helen's body arched as she struggled to reach her climax. Her lover's touch was skilled and relentless, bringing her again and again to the very brink of ecstasy.

She began to gasp, tiny diamonds of sweat breaking out on her top lip and between her breasts. 'Please,' she begged, in a sobbing excited voice, 'please, please . . .' She started to twist, writhing with passion – Max desperately sucked in a breath. He could almost feel the sensations coursing through Helen, and, at the same time, taste her musky salty excitement on his lips. Suddenly he saw the tension sweep through her, her face contorting with sheer pleasure as she let out a wild animal moan of satisfaction and ground her sex into her lover's face.

Max slumped forward almost as if the orgasm had been his own, but, in the room beyond, Helen's lover had not finished with her. He clambered up, stripping off his own clothes as he did so. He picked Helen up as if she were weightless and slid his hands round her thighs, lifting her up so that she encircled his waist with her long slim legs. Max found himself unable to tear his eyes away.

In the laundry room, Helen bucked and Max knew the man, her dark eager lover, was sliding deep inside her, his cock pressing into the slick fragrant depths of her body. Her head rested on her lover's shoulder as he drove home again and again. Helen's expression was almost vacant as if she were being consumed by their love-making. The man pressed his cock into her again and suddenly she began to move with him. Her eyes opened to reveal glittering pools of pleasure as his movements rekindled her desire.

Max tried to work out which one of his friends could possibly be so taken with his little sister-in-law. Who, amongst all the people he had invited, had been sensitive enough to detect this hidden well of sexuality beneath Helen's calm, almost prudish, exterior?

As he thought it, the man turned a little to ease the weight of Helen's eager body – and instantly Max recognised the profile. Memories of the previous evening came flooding back in vivid detail. Max gasped in horror. 'That bloody tinker,' he hissed in disbelief.

As Max tried to take in the full implications of what he was seeing, Jack Hartman let out a great wild, shuddering sigh and tightened his grip on Helen's body. She threw back her head and howled like a wolf as Jack's climax swept them both away.

Helen shuddered as Jack let her slip to the floor, her legs still trembling with excitement.

Jack grinned, stepping forward to kiss her. 'I'm glad I came back to see you,' he said.

Helen snuggled against his body, 'Me too, Jack Hartman. Whatever the risk, I'm glad you came. But you have to go. I've got to get back to Charles, he'll be worried.'

Jack snorted in derision but Helen lifted a finger to his lips to silence him. 'Not a word, Jack. What we've had is a world away from real life.'

Jack nodded wordlessly but his face still registered his contempt for Helen's husband. He reached for his clothes. 'Best if I'm away then, lady,' he said softly.

Helen nodded, torn by her impossible desire for him to stay. 'Will you come and surprise me again?' she said unsteadily.

The rough man grinned and pulled her to him, 'Aye, watch out for me, woman. I'll be back soon.'

They dressed quickly, and Helen took Jack by the hand. 'It would be easier if you went out through the kitchens. I'm not sure what time Liddy's guests will be leaving but I know some are going home tonight. It would be better for us both if you weren't seen.'

Jack nodded and didn't protest as Helen led him through the dark corridor towards the kitchen door. At the threshold he pulled her to him, his features dark and brooding in the gloom. 'I would set you free, Helen Garrison—' he murmured.

Helen returned his kiss, his eagerness rekindling her need. 'You already have,' she said softly. He slipped out into the strange snowy light. Helen shut her eyes and closed the door quickly behind him, fearing that she might be tempted to go with him.

'What a very touching scene,' said a voice from the shadows. Helen cried out in astonishment, as Max Garrison stepped out from the darkness of the corridor.

Helen felt herself blush and fought to regain her composure. 'Max—' she began.

But her brother-in-law raised a hand that silenced her. 'Don't say anything,' he murmured darkly. 'I've already seen you in the laundry room with your tinker friend.'

Helen felt every ounce of her resilience slipping away. 'What are you going to do?' she murmured, imagining Charles' tight angry face.

To her surprise, Max smiled. 'That rather depends on you,' he said cheerfully. Helen shivered as he moved closer. 'I thought I had weighed you up,' he said softly. 'You've really surprised me.'

She could see the desire in his eyes and the realisation that it was her that had lit this fire made her quiver. 'What do you want?' she said evenly.

Max was barely a stride away from her now, his eyes moving slowly across her body, 'I want you,' he murmured.

Helen held herself steady. 'Is this blackmail?' she said coldly.

Max lifted his hand to caress her bare shoulder. 'Oh no,' he said smoothly. 'I'm far too sophisticated to sink to that, Helen. No, I want you to come with me because you intrigue me.'

Helen shivered. 'Or you'll tell Charles?' she murmured, almost to herself.

Max ran a finger along the soft sensitive skin of her throat. 'If that's what you want to believe,' he said softly. He extended a hand to her. She glanced down at his open palm and then back up into Max's eyes. His gaze was steady and even.

'And if I don't come?'

Max shrugged. 'It's your choice.'

Helen wasn't fooled; there was a glint of menace in

his apparently calm expression. She looked away as he traced a finger around the outline of her lips. His caress was electric. She could feel the low hum of desire in his touch.

She looked back up at him, and nodded. 'All right,' she said softly, 'what is it you want from me?'

Max's expression was triumphant. 'Oh, I've got something special for you, my dear,' he purred, 'something you very much deserve.' He turned away from her and then glanced back over his shoulder. 'Come with me,' he whispered, 'and I'll show you.'

Mesmerised, Helen fell into step behind him.

Chapter 3

The Menagerie

At the door leading from the servants' quarters into the main hall, Max paused and looked back at Helen. 'You have truly astounded me,' he said, smiling narrowly. Helen didn't share his good humour. She shivered as he opened the door for her.

'Before we go upstairs, I'd like to show you my little hobby, Helen,' he said, indicating that she should go first.

She pulled a face, 'Hobby? I don't understand what you mean, Max.'

Max grinned, heading across the huge hall, 'My famous little soirées. I must ask you to be very quiet,' his eyes glistened. 'But I think you've realised if you want me to keep your secret, the least I expect is that you help me keep mine.'

Helen hesitated. The last person she wanted to be obligated to was her dissolute and corrupt brother-in-law. She imagined Charles' strained angry face and shuddered; there was really no choice.

At the door to the dining-room Max signalled her to

be quiet. She sighed; she already knew what lay inside and wondered what he expected her to do. To her surprise, Max led her next door into the little room where Liddy had set up her gramophone.

The room was dimly lit, the remains of the fire just a pile of orange embers in the grate. Max moved quickly across to a large painting on the wall and beckoned for Helen to join him. As she reached his shoulder, he slid the painting to one side. It moved silently on narrow rails and behind it were a series of holes cut into the wall. Helen gasped.

In the elegant dining-room beyond, the bald man she had seen earlier, was lying naked across one of the side tables. His blonde companion was kneeling above him, her heavy breasts picked out in the glow of the candlelight. As they watched, she trailed her hair across the man's chest, touching and teasing his hot sweating body. Her lover moaned as the woman stroked the puckered folds of his balls with one long, perfectly painted fingernail. Above, arching up onto his hairy belly, the man's meaty phallus jerked with pleasure.

Helen glanced at Max, feeling the colour rush to her cheeks.

He smiled. 'Keep watching,' he purred, pressing his face to the spy holes. 'It gets better.'

Inside the room, the woman's scarlet-painted lips closed over the end of the man's cock, nibbling and lapping at its livid purple head. Her tongue and lips worked him relentlessly, making the little man shiver and snort with delight. He whimpered as her fingers drew his foreskin back and forth, an electric counter-point to the rhythm of her mouth. The bald man seemed helpless, writhing and gasping under her caresses. He didn't seem to be able to move. Suddenly Helen felt the pulse roar in her ears as she spotted the leather straps around his ankles and wrists and realised that he was tied to the table.

She couldn't resist the compulsion to move closer to the spy hole, watching mesmerised as the blonde crept up over her lover's face, holding her body just out of reach. Her shapely body, arched above him in a perfect hourglass was an erotic masterpiece. Above them, on the high pale walls, the candles recreated the lovers' exertions in strange exotic shadows.

Helen could make out the man's tongue, straining to taste the woman's gaping sex. She could see the open moist lips of the woman's body, teasing him, held just inches above his waiting mouth. Slick moisture clung in tiny droplets to the light covering of blonde hair around her pussy, reflecting the candlelight.

Helen had never seen anything like it in her life. She swung round to face Max, knowing that her eyes would betray the little flurry of excitement the tableau had awoken in her. It was impossible not to be moved by the electric images of the couple's desire. 'You like to watch all these people?' she whispered in disbelief. 'Is that your hobby? I thought they were your friends.'

Max, his expression almost obscured by the gloom, nodded. 'They are my friends,' he said quietly. 'I love to see them like this; the noises they make – all their interesting, tantalising little foibles. So much more fun than their awful dull conversation.' He nodded towards the viewing window. 'He's a member of the House of Lords. Stood up against that bounder Lloyd George. Damned fine chap.' He paused and Helen saw him lick his lips. 'Look now—'

In spite of herself, Helen glanced back. The blonde had dropped her hips and was grinding her sex into the man's face. Her long fingers stroked at his arching aching cock and the tightly gathered sensitive flesh behind. Helen could see the man's legs tensing, trying to hold on, trying to hold back. His fists clenched rhythmically as the woman circled on his lips again and again. Even through the spy hole Helen could make out the woman's soft animal moans combined with the man's deeper, throatier gasps of pleasure.

Just as Helen thought the little peer could take no more, the blonde woman wrenched herself off him and slipped easily from the table. She stood, looking down at the prone man, her eyes alight with passion. Before she moved away she brushed her erect nipples along his hairy belly, planting a single kiss on his throbbing phallus.

'You damned vixen,' the man whimpered and struggled desperately against his restraints. His lover grinned, stuck out her tongue provocatively and then padded across the room towards the sideboard. Her lithe body seemed to shine in the delicate glow of the candles.

In the sitting-room Max grinned, his teeth white and wolfish in the low lights. 'They carry on like this for hours. By the time he comes he's nearly mad with excitement. Isn't she magnificent? Just look at the way she moves.'

Helen turned away, feeling that she couldn't watch any more.

Max stepped closer to her, his eyes gleaming. 'What, bored already, little one? Aren't you interested in the grand finale? In a minute or two, she'll splash iced champagne onto him. He will call out, writhing and straining, and then she'll lap it off – every last, single, tiny droplet. Sliding across him, stroking him with that wicked, wicked tongue of hers. He loves every second of it. Can you imagine how wonderful she must taste then, the subtle mixture of good wine and excess excitement. My God, how delicious.'

Max moaned appreciatively at the thought as Helen began to walk across the room towards the door. 'I think I've seen enough,' she said unsteadily.

He hurried after her, 'Oh no, no you haven't. There's so much more, and you still haven't given me what I want.'

Helen felt a cold chill creep over her, 'Tell me what is it you want then, Max.' She wanted it to be over and done with, anxious now to get home and away from the wild erotic atmosphere of the hall.

'Come, come, Helen, don't be so hasty. You didn't seem in that much of a hurry with your dirty tinker, did you? Tell me, what did he feel like when he was inside you? You don't have to tell me it felt good. I could see that by your face.' He tipped her head back so her eyes met his. 'I'd never noticed what a sensuous little mouth you had before. If I kissed you now, would

I taste the perfume of your quim on those full pink lips, mixed with the kisses of our peasant friend?' He moved a fraction closer.

Helen could feel his hot breath on her cheek. She shivered, feeling her colour rising. 'Please don't . . .' she whispered uncomfortably.

Max smiled again. 'Don't be so coy. I saw it all, Helen.' He nodded towards the viewing window into the dining-room, 'Perhaps you might be good company for our little bald friend in there but could you make him wait, I wonder? It seemed to me that you wanted it almost more than the tinker did. You really have turned out to be quite a surprise. I'd always wondered what it was that Charlie saw in you.' He stroked his finger around her lips. 'But now I understand. Inside that tight-lipped little wife there beats the heart of a true courtesan.'

Helen pulled away from his touch. 'What else do you want to show me?' she said, trying to hide her emotions. She didn't want him to see the bright tears that glistened in her eyes. If Charles had only fulfilled the dark raw need in her belly, Max would never have had the chance to catch her with Jack Hartman.

'Next, I think we will go to visit the major in the ballroom.' He extended her his arm. 'Will you permit me to guide you on a tour of my menagerie, my dear?' he whispered archly.

Without meeting his eyes, Helen slipped her arm through his. As they made their way back across the hall, he pulled an ornate fob-watch from his waistcoat, 'I do hope we aren't too late for their grand finale.'

At the top of a flight of stairs, Max led Helen onto a

small balcony which overlooked the polished wooden dance floor below. He tucked a chair beneath her and settled himself down in the shadows, his eyes bright with anticipation.

Helen had only been in the ballroom once before – at Christmas, at another of Max's parties – when the little balcony had housed a small orchestra. The room was magnificent with great swags of gilded plasterwork and a central row of ornate crystal chandeliers.

It occurred to Helen, as she glanced out onto the ballroom below, that she and Charles had left early on Christmas Eve. Had Max's friends indulged their passions that night? She let the memories filter back: the beautiful Christmas tree, the candles, the glittering elegant dancers as they had glided around the floor to the lilt of a Brahms waltz. She had felt overawed by the rich beautiful people. Thinking back now she also remembered the half-glimpsed looks between the couples, the soft murmurs behind raised hands, the way they had moved – yes, of course, they had been planning their discreet indulgences. How could she have been so naive as to miss the signs?

Max seemed unaware that her mind was elsewhere. His glittering eyes fixed on something at the far end of the huge room. A strange shape moved gracefully in a circle of lamplight. As Helen focused her attention on the shapes she nearly called out when she realised what they were.

Three shadowy figures moved in a delicate erotic ballet. A naked woman, crouching on all fours, was being impaled at the rear by a large red-faced man. He grunted with pleasure at each stroke. Helen instantly recognised him as the major Max had referred to. In the woman's mouth rested the sizeable cock of another man, who Helen had met briefly at dinner.

The woman was voluptuous, with a mass of golden tumbling hair that hung in slick damp coils over her shoulders and back. She arched upwards, revealing her large swaying breasts, bringing the man in her mouth with her. He moaned softly, pressing himself deeper between her moist lips. She seemed completely absorbed in the heady task of bringing her two riders to the edge of heaven. Each man had his eyes firmly on the other, as if they were drinking in each other's pleasure. The major's hands stroked the woman's ample hips, much as he might stroke a favourite horse, whilst his tall partner toyed distractedly with the woman's engorged nipples.

Max pulled Helen closer so that he could whisper in her ear. She flinched as his fingers closed tightly around her arm. 'I've often thought these chaps would prefer it if there were no filly between them,' Max murmured, 'but you know how strange men can be about these things. This way they can convince themselves what a pair of bucks they really are. See how they look at each other—'

Helen's eyes were firmly on the tight muscular buttocks of the man with his cock in the woman's mouth. They clenched dramatically, pressing his phallus deeper and deeper between her compliant lips. The woman's eyes were closed in ecstasy, her expression blissful and enraptured as she matched the two men's thrusts stroke for stroke.

Helen realised, with a start, how narrow her experience of love and sex truly was. She had no idea things like this were possible. Until she'd met Jack, no man had used his tongue on her sensitive fragrant sex, nor did she have any idea that a woman could use her lips and mouth on a man.

She thought about Jack's mouth delicately pressed against her, his tongue prising her apart to seek out the little throbbing bud folded deep between her inner lips. She shivered, thinking what magic there was to be experienced – what heady delights were possible.

She wondered, as she watched the eager contorted expression on the tall man's face, what it would be like to take a cock into her mouth. The idea made her shudder with expectation – as in her mind she imagined Jack guiding her lips to his hard thick sex.

Below them, the two riders shuddered, both teetering close to the brink of release. The major suddenly let out a throaty triumphant yell and thrust deeper into the woman. It was too much for his fellow jockey, who threw back his head and, grabbing tight hold of the woman's breasts, pulled himself closer, his face contorted by pleasure.

Helen could see the waves of their mutual orgasm sweep through the trio. The woman instinctively dropped her belly. Her body was flushed and hot as she pressed back against the major's thighs, drinking in each last flurry, each last ripple of his delight. Meanwhile her tongue and lips worked desperately on his companion. Each thrust and counterthrust of the three lovers became exaggerated and fierce, as if they were intent on destroying each other with pure passion.

Helen could feel the heat growing between her legs, as if she could feel the deep press of the major's cock sliding into the deepest recesses of the woman's sex. She licked her lips, suddenly transported into the plump woman's body. This time she did not flinch when Max lifted his fingers to stroke her throat. She was almost unaware as his hands dropped lower, stroking softly at the hard peaks of her nipples where they brushed against the thin fabric of her dress.

She heard him sigh with pleasure and instantly snapped back to reality, blushing when she realised Max was watching her with undisguised interest. His fingers, teasing at the soft curve of her breasts, only heightened the sense of excitement that was growing in her belly. Their eyes locked.

Beneath them, on the ballroom floor, the trio collapsed down onto each other, the air heavy and alive with their sobs and stifled cries of pleasure.

'Come along,' Max whispered, holding out his hand. 'Time we moved on, I think.' Gratefully Helen slipped away from him and headed back out onto the landing.

As they walked through the huge house, it seemed to be silent and empty. Helen looked down into the great shadowy hall, knowing that hidden behind the closed doors of the sumptuous rooms, Max's friends were all chasing their own particular wild brand of pleasures. She shivered. The conflict of her curiosity and embarrassment made her feel uncomfortable and ill at ease.

Max sensed her hesitation. 'Well, what do you think of my little zoo, then?' he said softly. Helen shook her head wordlessly and fell into step behind him. There was nothing she could say.

Next they moved to one of the guest bedrooms. Even from outside Helen could hear strange cries of excitement. Max guided her towards yet another vantage point; a small grating set into the wall on a servants' corridor. He pulled Helen close to him, so close that she could smell his cologne and a hint of cigars and brandy.

'Here we are,' he whispered. 'Our beloved judge. Wouldn't you agree his new outfit becomes him better than his silks and that awful dusty old wig?'

Helen pressed her face against the grille, knowing that she was truly curious to see what was going on inside. She took in the scene in seconds and then swung away, her face flushed crimson. 'Is this some kind of joke?' she managed to stutter.

Max grinned, moving closer to the grating, 'Not as far as our dear friend the judge is concerned.' As he spoke he flinched, as from inside the room they heard a short yelp of pain. Helen looked again, shaking her head in disbelief.

Inside the room, a distinguished-looking gentleman, wearing nothing but a school cap and stout boots, was bent double over a piano stool. His large fleshy buttocks glowed pink in the lamplight while, behind him, a formidable woman still in her evening dress, was administering a blistering spanking with a carpet slipper.

At each stroke the judge yelped ferociously and then said how sorry he was that he'd caused the woman so much trouble. The woman's only response was to draw the slipper back again and bring it down with a resounding crack on his already livid buttocks. As the slipper found its mark the judge snorted, every part of him tensing. His face grew redder as he mumbled his apology again and braced himself for the next blow. Between his legs, his excitement was obvious. The woman's face was impassive, only her bright eyes revealing her delight.

Shaking her head, Helen turned away. 'You have some extremely strange friends,' she said to Max, who was still glued to the grating.

Max grinned. 'My very own menagerie of delights,' he whispered and took her hand. They walked back towards the main stairwell.

Back on the landing Max hesitated for a few seconds, 'I wonder,' he murmured. 'I'm sure Liddy will have finished with that blistering bore, Bracken. She's probably back in her own room by now.'

Helen stared up at him. Lydia had to be involved in his strange obsession. There was no way it could take place without her involvement or her approval. Helen blushed, 'Liddy? Are you going to check up on her?'

Max raised an eyebrow, 'Not exactly; come with me.'

On the next floor, he opened another door and they stepped into what looked like a little boxroom. It was soon obvious to Helen that in fact they had stepped into a viewing area through which Lydia's bedroom was clearly visible.

'Is this another painting?' she whispered, pointing to the sheet of glass that divided the room from Liddy's bedroom beyond.

Max shook his head, 'No, it's a two-way mirror. It looks perfectly ordinary from the other side.' As he spoke, Liddy appeared from a side door, dressed luxuriously in a cream silk nightgown, trimmed with feathers. She peered into the mirror and pulled a face, slipping two clips into the little curls either side of her face. It seemed that she was oblivious to the fact that she was being watched. She moved across to her dressing-table and took out a large pot of face cream.

Max touched Helen's arm. 'Unfortunately we have missed the main event here,' he whispered with a trace of regret in his voice. 'I think you would have enjoyed watching Liddy. She is extremely impressive when she is in her element.'

Helen shivered, wondering what it might be that Liddy did which fascinated her husband so much.

Once out into the main house again, Max seemed preoccupied and Helen wondered if she would be able to slip away. Just as the thought formulated in her mind, Max swung round. His eyes had darkened to intense glittering pools. 'Ah well,' he purred softly, almost to himself. 'It seems that it is just you and I now. Nothing else appeals to my sense of adventure tonight.' He looked her over thoughtfully and repeated slowly, 'Just you and I.'

Helen shuddered under his undisguised scrutiny.

'I think it's time, dear Helen, that you paid for your little indiscretion this evening.' He paused, letting his eyes move slowly over her body.

Helen stepped away from him, a sense of panic growing in her stomach. 'Doesn't all this count as an indiscretion?' she said, lifting her hands to indicate the Hall. 'All your friends, busy – ' she faltered, trying to find words to describe the events that were going on under his roof, ' – indulging their strange passions.'

Max smiled thinly, 'Ah, but there is a difference, my dear. All my friends are *very* discreet. We belong to a closed group, a select band of hedonists, a class apart – unlike your dalliance tonight with that tinker. Or perhaps he is closer to your mark than you'd have us believe. Do you prefer your lovers to be a little rough?'

Helen flushed scarlet with anger. 'How dare you?' she snapped. 'Are you and Charles both so ashamed of me? Does my background upset you so much?'

Max gave her a puzzled look and then laughed, 'Ashamed of you, is he? My God, I wouldn't be ashamed of you if you were my wife. I would relish and encourage your little foibles. I can't believe young Charlie is such a snob. Do you really think he is?'

Helen reflected. The answer to Max's question was 'yes' but now, after her antics with Jack in the laundry room, Charles would have every right to be ashamed of her. His name brought the image of his strained face into her mind. She couldn't imagine what he would have said if he'd discovered her making love to Jack.

She looked back at Max. 'I don't think he would be so amused,' she said flatly.

Max threw back his head and roared with laughter. 'Then best we get on with what I have in mind for you.

Once it's over, we will consider the little matter of the tinker closed. Though –' he paused and let his eyes move back over her body, ' – perhaps next time Liddy and I have a party you might care to join us? I'm sure there would be several of my friends who'd be only too delighted to take you under their wing. They're always keen to welcome new blood—'

Helen shivered.

Max took her hand and led her along the panelled corridor. Helen tried to control the growing sense of unease building in her belly as Max unlocked a heavy door and drew her inside. She swallowed hard, looking around the shadowy room as Max closed the door quietly behind them.

'Here, let me help you take off your clothes,' he whispered, stepping closer. She could feel his hot breath on her bare shoulders and shuddered.

'Max—' she began, wrapping her arms protectively round her body.

His voice was colder now, with a brittle edge. 'That was not a request, Helen. Come here.'

She felt a surge of fear, knowing that Max didn't intend to leave her until he had exacted his punishment. She whimpered nervously as his fingers struggled over the fastening of her dress. He worked slowly, his mouth pressing against her neck and spine. The touch of his hot wet lips on her naked skin made her quiver.

As the dress glided down over her chest she grabbed it, trying to cover herself. Max sighed. 'Let it fall,' he said very quietly. Looking down at the floor, hot tears welling up in her eyes, she let the fabric slide down between her fingers to the floor.

His hands cupped her small uptilted breasts. His touch was almost cold. He began to nip at the delicate buds. She gasped, afraid and at the same time astounded as her nipples hardened under his fingers. Deep inside she could feel her excitement stirring.

Self-consciously she stepped away. 'Please Max . . .' she whispered. 'I really can't do this. Please let me go.' She glanced at him, afraid to catch his eye in case her face betrayed the bright flares of excitement glowing inside her. 'I have to go,' she began again.

He ignored her voice; instead his eyes roamed across her breasts and slim figure with proprietorial pride. 'My God, you are so beautiful,' he hissed on an outward breath, drinking in her exposure. Helen blushed furiously, her hands instinctively lifting to cover her breasts.

'No, don't do that,' Max snapped, 'I want to look at you. Turn round. Slowly.'

Helen lowered her eyes, unable to deny him what he wanted. Flushing scarlet, she let her hands drop and began to turn round. As she did so, Max turned up the lamp. She could feel his eyes on her, travelling over her, down to the soft swell of her sex, outlined against the thin silk of her knickers. She felt like a trapped animal, desperately aware of her vulnerability and yet at the same time strangely excited. The paradox unnerved her.

'Come to me,' he whispered.

She bit her lip and moved closer, fighting the

compelling instinct to run away. He slipped his fingers into the soft folds of her drawers, sliding them down over the swell of her hips. They slithered down over her thighs, gathering in a soft puddle round her feet. He took her hand and she stepped out of them.

'There,' he said. 'Now, that wasn't so bad, was it?' She looked up at him, trying to control her trembling body. He grinned. 'Why, Helen Garrison,' he said softly, 'I do believe you might actually be enjoying this.' She closed her eyes and bit her lip, horrified that he could detect the white-hot pulse of excitement amongst her fear and confusion.

'Don't fight what you feel,' he murmured, 'there is no shame in taking pleasure, Helen. Give yourself to me. Let me posses you.' His fingers traced the tight dark buds of her nipples, caressing her belly, her shoulders, as he circled round her like a tiger.

She swallowed a sob as she felt his eyes and fingers examining every part of her with great interest. It felt as if he were a collector and she was an exhibit. She gasped as his fingers closed over her sex and realised, with blinding clarity, that he saw her as another part of his exotic menagerie. She was just one more creature for him to observe and enjoy.

As he slid a finger inside her she whimpered. Inside the soft sensitive folds she knew she was still moist from Jack's lips and love-making.

Max grinned, wiping the juices over her thighs. 'You will really have to pay for all this excitement,' he purred. 'Here, let me have your hands.'

Helen held them out in front of her, lifting them

slowly, desperately trying to keep them steady. Max slipped his hand into his pocket and produced a long leather strap.

Helen gasped, feeling a subtle mixture of fear and anticipation. The thought of being bound excited something deep inside her and – at the same time – the realisation shocked her. Instinctively, as he moved closer, she pulled away, fighting her own excitement as much as Max's intentions.

Far from annoying him, it seemed to delight Max more. His eyes sparkled as he grabbed her, holding her wrists tight in one hand, while with the other he started to loop the soft leather around them.

She struggled without thinking, feeling the strength of Max's body as he fought to hold onto her and the soft caress of the leather. She screamed out, dragging herself away from him, her breathing coming in ragged gasps. Max gritted his teeth, his expression grim and determined as he jerked her closer. She wriggled, pulling backwards and forwards against his grip on her.

Finally, he succeeded in sliding the loop of leather tight, binding her hands together at the wrist, then wrapping it around again and again until she was totally helpless. He looked across at her triumphantly, sensing her fear and also – she realised once again – her growing sense of arousal.

'There we are,' he said, panting from his exertions. 'Now you are truly mine. Truly free.'

'What do you mean?' she gasped. 'How can being tied up make me free?'

Max grabbed hold of the leather thong and dragged

her into the centre of the room. He grinned. 'You shouldn't underestimate the freedom I'm giving you, Helen. You have no choice now. No control – you're free to enjoy what I have to give you.' He glanced up above her. Helen followed his eyes. Set into one of the ceiling beams was a large meat hook; beneath it stood a low solid wooden block.

She let out a thin high-pitched squeal. Her eyes were bright with terror as he grabbed her around the waist and lifted her onto the platform, dragging her arms above her head so that the hook slipped between the leather strap. The metal felt cold against her hot skin. Secured, standing on tiptoe, her shoulder muscles screamed out in protest.

Max stepped back to admire his new creature, his face reverting to an impassive mask. Only his eyes betrayed his excitement. He stepped away from her, slipping off his dinner jacket. 'My, my, aren't you a pretty sight?' he whispered, appreciatively. 'I can't imagine why I didn't see the possibilities in you before. You really are quite delightful.'

Helen jerked her hands against the hook. There was no way she could resist Max now. He grinned as she felt tears stinging her eyes. She was confused by the strange sense of elation and excitement her exposure and the bite of the leather lit in her belly.

She watched with peculiar fascination as Max undid the buttons of his shirt and slid it over his broad shoulders. His skin was lightly tanned, his strong muscular torso covered with a sprinkling of dark hair, belying his dissolute lifestyle. She swallowed hard;

Max's body was magnificent and she knew then that she was lost. The subtle blend of fear and arousal was almost too much to understand. She shivered, unable to tear her eyes away from his body.

'You rather like what you see, don't you?' he said softly, stepping into the pool of light that surrounded the block. 'You can't deny it, I can see it in your eyes.'

Helen swallowed again, embarrassed that her face so easily betrayed her. She struggled to retain her composure.

Max stroked her naked skin, touching her breasts, circling her flat stomach. She shivered as he knelt in front of her, his fingers running over the swell of her calves, moving across her thighs. She closed her eyes and finally let the sensations take her completely; the compulsion to surrender to Max's caresses was overwhelming.

Max Garrison smiled as he felt Helen's body relax beneath his fingertips. He drank in the heady possibilities of her willing surrender. She truly was a surprise. Her blue eyes had betrayed her fear and, yes, the unmistakable signs of excitement. How delicious.

She was still wearing her stockings, tied tight around her slender thighs with little blue lacy garters. He pressed his lips to the frills, thinking about the tableau in the laundry room with the tinker, when she had been similarly dressed. The constriction of her pale flesh delighted him and, below, those little high-heeled boots. He sighed, and wondered how it was he had not recognised her appeal before. He lifted her feet, one at a time, slipping off the boots, pleased that he had left the little leg chains beside the block.

She did not resist him as he slipped the restraints around her ankles. Carefully he adjusted the block so that she was resting on the balls of her feet. No need, he thought to himself with amusement, for her to be too uncomfortable. Secured either side of the plinth, the chains held her legs apart, giving him free access to her body – a delightful thought.

Beneath his fingers he could sense the delicate tremors of her fear; her breath was shallow and expectant. She *was* excited by his ministrations, however much she tried to hide it – and he would take the greatest of delight in showing her the pleasures that lay ahead. Kneeling between her legs he could smell the heady ocean musk of her sex. Clinging to the dark shiny hairs around her quim were tiny beads of creamy moisture. He lifted his fingers to caress her there, opening the heavy outer lips to reveal the moist pink folds within.

He was charmed that his caresses should follow so close after those of the unknown tinker. He planted a single moist kiss at the junction of her lips, just letting his tongue slide for a split second between them. She tasted divine.

Above him, Helen jerked against the ties, a thin silvery moan trickling from between those plump pink lips as he found her clitoris. Her eyes were closed, her face wearing the same ecstatic expression he had seen in the laundry room.

He sighed sadly. He may be a cad but he drew the line at making love to his brother's wife – however great the temptation – and Helen really was a temptation. But there were other things he could do to her. Things that would show her who was truly the master of Garrison Hall, things that would ensure that instead of turning her attentions to strangers, she restricted her games to those in his circle.

He could imagine her with Bracken and then there was the peer downstairs in the dining-room with the blonde woman and, of course, there were the others. He smiled at this new turn of events. Even if he couldn't allow himself to enjoy her hot eager little body he could certainly benefit from her obligation to him in other ways. First though, he would punish her for the scintillating little misdemeanour with the tinker; she had to know what was acceptable sport.

He pushed himself to his feet, tearing his concentration away from the temptation of her gaping and engorged sex, and picked up his dinner jacket. Inside one pocket was a large paisley handkerchief. Much as he wanted to watch her face he thought it would add another little *frisson* to the proceedings if his little sister-in-law were blindfolded.

She whimpered when he stepped up beside her and slipped the cloth over her eyes and struggled deliciously against her restraints. Each twist revealed another delicate secret place. Her little rounded breasts were flushed and swollen, her nipples dark and erect. Oh yes, he could find a lot of ways to enjoy her for a very long time to come and he sensed – despite her struggles

– that she might well enjoy the obligation of being at his beck and call.

Slowly he stepped across the room and poured himself a drink. It would do her good to wait. Helen strained against the leather ties. He smiled – this really was going to be very enjoyable. Sipping his drink, he opened one of the cupboards in the room. Inside were a selection of whips and riding crops. He let his fingers stroke each one speculatively; most were old friends. Best, he thought, if he chose something light and delicate. He didn't want to hurt Helen too much, just to teach her a lesson she wouldn't forget. Besides, what would she tell Charlie if he left her bruised?

He selected an old favourite, something he had bought when he'd first married Liddy. He grinned – it was ironic that he should break both of them in with the same whip. He flexed it gently. Its end was split into chamois strands, so soft to touch that it almost tickled as he ran his fingers through it, but oh, how it stung when used in the right way.

He stepped back to the block and the enticing image of the bound, blindfolded Helen. She stood very still, trying to listen to him, her whole body tense and knotted. Between her breasts he could see a light gloss of perspiration rising.

As he let the end of the whip trail across the pert upturned peaks of her nipples, she gasped. Her whole body seemed to concentrate on its soft teasing caress. He let it trail around her. He stroked it across her waist, around her hips, down over the swell of her sex, walking around her as he did so, relishing her reactions as she

87

tried to work out what the touch was.

Could she guess? He thought not. As he stepped behind her she suddenly began to struggle, desperately trying to turn around. It was as if she thought facing him would let her see what he was planning.

For an instant it seemed as if her body relaxed. In that split second Max drew the end of the whip back and flicked it around in a sharp tight arc, landing the first blow squarely on Helen's ripe rounded buttocks. She let out a strangled scream of terror and pain, her body thrashing around as he laid the head of the whip back for the second stroke. Her body jerked forward, exposing the open moist lips of her quim, pink and soft above the tight puckered closure of her backside. Max licked his lips and brought the whip down again.

Inside Helen's body and mind, the first kiss of the whip exploded like a pistol shot, sending a searing white-hot pain through every fibre of her body. The pain was like a liquid burn, spreading out in a great wave from where it had landed.

She lunged forward, away from its bitter caress, losing all control as her instincts took over, bucking and thrashing to escape Max's punishment. Deep inside her mind she struggled with the growing sense of paradox; the pain and the humiliation were exhilarating. Tears flooded down her face, soaking the handkerchief, as the excitement mounted in the pit of her belly. She sobbed with fear and desperate confusion but before she could gather her thoughts the whip struck again. Its blistering kiss momentarily drove away all logic and she surrendered to the engulfing sensations.

All her consciousness seemed to centre on the raw glow in her buttocks and the electric charge that was growing between her legs. The whip found its mark again and she screamed, submitting totally to Max's punishment and her own desire. Behind her, above her sobs, she could hear the whip as it cut through the still air and she cried out as it bit, once again, into her tender flesh. All rational thoughts finally ceased as she concentrated on the hiss of the whip head as Max swung it again and again.

At last there was stillness. She strained to listen to her captor, still bracing herself for another blow, her breath raw and gasping. Her whole body felt as if it was alight and glowing. Behind her she could hear Max's breathing as he moved closer and closer to her. She tensed, waiting for his next move and was startled to feel him reaching up to undo her hands. She could smell the bitter scent of his sweat and shivered as his chest brushed against her naked back.

'It's all right. Gently, gently,' he whispered, as she felt his fingers moving up over her.

Once free she had to struggle to stop herself from falling. Every muscle in her back and arms screamed in protest. Max's hands moved back over her body, holding her tightly under the arms, guiding her down onto all fours on the plinth.

Helen thought it was over and sighed. He would free her feet next – she clutched the side of the wooden plinth waiting to feel his fingers on her ankles. Instead she sensed him moving in front of her. She heard the sounds of his fly buttons being undone and froze. Her mind was flooded with memories of the woman in the ballroom.

'There we are, my dear, your final prize for tonight's little crime,' he purred. Slowly he began to move towards her.

She gasped but did not resist as Max tipped her head towards him and brushed his thick swollen cock against her lips. Without thinking she opened her mouth to take him in. From above she heard a little grunt of satisfaction and was immediately shocked at how hard his cock felt in her mouth. The moist salty taste of his excitement on her tongue made her shiver.

Instinctively she lifted her hands to caress him. Her fingers folded tight around the base of his shaft, cupping his balls, working his foreskin back and forth along his slick engorged phallus. She drew in the recollections from the ballroom, thinking about the woman's face and engulfing lips – and aped the movements without hesitation.

Above her, she heard Max moan and renewed her efforts, nibbling, sucking, taking more and more of him between her lips. She relished the sensation of submission; not fighting the strange fantasies that bubbled up in her mind of master and maid, slave and lord. She felt her own excitement growing and began to move her whole body rhythmically in time with her mouth and fingers.

Max let out a long shuddering sigh of pleasure and pushed fiercely into her caress. 'My God, you're good,' he hissed.

Finally she tasted the salty prelude of his orgasm pressing up between her lips. Pushing aside her fear, she lapped at him, running her tongue around the slick engorged crown, drawing it deep into her mouth. She felt him buck, heard him gasp and lock his fingers into her hair.

'Yes,' he snorted. 'Yes . . .' jerking her closer still.

She was rewarded a split second later by the hot splash of his seed flooding her mouth. Beneath her fingers she felt the electric throb of his orgasm shuddering through her.

After a few second he slipped from her mouth and at once she felt exposed and ashamed. She was aware again of the glowing ache in her buttocks and the desperate soreness in her arms and shoulders – but, above every other sensation, she was aware that her body demanded satisfaction.

'Please,' she whispered, between her slick lips, 'please, Max. Don't leave me like this.'

Close by she heard Max's dry breathless laugh. 'You want more, do you, Helen? My God, I really am sorry I didn't discover you years ago,' he said throatily.

Helen, despite her blindfold, felt herself blush. She knew no words to describe what it was she wanted, but her body knew. It cried out for completion of the spiral of excitement Max had started within her. Her breasts ached to be caressed and longed for the feeling of a lover's lips closing around their swollen peaks. Between her legs, she could feel the slick juices of excitement trickling out onto her thighs, her clitoris was alight and throbbing. She whimpered unhappily.

Max laughed again, running his hand across her naked back. 'It does seem a great shame to leave you high and dry like this, but even I draw the line at rogering my brother's wife – however tempting. Here, let me get your legs free.'

She sobbed, horrified that he was denying her satisfaction.

Max pressed a tender kiss between her damp shoulder-blades. 'Let's call it the last of your punishment, shall we, Helen?' he said thickly.

Tenderly he undid the paisley scarf and the restraints around her ankles. She collapsed onto the block. With gentle hands Max turned her over, his eyes heavy with tiredness and sated desire. 'The game's over now. You'd better get yourself dressed and hurry home to young Charlie. I'm sure he'll give you what it is you need so badly.'

Helen felt the pulse rise in her throat as she struggled unsteadily to her feet. 'Oh no,' she muttered, blushing furiously, 'No, I can't go home tonight.'

Max looked at her with surprise and his expression held a question.

Helen hurried around the room, still naked, picking up her clothes. 'I really can't go home,' she repeated in desperation. 'Please, Max, can't I stay here tonight?'

She saw the truth dawning slowly on Max's face. 'You're not like this with Charlie, are you?' he said steadily, watching his sister-in-law with renewed interest.

Helen froze, standing up slowly to face him. She shook her head, tears pricking up in glistening shards behind her eyes. 'No, but Charles is not like this with me either,' she said unsteadily, glancing back at the block and the discarded whip.

Max smiled thinly. 'What a dreadful waste of talent,' he said. 'I can see now why you were tempted by the charms of our little tinker friend. Here, would you like a drink?'

Helen took the glass from him, her hands unsteady, her eyes anxious and bright. 'I really can't go home tonight,' she said softly, draining the glass.

Max took it from her and stood it back on the tray. 'No, perhaps not,' he murmured thoughtfully.

Tears began to trickle down her face, 'I need . . .' she began, still unable to find a word that expressed the hot glistening desire that still burnt inside her. 'I need more,' she spluttered unhappily.

Max nodded and opened his arms to her. 'I understand. Come here, Helen. Let me take you where you need to go,' he whispered. His voice was low and gentle.

Helen shuddered and stepped into Max's waiting arms. Even if her rational mind denied it, she knew that Max understood exactly what it was her body cried out for. She felt the press of his cock, renewed and eager, against her belly and groaned in anticipation.

He pulled her closer, his mouth seeking hers, his tongue prising her lips apart. His fingers moved to her sex, slipping inside her, seeking out the hard engorged ridge of her clitoris. She whimpered as he brushed over its sensitive hood and closed her eyes, letting the heady sensations engulf her. Blinking back the tears, she sank slowly to the floor, grateful to be in the arms of her unlikely ally.

Something disturbed Helen, even though she knew she was asleep. A change of light, the sound of breathing close by, something pulled her away from her dreams. Instantly she was awake and aware that she was lying in a huge ornate bed in one of the guest rooms at Garrison Hall. Every muscle in her body ached and her waking mind was instantly flooded with intense memories of the previous night.

Her final recollection was of Max bringing her to the guest room after they had made love and gently pulling the blankets up around her shoulders before he'd gone back to his own room.

From the window opposite the bed, a broad shaft of early morning sunshine filled the room with a peculiar snow-kissed light. She took a deep breath and turned over slowly only to come face to face with the brooding stormy eyes of her husband.

Charles Garrison, glowering at her from the bedside, was dressed in his outdoor clothes. His hat and muffler looked incongruous against the backdrop of the luxurious bedroom.

'Would you kindly like to explain to me what is happening to you, Helen?' he said slowly. 'Why didn't you come home to the Lodge last night?' His voice was tight with repressed anger. Helen felt her colour drain, while beneath the heavy coverlet her body ached from Max's attentions.

Chapter 4

The Lodge

Helen pulled the linen sheets up around her shoulders, trying hard to control her emotions before she spoke. What could she say to him? She was afraid that Charles would be able to guess by the way she moved or the way she spoke that she had betrayed him. She licked her lips, her mouth felt dry and tense.

Charles moved closer, his face contorted with fury. 'My God,' he hissed. 'Are you wearing a nightgown underneath that sheet?'

Helen shook her head.

Charles threw his hat on the bed, 'Well, that just about takes the biscuit, Helen. What in heaven's name would Liddy or Max think if they could see you like that? What were you thinking of?'

Helen stared at him incredulously. 'What?'

'What sort of woman do you think goes to bed like that?' He paused, the colour rising in his cheeks. He flapped his hand in her direction, 'You know, with nothing on.'

Helen swallowed hard. This is totally ridiculous, she

thought, pulling the sheet up higher around her bare shoulders. 'I can't believe you said that, Charles. What was I supposed to do?'

Charles bit his lip, struggling to keep control of his anger. 'Come back to the Lodge as you said you would, you knew I wasn't feeling well,' he hissed. 'At the very least you should have asked Liddy to find you something to wear. What if someone had come in during the night? Did you think of that? The Hall is full of their friends, anyone could have walked in. I suggest you get yourself dressed and come home with me.' He glanced at his watch. 'You realise, of course, that I've missed the eight-thirty service because of you.'

As he spoke there was a knock on the bedroom door. Charles jumped as if he'd been shot. 'I'm afraid you can't come in,' he snapped, glaring at Helen. 'My wife isn't decent.'

The door swung open slowly to reveal Liddy, standing in the doorway, dressed in a blue silk pyjama suit. Helen couldn't help noticing how Charles' eyes moved quickly across the other woman's body, drinking in the details of her undress.

Lydia puffed greedily at her cigarette in its holder and smiled at her brother-in-law. 'Oh, for goodness' sake, don't be such a stuffed shirt, Charles, darling,' she whispered disarmingly.

Charles blushed scarlet and started to fiddle with his scarf. 'Er, good morning, Liddy, dear,' he muttered.

Lydia smiled. 'Don't I get a morning kiss?' she said, tipping her head provocatively in his direction.

Helen watched as Charles, scarlet with embarrassment, stepped forward and brushed his lips lightly against her cheek.

Liddy turned towards Helen. 'Good morning,' she said pleasantly. 'Max told me you'd decided to stay overnight and all the sorry, sorry details.'

Helen suppressed a gasp, wondering what it was that Max had told her.

Lydia continued, poking Charles teasingly in the chest. 'Helen was a great help last night. Apparently Max didn't feel very well either.' Lydia paused. 'I wonder if perhaps the salmon was the problem. I'll have to have a word with cook. Anyway, by the time she'd helped sort him out, she asked if she could stay here as it was so late. The dedicated little creature was worried she'd wake you up if she got someone to drive her home.' She glanced at Helen's naked shoulders, 'You could have popped along to my room and borrowed what you needed.'

Helen let out a sigh of relief. 'I didn't want to disturb anyone,' she said carefully.

Liddy looked back at her. 'Oh, you wouldn't have done that, darling,' she purred.

'I told you, didn't I?' Charles blustered at Helen. 'I can't believe she slept in the buff. I mean, I ask you.'

Liddy rolled her eyes heavenwards, 'Charles, darling, don't make such a fuss, there's no harm done. Besides, sleeping as nature intended is all the rage in Paris. Why don't you and I go and find Max and let Helen get dressed in peace?'

As she slipped her arm through Charles' and guided

him from the room she glanced back over her shoulder at Helen. 'I've had my maid sort out something for you; your party dress is hardly suitable for Sunday breakfast.'

With a quiet click the door closed behind them and Helen threw herself back amongst the deep pillows, hardly able to believe that Liddy and Max, of all people, had come to her rescue.

A few seconds later there was a discreet knock on the bedroom door and the sound of Liddy's maid's voice. 'May I come in, ma'am?'

Helen smiled to herself. 'Yes, please do,' she said softly.

Breakfast was quite a subdued affair. By the time Helen had had a chance to wash and dress, most of the guests were sitting around the dining-table, cradling cups of tea and – apparently – quietly nursing the after-effects of the previous evening's revels.

As Helen helped herself to food from the sideboard she couldn't help notice the faces of the people she and Max had watched from their hidden vantage points. The judge, now sombrely dressed in a country suit, was picking at a plate of kedgeree. He looked the epitome of an English gentleman. His female companion, to his right, cradled her tea between large capable hands and stared out into the park. The trio of lovers sat close together but none spoke, while, at the far end of the table, the little peer and his blonde mistress were tucking into a hearty breakfast.

Helen smiled ruefully. They weren't the only ones

who needed time to recover. Her whole body was stiff and sore from Max's ministrations with the whip and between her legs she felt raw and bruised.

Max, Liddy and Charles were nowhere in sight. As Helen was about to take a seat at the table, the subdued air was suddenly broken by the sound of a raucous laugh from the hall, and the sound of Liddy's high-pitched, cultured voice. 'Oh Charles, you can be so silly,' she giggled. The doors of the dining-room flew open, framing the three other members of the Garrison family.

Max and Liddy were arm in arm, both laughing wildly, whilst Charles stood to one side, his expression strained and uneasy. Liddy lifted her arms to the assembled company. 'Good morning one and all,' she said warmly, 'I hope you all slept like babies.' There were murmured responses.

Max grinned as he picked up a plate, his gaze moving quickly around the table until his eyes rested on Helen. She felt herself colour, memories of the previous night filling her mind. She looked away quickly and concentrated on her plate but not before she saw his eyes twinkling mischievously. She swallowed hard. It was essential that she did not betray herself in front of Charles. Taking a deep breath, she returned Max's gaze.

'Good morning, Helen. I've just been telling Charlie how good you were to me last night.' Max lifted an eyebrow in amusement as she struggled to maintain her composure. 'I told him he really doesn't know what a lucky chap he is.'

Helen lifted her cup in salute. 'I hope you're feeling much better,' she said evenly, determined to keep her hand steady.

Max seemed delighted by her response. 'Indeed I am, my dear, the tonic you gave me last night seems to have cured all my ills.'

Liddy looked at them both with her sharp bright eyes. Helen could see that she was considering the possibility that Max's story was a fabrication. Helen held her gaze steadily and felt as if she almost sensed the instant when Liddy dismissed the idea she had been toying with as ridiculous.

Charles began to load his plate with sausage links. He glanced over his shoulder at the odd assortment of guests, 'There's a mid-morning service at St Luke's if anyone wants to come along with Helen and I.' No one moved or spoke. Charles slipped a grilled kidney alongside the sausages, 'The local rector is an absolutely wonderful chap, excellent sermons.' Still no one moved.

Max slapped him heartily on the shoulder, 'For goodness' sake, come and sit down, Charlie, and eat your breakfast while it's hot. I've been telling the judge about my new hunter, Saracen. I thought you might like to come down and take a look at him with us after breakfast.'

Charles pulled a face. 'I missed the early service,' he said, adding as if by way of explanation, 'Helen and all that.'

Helen smiled. 'I don't mind going on my own, Charles. It would do you good to get out for once without worrying about the farm. Don't you agree, Liddy?'

Liddy looked up from her conversation with a tall dark-haired woman at the far end of the dining-table. 'Oh yes,' she said, unaware of what she was agreeing to, 'absolutely.'

'Well, that's settled then,' said Max, picking up his knife and fork.

Helen glanced at him with gratitude. The last thing she needed was to be alone with Charles on the long cold walk to church. She desperately needed time to think.

'What sort of tonic was it Helen gave you?' Liddy was watching Max's face in her bedroom mirror as they both changed to go out into the grounds.

Max was struggling with his collar. 'Damn,' he snapped, as the tiny stud shot across the room.

Liddy smiled indulgently. 'Come here and let me help you.'

Max grinned, 'What would I do without you?'

Liddy snorted, patting her sleek blonde hair into place, 'Run off with a showgirl I should imagine.'

Max rested his hands on her shoulders, relishing the sensation of her cool alabaster skin beneath his fingertips. 'Helen didn't give me any medicine. I just said that to stop Charles whining. Did you see where that damned stud went?'

He dropped to his knees and felt under the dressing table, watching whilst Liddy leant forward to apply her lipstick. He smiled. Liddy was beautiful, there was no doubt about that, but he wondered reflectively what it would be like to be married to a woman who shared his intellect – as well as his hedonism. Helen's tiny features and shapely compliant body focused in his mind. She had been truly magnificent.

As if reading his thoughts, Liddy caught his eye in the mirror's reflection. 'You *are* telling me the truth about last night, aren't you, Max? You didn't have to prise Helen away from one of the gang, did you? I didn't think she looked herself this morning.' She watched his face closely.

Max crawled beside her and handed her the collar stud, 'Oh, come off it, Liddy, you're beginning to sound just like Charlie. I wouldn't look myself either if he'd been sounding off at me in that self-righteous tone of his.' He shivered as her long fingers stroked at the curve of his muscular neck. 'Besides nobody here would give Helen a second glance.' Which is their loss, he thought mischievously. 'Anyway, what are your plans for this morning?'

Liddy lifted a perfectly plucked eyebrow and then pouted playfully, 'A friend and I have planned a little stroll. I've asked the gamekeeper to light the fire over in the gun cottage.'

Max smiled, sliding closer to her. 'Really, are you and your friend planning to stop off to warm yourselves?' he purred.

Liddy giggled as he stroked her ankles, 'We might be.'

'Would you mind awfully if I happened to come that way and take a little peek later?'

Liddy stretched like a sleek wild cat, her eyes glistening. 'Mind? I was rather expecting it, darling.'

She stroked his cheek, 'Knowing I'm being watched and adored always adds a certain extra something to my passion. But what about Charlie and the judge? You did say you'd take them down to see Saracen.'

Max stood up to admire himself in the mirror, pulling his tweed jacket straight. 'I'll soon be done with those two. We'll take a quick walk down to the stables. I might get the lad to turn Saracen out for us and then I'm planning a long solitary walk, that – by sheer coincidence – will take me right past the gun cottage.'

Liddy smiled and stood beside him, admiring her own reflection. 'Will I do?' she purred, leaning provocatively against him.

In the mirror he could see her high uptilted breasts, outlined through the soft wool of her cream sweater. Liddy was a sensual masterpiece; the pale wool suit accentuated every curve of her ripe body. He slid his hands up over her thighs, dragging up the fabric as he moved closer. Beneath the narrow skirt, her sex was clearly visible through the sheer shimmering silk of her drawers. Max moaned softly, sliding his hand between her legs, relishing the heat and the promise of the moisture that lay beneath his fingertips.

'You really are magnificent,' he groaned, pressing his lips to hers. She returned his kiss, sliding her little tongue between his lips.

Max grimaced, feeling the familiar stirring in his groin.

'Ummm,' she gasped, stroking the hardness through his trousers. 'You must have had a good night, before you felt poorly.'

Max laughed, sliding his hand up over the mound of her quim. 'Oh, I did,' he whispered, 'a very, very good night. How about if we make our friend the judge and young Charlie wait a little while longer. Let me show you just how good it was?' He caught hold of her arms and steered her back towards the bed.

Liddy shivered deliciously and wriggled away from him, her eyes sparkling. 'It's such a shame, but I really am spoken for this morning. Though I am quite tempted to stay and take you up on your kind offer.' Her tone was teasing and affectionate. She picked her gloves up off the bed and turned toward him, 'Maybe later?'

'I'll hold you to that,' he said to her retreating figure.

She glanced back over her shoulder, 'I rather hoped you would.'

In the guest bedroom Helen found her clothes from the dinner party neatly folded and packed inside an overnight bag. She picked it up and glanced out of the window. She didn't want to see Charlie again before she left.

All that nonsense over the nightdress had completely thrown her. She shook her head, wondering what on earth could have been going through his mind. He had seemed far more concerned about her clothes and what people might think, than what might have happened to her. It hurt her that he was more upset by the inconvenience of coming to find her and missing church than whether or not she was safe.

On the landing she watched the guests as they left the dining-room. There was a low hum of conversation.

They all seemed so ordinary in daylight. The judge, with his arm linked through his female companion's, caught sight of her and lifted his hand in greeting. Helen smiled, wondering if Charles had any idea what went on in his brother's house after his famous dinner parties. Surely he must suspect something. How could he be unaware of the stolen glances, the whispers? She shivered, thinking about what his reaction might be if he knew the truth.

She hurried downstairs, ignoring the dull ache in her legs and back. Finding her coat hanging in the hall cupboard, she realised with horror it had been left down in the laundry room the night before. Without looking back, she hurried out into the snow and the avenue that would lead her home to Garrison Lodge.

Once clear of the Hall she slowed down, thinking about Max and wondering if perhaps Jack Hartman might still be somewhere around.

The morning was bright and crisp. Helen found her eyes drawn again and again to the bare trees that framed the park. Beyond the main open vista they spread into a copse. Perhaps Jack was still there, waiting for her.

She shivered. In her mind, the images of Jack and Max had blended to create a tantalising third imaginary lover. She pulled her coat tight around her and forced herself to look at the road ahead. In the distance she could see the smoke from the Lodge chimneys. Concentrating on the curling grey plumes rising in the still winter air she hurried home.

* * *

'Annie?' In the hallway Helen stood her case on the floor and slipped off her gloves.

Their maid bustled out from the kitchen, wiping her hands on her pinafore, 'Morning, Mrs Garrison. We were real worried about you last night. Are you all right?'

Helen lifted a hand in greeting, thinking how strange it was that her housemaid seemed more anxious about her than her husband. 'Thank you, but I'm fine, Annie, really.' She glanced up at the hall clock, 'I'm going to walk to the church. I should make it if I hurry. Mr Garrison's gone out to look at a horse with his brother. I'd be very grateful if you could light the fire in his study. I'm sure he'll be cold when he gets back.'

Annie nodded, 'Right you are, ma'am. Will there just be yourself and Mr Garrison for lunch?'

Helen nodded and then hurried upstairs to change.

Charles threw open the front door of the Lodge. 'Helen!' he called from the hallway.

He was frozen to the very core. The damned judge had insisted on seeing Max's new hunter put through his paces on the bottom paddock. God, it had been so cold out there.

Charles stamped the snow off his boots and glanced up at the hall clock. Even if he hurried now, by the time he'd changed, he would still miss most of the morning service.

'HELEN!' he bawled again into the shadowy house. The woman was really becoming quite impossible. She'd left the Hall before he'd had a chance to talk to her and now, when he needed her, she had vanished.

It was such a shame she wasn't more like Liddy. Now there was a woman who knew how to behave herself. She plainly adored Max and was always pleasant, never disconcerted by anything – and she always looked absolutely stunning. He thought about the little pyjama suit she'd been wearing up at the Hall that morning. Perhaps it was a little *avant garde* for his taste but even so – he licked his lips, thinking about the way her breasts had moved, fluidly, beneath the delicate shimmering silk. Quickly he took control of his thoughts; after all that was no way to think about his brother's wife, however damned tempting. Where had Helen got to?

He slipped his coat off as someone appeared in the hall. 'Finally,' he snapped. 'Where the hell have you been?'

Annie, the housemaid, stepped out into the light. 'I'm sorry, sir,' she began, her large brown eyes filling up with tears. 'I was in the kitchen helping cook.'

Instantly Charles felt contrite; he had no wish whatsoever to upset Annie, dear plump, compliant Annie.

She looked up at him anxiously. 'Mrs Garrison's already left for church, sir. She told me to light the fire in your study.'

Charles smiled thinly. 'Did she? Right, well in that case—' He paused, considering the possibility that Helen might well be gone some time. 'Did she take the car?'

Annie, still looking uncomfortable, shifting her weight uneasily from foot to foot, shook her head, 'No, sir, she said she was going to walk.'

Charles nodded, 'Good, very good. Well, in that case, Annie, I'd like you to come with me into the study for a little while. You do understand, don't you?' He thought fleetingly of Helen's prim face and her utter foolishness. He would show her just who was the boss.

The girl's eyes grew wider, 'Yes, sir,' she said flatly. 'Cook's now getting the dinner ready. I'll just have to tell her you'll be needing me for a little while—'

'Lunch, Annie,' corrected Charles, relishing the way she looked at him with a mixture of fear and awe. She nodded and scurried off into the depths of the house.

Charles slipped off his jacket and hung it up.

In his study there was a glorious fire roaring in the grate. He settled himself comfortably in his favourite arm chair and waited. Images of Annie's comfortable body filled his mind.

He shivered. Well, he thought, even if Helen had changed beyond all recognition he knew he could always depend on Annie to provide him with what he needed. He stretched and waited. He would deal with his wife later. From his chair he could hear the tip tap of the maid's feet coming along the corridor and then her timorous knock. 'Come in,' he said slowly, 'we have plenty of time.'

In Garrison Hall, Max was changing his wet boots. Damn the blasted judge. He knew Liddy was planning to leave just after they had gone down to the paddocks, but then again she didn't like to rush her pleasures. There should be plenty of time for him to catch up with her and her lover. He stretched and looked outside. The wide expanse of snow reflected the bright sunlight. An ideal morning for a brisk walk, he thought, grinning.

Above the trees he could see a curl of smoke that let him know Liddy was in the gun cottage; she liked to be warm and it looked as if she and her companion had just made up the fire. Plenty of time, he thought, and slipped off his damp socks. All in all, it was proving to be a very entertaining weekend.

Helen, sitting in St Luke's church, was stunned to find that the rector was just finishing his final blessing. The organist was playing an anthem and the congregation had already begun drifting from the pews towards the open church door. She looked around in surprise, realising with horror that she had spent the whole service deep in thought and certainly not thoughts that were appropriate in a church. She blushed, wondering if she had managed, somehow, to kneel and sing in the right places. No one seemed to be giving her a second glance so perhaps she hadn't disgraced herself after all. She began to gather her things together.

'Mrs Garrison?' Helen glanced up at the sound of her name. Dr Roberts, the local GP, smiled pleasantly down at her from beside the family pew. 'How nice to see you this morning.'

Helen nodded, 'Good morning, Doctor, how are you?'

The doctor, a man in his late fifties with a jovial comforting demeanour, smiled, 'Fit as the proverbial fiddle, my dear. I can't afford to be otherwise in my profession. I was wondering whether you might like a lift home? I'm on my way to the Vantons' Farm, it'll take me right past the Lodge.'

Helen smiled, 'That would be wonderful, if you're sure it's no trouble. It's very warm in here this morning.'

The man extended his arm, 'My pleasure, Mrs Garrison. It does seem as if the verger has finally mastered the vagaries of the boiler. What did you think of the sermon this morning?'

Helen blustered, 'Oh, I thought . . .' She paused, realising she hadn't heard a single word of it. 'I'm afraid I have to admit I wasn't paying much attention.'

The doctor chuckled. 'You didn't miss much, I always think our rector's oratory is a little over-rated. Wonderful news about my housekeeper's daughter though, don't you think?'

Helen flushed scarlet and the doctor smiled again, 'Don't tell me, your mind was elsewhere, so you didn't hear that either. Is there something I can do perhaps? Are you feeling indisposed?'

Helen shook her head, 'No, not at all, but it's very kind of you to ask. I was just thinking about other things.'

Seeing that Helen wasn't going to elaborate, the doctor nodded sagely and continued, 'She's got herself a job teaching English in Florence through some agency in London. It's a wonderful opportunity for her, wouldn't you say? Her mother is absolutely delighted.'

Helen nodded, 'I can imagine. Perhaps Charles mentioned I used to teach?'

The doctor smiled, 'No, though he did tell me once you'd met while working with the Red Cross.'

By now the congregation had thinned and Helen and the doctor made their way outside. The brightness came as a sharp contrast after the gloom of the church. The doctor led Helen to his car and, with remarkable speed, they set off along the winding country road that led back to Garrison Hall and the Lodge.

On Helen's insistence the doctor dropped her at the top of the Hall driveway, rather than take her right up to the house, so that he could go straight on to his call.

Helen stuffed her hands deep into her pockets and headed home. As she walked, her thoughts strayed back to the days she had spent in London before she met Charles.

It seemed such a long time ago now, a lifetime away. How could she have been so wrong about him? And then there was Max. She shivered, remembering the hypnotic hiss of the whip as it cut through the still air and the hot bite as it kissed her body. Every step reminded her of his attentions. And then there was Jack Hartman, with his compelling touch and his dark haunting eyes.

She stopped for a second and looked around at the familiar scenery and the elegant square lines of the Lodge. It felt as if, during the last two days, her whole life had suddenly been torn away and she'd been left with nothing but chaos and confusion and, even more unsettling, the strange knowledge that she relished the unexpected changes.

At the Lodge she opened the door quietly. If she was

lucky, perhaps Charles hadn't arrived home yet, or maybe he was safely installed in his study with the Sunday papers.

The house seemed very quiet, the clock's tick unnaturally loud in the empty hall. On the hall stand were Charles' coat and jacket. She sighed uneasily. No doubt he was holed up in the study waiting for her return, ready with another lecture.

She walked quietly along the corridor. Annie was nowhere in sight. It was strange that the girl hadn't heard the front door open.

'Please Mr Garrison, sir . . .' The words echoed along the corridor beside the stairs.

Helen froze. The voice was Annie's but the tone was peculiar, throaty and desperate. Helen slipped off her boots and crept closer to the door of Charles' study, which stood slightly ajar. What she saw inside made her head spin. She stared, unable to believe her eyes.

Annie, the maid, was naked, crouching on all fours on the hearth rug in front of the fire. Her heavy pendulous breasts swayed dramatically. Behind her, fully dressed, Charles knelt between her open legs. His fingers worked between the girl's meaty thighs, probing and pressing into the secret places of her body. As Charles moved closer, Annie shuddered, a guttural moan trickling between her open lips.

Helen felt a wave of horror and disbelief flood through her and almost gasped as she watched Charles unbutton his fly and guide his angry cock deep into Annie's firm body. Beneath him, Annie started to pant, her face contorted and fearful. Her capable hands clutched at the tufts in the hearth rug, bracing herself as Charles pushed himself deeper and deeper.

Charles' fingers locked in the girl's dark hair, encouraging her to take more of him into her. Annie wailed miserably.

Charles' glassy eyes fixed on the door. Helen stepped back, afraid that he might be able to see her, although she suspected his concentration was firmly on chasing his pleasure. His bright feverish eyes were unseeing and distant.

In the shadows Helen began to sway unsteadily, feeling faint and sick. The most startling image of the scenario was Charles' expression. There was a look of pure lust and pleasure on his usually closed and angry features. Helen rested against the door frame while, in the study, Charles pressed into Annie again and again, sliding his hands down to grab hold of the girl's rounded hips. His lips were open and slack, beads of sweat trickling down his face.

Helen pressed her forehead against the cool wood, trying to fight the hideous compulsion to keep watching. When she looked back, Charles, close to the point of no return, let out a long sobbing moan and tightened his grip on the girl's body.

Hearing his desperate excited cry, Annie stiffened, her dark eyes suffused with panic. 'Oh please, sir, no more, you'll get me caught,' she begged anxiously from beneath him. Charles jerked her back once more, his rough tweed suit a stark contrast to the pale curves of her ample thighs.

He looked down at her back with a mixture of

contempt and lust. 'Shut up, you stupid little bitch. I'll do exactly what I want with you, do you understand?' Charles snapped, and for one blinding moment Helen wondered if the words were meant for Annie – or for her.

Annie began to sob, trying to wriggle out from under Charles as he fought his way towards his climax. His fingers bit deep into her flesh, sliding forward to grab at her heavy hanging breasts. He seemed possessed as he plunged on and on, forcing the girl down onto her belly to accept him.

Helen watched with growing horror as tears flooded down Annie's face. Charles let out a strangled scream and lunged deep inside the girl. Helen held her breath as he wrenched himself out of her body and a great splash of thick silver seed spurted over Annie's ripe dimpled buttocks.

Gasping, he slumped back onto his haunches, his face sweating and flushed. 'Now get up and get dressed,' he mumbled to the stricken girl, who had collapsed onto the hearth rug. 'Clean yourself up. My wife will be home from church soon.' As he spoke he wiped his flaccid cock and tucked it back into his trousers.

Helen, totally stunned, stepped back into the shadows and picked up her boots. She had no desire to be discovered by either Annie or Charles. Glancing behind her to make sure neither of them had left the room, she rushed to the front door as quietly as she could, and let herself out.

She ran to the end of the driveway, her face livid, her eyes full of tears. 'How could he?' she murmured again and again, feeling an uneasy sensation in her gut. She couldn't forget the terrified face of their maid pinned beneath Charles. And as for Charles himself, she would never have guessed he was so full of lust. It was totally at odds with everything she believed about him and their life together. She let the tears trickle down her face. He had taken Annie, without thought, without feeling, dominating her because he saw her as a servant, a lesser mortal who he could use for his desires.

She shuddered. Had he anticipated doing the same to her? Is that why he had married her, only to discover that he couldn't bring himself to turn his wife into a compliant whore? It would explain his embarrassment in bed. Did he think about Annie when they made love? Or did his thoughts go elsewhere when he turned to her in the middle of the night?

She leant heavily against the gates of the estate, trying to regain her composure. The tears wouldn't stop. Everything had changed – everything. She glanced at her watch. After ten minutes she wiped away her tears and then very slowly retraced her steps to the Lodge.

At the front door, before she opened it, she called hello loudly into the quiet waiting house.

Annie stood in the hallway, now fully dressed, busy rearranging the coats on the hall stand. Helen found it hard to meet the girl's eyes; instead she said very quietly, 'Will you please tell my husband I've arrived back from church and that I've gone for a walk as the morning is so pleasant. I'll be back in time for lunch.'

Before Annie had time to reply, Helen shut the front

door and walked away, her face scarlet, her heart thumping in her chest.

Once out of sight of the Lodge she veered off under the cover of the trees. Her thoughts were jumbled and disjointed. Part of her still found it hard to accept what she'd witnessed in Charles' study. The Charles she knew was closed and dry, a passionless animal who left her feeling frustrated and alone. But the Charles she had seen in the study – she shivered, thinking again of his wild glassy eyes and his cock sliding home into Annie, cowering naked beneath him. It seemed as if everything she had believed to be true was just a series of lies.

The trees crowded in around her. Walking blindly, she suddenly realised she had no idea where she was. She had left the pathway and her progress was barred by a wet tangle of brambles. She glanced left and right. Surely it wouldn't be hard to retrace her steps?

Charles' angry face instantly appeared in her mind, quickly replaced by the expression of lust she had seen in the study. She didn't want to retrace her steps; she needed to be alone. She couldn't risk him finding her yet.

She turned along beside the brambles, in the direction that she thought might take her out into the main park, and tried hard to concentrate on finding a path. Between the trees she caught a glimpse of the Hall's roofs and, once sure of her bearings, turned back into the woods – she had no great desire to be discovered by Max either.

Deep in the copse she found a path that she knew

led to a little building known as the gun cottage. Max and Liddy used it as a base to serve lunch for shooting parties. What was it Jack had said? He'd been to the estate before to work as beater on the estate shoots. She felt a flicker of hope; he'd certainly know where the gun cottage was – perhaps he was there. Even as she thought it she saw the outlines of the little building between the trees and from the chimney rose a faint curl of smoke. Her heart leapt – he *had* decided to wait for her – she was certain of it now.

She broke into a run, hurrying between the trees. It was reckless of him to have lit the fire, someone might notice up at the Hall. Images of the fire made her think about their night in the pump house, the smell of wood smoke, the feeling of his body in hers. She took a deep breath, she needed him—

At the cottage door she hesitated, tidying her hair, trying to get a grip on her thoughts. Then from inside she heard a high-pitched throaty laugh – a female laugh – a laugh she would have recognised anywhere. Her hand froze on the door knob and she knew for certain that Jack wasn't inside. It was Liddy. She crept closer to the window, wondering if some strange twist of fate was leading her from one disturbing discovery to another.

Inside, the flames of the fire roaring in the grate highlighted the naked body of Liddy and, in her arms, the lithe shapely form of the dark-haired woman she had been talking to at breakfast. They seemed to be dancing.

Helen watched in astonishment as Liddy leant

forward to kiss the breasts of her companion. She moved with fluid grace, her painted lips closing delicately on her lover's swollen nipples. As she guided the woman round the floor her fingers moved lower to caress the triangle of the woman's sex.

The dark woman moaned with delight, surrendering to Liddy's touch, pulling her closer so that Liddy drew the woman's breast deeper into her mouth.

'So, I've converted you to the pleasures of voyeurism, have I? You should have told me how much you'd enjoyed yourself last night and we could have walked down here together.'

Helen spun round. Max, dressed in a thick winter coat, smiled broadly. He had his hands thrust in his pockets and looked extremely pleased with himself. 'Well, what have you got to say for yourself? I hadn't got you down as a Peeping Tom, though I suppose after last night's revelations I really shouldn't be surprised.'

Helen felt herself colouring. 'I thought—' she stammered, but the next words died on her lips. She couldn't tell him that she thought Jack Hartman had been waiting for her in the cottage.

Max shrugged, 'It doesn't matter what you thought, but there's no need for us to freeze out here. Come with me.'

Helen followed him silently around the side of the cottage and into a lean-to. Once inside Max helped her climb a narrow flight of stairs into the cottage roof. Below, through the slats, the lovers were completely exposed. The soft strains of dance music from a wind-up gramophone filtered up between the boards.

Max grinned at Helen through the gloom. 'Make yourself comfortable,' he whispered. 'Liddy is a very talented lover, this may well take some time.'

Helen looked at him in disbelief, 'Is this what you wanted me to see last night?'

Max nodded and handed her a hip flask. 'This is my darling wife's true obsession. Look at them. Aren't they breathtaking?'

Helen glanced down. The two women were now dancing to the delicate lilt of a waltz. From this angle Helen could see their breasts touching and Liddy's hands, snaking around her female companion's waist, pulling them closer together. Helen bit her lip and took a deep swig from the flask. Below them the women moved slowly around the room, touching, brushing against one another in a delicate erotic ballet.

As the music stopped, Liddy guided her lover back to the hearth where a pile of fur rugs had been arranged in front of the roaring fire.

Liddy kissed the woman's mouth tenderly, her fingers moving over her breasts and then down to the dark triangle of her sex. She parted the heavy outer lips to reveal the soft shell-pink inner folds, her long fingers seeking out the bud of the other woman's clitoris. Helen held her breath as Liddy trailed a web of wet kisses down over the woman's breasts and belly. As her mouth closed over her sex, from below them the woman's soft throaty moan bubbled up between the floorboards, electrifying Helen.

She looked across at Max but his concentration was firmly fixed on the tantalising scenario developing beneath them. Liddy's companion began to roll from side to side, lifting her hips up to Liddy's mouth, her fingers joining Liddy's tongue to hold herself open for her exploration. The woman's eyes were closed, her whole body flushed and glowing with desire. One hand lifted so that she could play with her own nipples, teasing them back and forth between her fingertips. Helen was stunned, imagining the sensation Liddy's lips were creating deep inside the woman's body.

The woman caught hold of Liddy's head, pulling her onto her, pulling her down close and hard into her moist fragrant depths.

Beside her, Helen heard Max moan appreciatively as the women started to buck and thrash from side to side, washed away on a tidal wave of utter delight. Helen could imagine every kiss, every tiny, tight, glittering ripple of pleasure and was stunned to realise how excited the women were making her feel. She bit her lip, keeping her eyes on the floor, knowing that if she looked at Max her eyes would betray her arousal.

Finally Liddy pulled away and the dark woman slumped back amongst the fur rugs. Liddy lay down beside her and stretched across them both to produce a bottle of wine and poured two glasses. 'Here,' she murmured sleepily.

The woman took the glass gratefully and then reached up to encircle Liddy with one arm, pulling her closer, rolling her onto her side so that their lips met and pressed hard together. The wine splashed onto their naked bodies.

Liddy giggled delightedly. 'Careful,' she purred.

'Let's drink this, we've got as much time as we need.'
As she spoke she lifted her glass and her eyes towards
the ceiling – a silent toast to her unseen audience.

'Let me wind the gramophone up again,' she said
lightly, disentangling herself from her lover's embrace.
Once again the music filtered up between the slats of
the ceiling.

Helen, who had been holding her breath, let out a
slow shuddering gasp. 'My God,' she whispered
unsteadily, feeling the tight spiral of heat building in
her belly.

Max looked at her with amusement. 'I told you they
were wonderful, didn't I?' he murmured in an
undertone.

Helen nodded, afraid that her voice would reveal
her deep aching excitement. Max moved a little closer
to her and she knew she had no need to say another
word. He could see by her bright glistening eyes the
effect Liddy and her companion were having. His hands
moved slowly to the buttons on her coat.

Silently, in the gloomy attic, he undressed her – she
had neither the will nor the desire to resist him. His
lips closed around her nipples whilst his fingers brutally
tore aside the thin fabric of her drawers, clawing her
open for his invasive hot caresses. He slid his fingers
inside her. She knew, even before he sighed with
delight, that she was sopping wet. He lifted a finger,
slick with her own juices, and slid it between her open
lips. She sucked hungrily at it, imagining that the
heady ocean taste came from the women writhing
beneath them.

Finally, as he guided her down onto a pile of sacks, she opened herself wide for him, relishing the sensation as the broad head of his cock nuzzled between her sensitive inner lips. She gasped as she felt him slide inside her, her muscles tightened gratefully around his shaft, sucking him deep inside her.

From below them came the soft strains of the dance music and the muffled cries of pleasure from Liddy and her lover. In the dusty attic, Helen buried her face in Max's coat and bit into the thick tweed to stop herself from crying out, as her own body soared towards the stars.

Max's knowing fingers brushed back and forth against the sensitive hood of her clitoris, building the already electric excitement that glowed there into a raging flame. As the impending inferno of her orgasm threatened to engulf her she bucked again and again beneath Max's thrusts and caresses until she felt she couldn't take any more. She surrendered herself totally to him, pushing up onto his cock, matching him stroke for stroke – all thoughts of Charles and Annie lost in the desperate race for release.

At the very instant that she thought she would go mad if the pleasure lasted a second longer, she felt Max falter, his thrusts growing wild and ragged. She lifted her hips towards him once more and instantly felt the wild spiral of ecstasy roar through them both. Above her, Max gasped as he tried hard not to call out, whilst she bit down again and again on his coat.

Finally they lay still, collapsing onto the rough sacks. Below them the murmur of the dance music still echoed up through the boards. Helen let out a deep shuddering breath. 'I have to go,' she whispered unsteadily, rolling out from under him.

Max, breathless, nodded. Helen quickly slipped her clothes back on and hurried down the stairs with barely a backward glance. At the bottom, in the little lean-to, she was surprised to see that Max had followed her. His eyes were bright with passion. 'Would you like me to show you the quickest way back to the Lodge?' he said softly.

Helen laughed, lifting her fingers to his broad sensual lips, 'No, I think I can find my own way home.' She hesitated, regretting what she knew she had to say next. 'This can't go on,' she said flatly, letting her fingers fall from his mouth. 'It isn't right.'

Max looked uncomfortable. 'If you mean Charles—' he began.

Helen lifted a hand to silence him, 'No, not Charles or Liddy but you and I. This just isn't right for me.'

Max grinned. 'Consider it finished then and your little debt paid.' He paused, 'Seems like a damned shame though. There are so many exciting possibilities—' He looked steadily at her, an unspoken invitation hanging between them.

Helen shook her head and then pressed her lips to his.

'No. No more possibilities, however tempting,' she whispered, thinking about the sensations he and Jack had awoken in her body and the erotic kiss of the leather whip. Her newfound sexual desire could ruin them all.

Max kissed her with great tenderness and slid his arms around her waist. She winced as he touched the aching muscles in her back. He grinned, 'Good while it lasted though, eh?'

She nodded then regretfully stepped back and disentangled herself from his arms. 'This is something I have to sort out on my own, Max. But yes, you're right, it was good while it lasted.'

Max watched Helen disappearing into the woods and blew his cheeks out thoughtfully. Charles was a total fool, he thought reflectively. It was a great shame that Helen wanted to call it a day. Perhaps he could find a way to persuade her otherwise.

From the inside of the gun cottage he heard Liddy begin to moan. He grinned and turned back towards the staircase; his mind had already moved on to the next instalment in Liddy's erotic extravaganza.

Chapter 5

Sunday Lunch

Charles was waiting in the sitting-room when Helen returned from the woods. He sat stiffly in an armchair beside the fire, behind his Sunday paper, silent and unreachable. Helen glanced around the door and called hello before she made her way upstairs to change yet again.

It felt as if her whole boy still held Max's musky hot smell. Between her legs she could feel their slick juices trickling out onto her thighs. Her body and mind were full of images, dark sensual pictures that were impossible to escape.

Upstairs she slipped off her clothes and let them fall onto the bedroom floor, thinking of Annie picking them up. Pale frightened Annie writhing beneath her husband as he forced his way between her thighs. Begging him to stop . . .

She put on her robe and hurried to the bathroom. Running a sink full of hot soapy water she washed quickly, trying to clear away every trace of her embraces with Max. As she glanced in the mirror, she thought about Liddy's delighted passionate caresses and the haunting strains of the waltz filtering up into the dusty cottage attic.

'Would you like a sherry before lunch?' Charles' voice came up from the bottom of the stairs as Helen struggled with the zip of her Sunday dress.

'Yes please,' she called without expression. She wondered how on earth she would be able to face him at lunch. And then there was Annie – the thought of the girl serving their meal and her haunted eyes made Helen shudder.

The dining-room was cold. The table – another hand-me-down from the Hall – was too grand and a little too large for the panelled room. Helen sat at the far end in uncomfortable silence whilst Charles carved the joint of beef.

When she had lived at home, Sunday lunch had always been a relaxed affair, father carving, mother hurrying to and from the kitchen, her brother and sister laughing and joking about their week. Helen glanced away, blinking back the tears; her life was so different now.

When she had been nursing in London she'd lived for a while in a shared house with three other girls. They'd taken turns to cook lunch for themselves, laughing at their disasters, relishing their successes. One of them, she remembered, had made the most superb Yorkshire puddings— Helen glanced back towards Charles who was poised with the carving knife in one hand and a fork in the other.

'Well?' he said.

Helen blanched and bit her lip. 'I'm sorry, I was miles away. I didn't hear what you said.'

Charles rolled his eyes. 'What on earth is the matter with you?' he said, laying another slice of meat onto the plate beside him. 'Is that enough meat for you?'

Helen nodded. 'Yes, thank you. I was just thinking about Sunday lunches in London,' she said quickly, unfolding her napkin onto her lap.

As she spoke, Annie came in with a tray of vegetables and passed Helen her plate. Helping herself from the serving dishes, Helen tried hard to stop her hands from shaking. Annie meanwhile seemed oblivious, swaying gently from side to side as she held the tray.

'How was church?' asked Charles, sitting down and pulling his plate closer.

Helen hesitated. She had to be careful not to mention the doctor giving her a lift home and at the same time was struck by how normal Charles sounded. She wondered how long he had been using Annie as an outlet for his needs.

Swallowing hard, she forced a smile. 'There were quite a few people there this morning. It looks as if the verger has finally worked out how to get the boiler going. It was very warm.' She hoped he wouldn't ask her about the sermon.

He nodded.

'Dr Robert's housekeeper's daughter has got a job teaching English in Florence.'

'That sounds a little convoluted,' Charles said, pouring the gravy.

Helen tried to get control of her thoughts; the rector

had to have mentioned it during the service, or the doctor probably wouldn't have said anything. 'The vicar asked for us to pray for her success,' she guessed, hoping Charles wouldn't be interested enough to pursue the matter.

Charles guffawed lewdly, 'I should damned well think so. What's her mother thinking of, letting her go off to Italy on her own, for heaven's sake?'

Helen looked steadily at him, feeling indignant that Charles should immediately think the worst of the girl. 'She got the job through a perfectly respectable agency.' She knew her voice sounded snappy and instantly regretted it, as Charles' eyes flashed with annoyance.

He laid down his knife and fork slowly. 'Well, of course – that makes it all right, doesn't it?' he said coldly.

Helen's meal tasted like sawdust. She hated Charles' moods. Laying down her knife and fork, she thought the time had come for all the nonsense to stop. 'Charles, I really think we have to talk,' she said, as calmly as she could.

'Talk?' he snorted. 'What would you like to talk about? I'd be very interested in what you have to say about your behaviour over the last few days. You really are becoming quite impossible, Helen. What would you like to say to me?'

Helen sighed; it was pointless. She had no idea where to begin and needed him to understand. There was no safe ground from which to begin. She shook her head. 'Nothing, Charles,' she said quietly.

He nodded and sucked his teeth, 'I should think not.

The sooner things get back to normal around here the better. Where's that damned girl with the wine?'

Helen pressed her napkin to her lips, hoping he wouldn't notice the tears in her eyes. He wanted things to get back to normal, but what was normal now that she knew about Annie and his brother – and herself? There was no way of stepping back to a time when she had been oblivious to it all.

At the dining-room door, Annie appeared with a bottle of wine. Charles made a great fuss of opening and tasting, complaining that really it should have been opened earlier to let it breathe. Helen said nothing as Charles began to talk about his plans for the week and Max's expensive new hunter.

On Sunday afternoon Helen usually read but today she couldn't concentrate. The words in her book swum together in a confused blur.

There were letters she could have written to her family and some of the girls that she had nursed with – but she knew there was nothing she could say without betraying her unhappiness or the secrets about herself and the Garrison family.

Charles had taken himself off with a small glass of whisky to the study to finish the week's ledgers. Helen wondered if, while he sat there, he was also re-living the morning he'd spent with Annie in front of the fire.

She sighed, pacing the room like a caged animal. Something had to change. Watching from the sitting-room window she saw the steady stream of Max's guests leaving. She watched the judge, alone now, driving slowly along the gravelled drive. It was hard to reconcile the images she had seen in the Hall guest room the previous night, with the distinguished-looking man sitting behind his uniformed chauffeur.

She could hear voices in the hall and knew it was Charles talking to Annie. The temptation was to slip out and listen to the two of them. She clenched her fists, refusing to be reduced to deliberate eaves-dropping. Finally she hurried out into the hall and picked up her coat. Charles appeared in the shadows near the study door. 'Going out again?' his voice was flat and cold.

'Yes, I thought I'd go over to the Hall, to see if Liddy needs any help,' she said, pulling her coat closed.

Charles nodded, 'Good idea, but don't be too long.' He looked her up and down, 'I don't expect to have to come and fetch you again.'

Once outside in the drive and away from Charles, Helen felt as if a huge weight had been lifted off her shoulders. She hurried towards the Hall. In the distance the lamps were already twinkling in the fading afternoon light. Jack and Max – their names, their faces and their knowing handsome bodies pressed up behind her eyes. She glanced left and right, wondering if either of them were in the park waiting for her.

Liddy was stretched out in the sitting-room on the *chaise longue,* almost asleep, when Helen was shown into the room. Her bright eyes were heavy and dark-ringed. On the floor beside her stood the remains of a large gin and tonic.

She lifted her head stiffly when Helen came in and peered at her, 'Oh, it's you. Hello, you'll excuse me if I stay put won't you, darling? I'm totally and utterly exhausted. Entertaining is great fun but I'm always delighted when they all finally rush off home.'

Helen smiled, 'Of course I won't mind. I just popped over to see if there was anything you needed.'

Liddy grimaced, taking a long pull from her glass. 'Not on another of Charles' errands?'

Helen shook her head, 'No, I was just taking a walk.'

Liddy looked at her incredulously. 'Good grief. Look, why don't you join me for a g-and-t. Do you want to stay for supper?'

Helen declined, 'No, it's sweet of you to offer but I'll have a drink and then head home. You know how worried Charles gets.'

Liddy rolled her eyes heavenwards and waved her empty glass towards Helen, 'Get me another large one will you, there's a dear?'

Helen realised as she sat with Liddy that she felt equally as uncomfortable in the Hall. It seemed she could find no peace or calm anywhere anymore.

The Hall held the brooding possibilities of meeting Max, the park land held the promise of Jack Hartman. However tempting their charms, she knew that indulging her desires with them would only lead to disaster. She sipped her drink and looked out into the rapidly darkening night. She had to get away from them all – the sooner the better.

'So you're home then?' Charles looked up from reading

the Sunday papers when Helen returned. She nodded, folding herself into the armchair beside the fire. Walking home she had had an idea; now all she needed was the courage to put it into practice.

'I think I'm going to give the doctor a ring,' she said.

Charles looked up, 'Are you feeling unwell?'

'You said yourself that I'm not myself.'

Charles shook his paper and returned behind it, 'I'm not sure there's any need to disturb him on a Sunday evening.'

Helen smiled. 'No, perhaps you're right, but I think I'll give him a ring anyway.'

She slipped into Charles' study and quietly closed the door. Her hands shook as she picked up the receiver.

'Hello? Is that the doctor's house? No, actually I didn't want to speak to him. Is this his housekeeper? Perhaps you remember me, I'm Helen Garrison, Charles' wife? You do? The doctor told me this morning that your daughter has just got a job teaching in Florence? Yes, it's wonderful news, I'm sure you must be very proud of her. I wonder, could you tell me which agency she applied to?'

Helen wrote down the details on a slip of paper. Smiling, she folded it and put it safely into her skirt pocket.

Helen lay very still when Charles came to bed. She watched through half-closed eyes as he carried his clothes in from the bathroom and folded them carefully onto the bedside chair. Slipping off his dressing-gown he snapped off the light and slid into bed beside her.

For a few seconds they lay side by side like two statues. Helen felt the tension growing in her belly. In the darkness she could hear Charles breathing unsteadily.

Finally he turned towards her, his hand brushing her knees through her nightdress. 'You don't mind, do you?' he said. He sounded desperately embarrassed.

She whimpered and was instantly annoyed that she had. His fingers slid higher, raking her nightdress up to expose her body to his fumbling clumsy caresses.

She realised she was afraid to refuse him and was saddened by the paradox. Was there any way she could tell him what she longed for? Their needs were not that different. His fingers found the bruised aching pit of her sex and brushed the hair there, probing roughly to find a way in.

In the darkness, as his fingers sought entry, her rogue imagination fantasised that he was Jack or Max and, to her horror, she moaned softly under his touch. Instantly she felt Charles stiffen but it was too late – the tiny flame of desire had been lit. Her body understood now the pleasure love-making could give her and knew exactly what it was Charles had been holding back. As he moved again she felt her body opening instinctively to his caresses, sliding her legs apart to give him greater access.

Charles' breath quickened as his fingers slid inside her. She was rapidly getting excited and wet and there was no way she would be able to hide it from her husband. He seemed to hesitate and then began to slide his fingers rhythmically into the depths of her body.

Her aching muscles contracted tightly around him, drawing them into her, her hips eagerly lifting to meet him.

In the darkness she heard Charles gasp and then roughly he pulled his fingers out of her. There was a moment of total stillness before he snapped on the bedside light. She blinked, stunned by the brightness, and knew even before she caught his eyes, that her face would betray her.

It was too late to look away. Charles caught hold of her chin and jerked her face towards him. She swallowed hard, trying to retain a vestige of control. She had no idea what he was thinking but his eyes were glistening and dark.

'You're very different this evening,' he growled, maliciously pushing the bedclothes down off her body.

Helen's eyes widened. There was nothing she could say to him; her mind bubbled with panic. Charles stared down at the bed. Helen's legs were still open, the dark triangle of her sex exposed among the rucked gathers of her nightie. She felt as if she were frozen, her limbs leaden.

Charles watched her thoughtfully, as if he were seeing her for the first time. 'Well,' he said coldly. 'This is a strange turn of events.' His eyes moved across her. She shivered, still unable to move. 'Get out of bed,' he whispered.

Helen shivered. 'Charles—' she began, unsure what she was going to say but knowing that she must try to say something.

'I said, get out of my bed,' he snapped.

Helen was rooted to the spot. The air between them was oppressive, like the still breath before a summer storm. Charles' eyes flashed with anger and Helen slithered across the mattress. He moved more slowly until he was standing close to her.

'You little whore,' he whispered. Helen was about to protest when she saw the wild angry look in his eyes. 'I won't ask you who,' he said flatly. 'I really don't want to hear. Can you deny it?'

Helen shook her head dumbly, feeling her face flush crimson.

As he spoke he moved closer, and instinctively Helen flinched. Charles smiled thinly. 'So,' he said, 'this is what all this has been about.' As he spoke his hands lifted to the neck of her thin cotton nightdress, fists clenched round the *broderie anglais* trim. His face was level with hers, his eyes reduced to dark cruel pinpricks.

'No, Charles, please don't,' she stammered, but before she could say another word he jerked hard, ripping the thin fabric apart at the seams. It bit into her flesh and she yelled out in pain and terror, trying to claw the fabric back to cover her nakedness.

'What are you complaining about?' he snorted. 'I thought you'd like this sort of thing.' He paused, letting his eyes travel greedily across her naked shivering body. 'I know exactly how to treat whores,' he hissed. 'Lie down.'

Helen gulped, her first instincts were to run, but there was nowhere to go. She lay back across the bed, her face hot and red, the pulse throbbing in her neck.

Charles prised her legs apart with his knee. Stepping between them, he smiled malevolently. 'I would never have thought this of you, Helen,' he said.

His fingers moved over her body, exploring her, pressing invasively into the secret delicate folds of her sex. She trembled as he leant over her, his eyes locked on hers. 'Turn over,' he hissed.

Helen rolled onto her belly, relieved that she didn't have to look into his eyes. She felt him step closer; his fingers stroked her buttocks slowly. 'Get onto your hands and knees,' he whispered. 'Let me show you how I like to treat whores.'

Unsteadily Helen pushed herself up onto all fours. Before she was steady, he grabbed hold of her thighs, splaying her wide. She gasped in horror as his fingers plunged inside her, cruel and invasive, opening her for his attentions. Before she had time to gather breath she felt the brush of his cock against her legs.

'Is this what you want?' he snorted and drove it into her, forcing her face down into the soft mattress. She felt as if he were tearing her apart; her cries of shock stifled by the blankets as he plunged into her again and again. Each stroke was cruel and brutal, forcing the breath from her. He hunched over her, his hands seeking out her hips, furiously dragging her back onto him.

'Do you like it like this, you little bitch?' he snorted.

Her mind was flooded with the humiliating images of Annie, hunched beneath him as she was, unable to refuse Charles as he took his pleasure.

Helen's excitement at his touch had opened the

floodgates of his real desires. 'Charles please, wait, wait—' she screamed.

He ignored her, sliding his hands higher, cupping the weight of her breasts. His cold fingers, wet with her juices, tightened and twisted around her nipples. She struggled under him. Barely able to breathe as he thrust deeper and deeper, she gasped as his weight pressed her into the mattress. His hands locked into her hair, arching her body up against him.

She was terrified. 'Please Charles, don't do this, please – let me talk to you, please—' she begged as he pulled her back against him.

'Oh, I like it when they beg,' he snorted, his other hand fumbling with her breasts.

Helen let out a long empty wail of humiliation and then let everything go. Her mind becoming a dark swirling blank as Charles drove on, his fingers tearing at her unfeeling body. She sensed the change as his desperate strokes became instinctive. She sobbed as he suddenly pulled out of her, throwing her down onto the sheets. Behind she heard his convulsive gasps as he reached orgasm, followed by the wet hot flood of his seed splashing over her quivering thighs.

She froze as he collapsed down onto her, his sweat trickling over her naked back. When he peeled himself off her, his voice was icy. 'Get yourself cleaned up,' he said, and dropped the shred of her ruined nightdress beside her.

When she turned over, he was pulling the eiderdown off the bed. 'What are you doing?' she asked unsteadily.

Charles threw a pillow onto the rug beside their bed.

His expression was dark and set, 'You can sleep on the floor from now on. I don't make a habit of sharing my bed with whores.'

Helen looked at him with stunned disbelief.

'Or,' he said evenly, 'you can go back to whoever it was who made you one. It's of very little consequence to me.' He handed her the eiderdown and she took it wordlessly.

In his eyes there was a deep malevolent gleam, as if he had finally got what he wanted from her. Helen shuddered and lay down amongst the rags of her nightdress, tears welling up inside her. Silently, Charles climbed into bed and turned off the light.

As Helen lay in the darkness she tried to hold back the impending tears. Her whole body felt violated and cruelly used. If Charles had taught her to make love when they had first married she would have gladly been anything he wanted her to be. With Max and Jack, although she had submitted to them, it had been because she wanted to. Their dominance and strength had opened the door of her sexuality and brought her to the very pinnacle of ecstasy.

Above her, she could hear Charles snoring now and she shuddered unhappily; he had torn from her what she would have gladly given him. Sadly she drew the eiderdown up around her shoulders and tried to sleep.

When she woke Charles had gone. Beside her, lying on her pillow, was a crisp folded five-pound note – her fee for Charles' pleasure. Helen picked it up and turned it over slowly in her fingers before bursting into tears.

* * *

'I'm not sure as I can give the information you want, Mrs Garrison.'

Helen stood stiffly by the bar in a small unsavoury pub called The Dog on the outskirts of Ferrybridge. Her expensive clothes looked out of place amongst the shabby surroundings.

The bar-keeper dried the glasses thoughtfully. 'Jack Hartman, you say? I know he lives out on the Fen, but get you there?' He blew out his lips, 'I'm not so sure. Most likely bloke I can think of who'd be able to help you is Nip Hunter, but he ain't been in today.'

Helen nodded, laying a few more coins on the bar. It had taken her most of the morning to find anyone who had heard of Jack and almost another hour to find someone who might know where he would be. 'Can you tell me where to find Nip Hunter?'

The old man pulled a face. 'Might be able to—'

Helen added another coin.

The bar-keeper grinned, 'Seems as if you're pretty keen on finding this Jack, missus.'

Helen tried hard to keep a poker face. It wasn't so much that she wanted to go to Jack but she had to get away from the Garrison estate. She needed time to think. 'I need to see him and I have no idea when he'll be back this way.' She hardened her voice, sliding her hand over the pile of coins on the bar, 'Now, can you help me or will I have to ask elsewhere?'

The barman laid down the glass he was drying. 'No need to be hasty, ma'am,' he said, smoothly sliding the coins towards him. 'I'll send one of my lads out to Nip's cottage. If you'd like to take a seat in the other bar, I'll have me wife bring you out a pot of tea.'

Nip Hunter was a short wiry man with shifty eyes and a strange high-pitched voice. He looked at Helen with open curiosity as they sat together at a table in the dimly lit snug bar.

'It's a long way,' he said, sipping his beer. 'It'll take most of the day to get there.'

Helen nodded, 'I'll pay you well if you'll take me up the river to him.'

Nip grinned, revealing blackened uneven teeth, 'Are we talking about something a bit fishy here, missus? I'll be honest, I've no wish to get meself in Hartman's bad books. He's not the sort'a fella you'd want to cross.'

Helen met his eyes, 'It's no business of yours why I'm going. Will you take me or not?'

The man nodded, 'Aye, but it'll cost yer, it's a fair old way.'

Helen sighed. 'I'll pay well. Can we leave today?'

The man shook his head. 'Too far to make the trip this afternoon. No, if it's fine I'll take you tomorrow, around seven. Will that suit you?'

Helen nodded, 'Yes, I'll meet you down by the bridge.'

'Right enough,' said the little man and finished his beer before hurrying away.

Helen looked at the empty beer glass and sighed. 'One more night,' she said softly and picked up her handbag.

When she arrived home, Charles was in his study. As she closed the front door he came out to meet her, his eyes glistening. 'I've given the staff the rest of the day off,' he said evenly, watching her face.

Helen shivered as he moved closer.

'I'd like you to come into my study,' he said, 'and take off your clothes. I haven't finished with you yet but I suppose you'll have to learn that whores are at the beck and call of anyone who can pay their price.' He ran his fingers over her breasts, 'I'd say marrying you was a high price to pay.'

It was barely light when Helen stepped down into Nip Hunter's boat.

She had submitted without question to Charles as he had demanded that she let him take her again and again until, finally, he had collapsed exhausted into their bed.

Lying on the bedroom floor beside him, she hardly closed her eyes all night for fear that she would oversleep. While it was still dark she had crept out of the Lodge, leaving Charles asleep in the bed he would no longer let her share. Cramming a few possessions into an overnight bag, together with what money she had, she'd hurried out into the cold unwelcoming morning.

Nip took her hand and guided her towards a small padded bench in the little cabin at the prow of the boat, 'Better make yourself comfortable, Mrs Garrison, it's a real long way.'

Helen nodded and peered out into the gloom as Nip pushed the boat away from the jetty.

* * *

At Garrison Lodge, Charles stretched and glanced at the clock; it was still early, the sun barely up. He smiled to himself. Time enough to make use of Helen's newfound obedience before he went to the farm. He stretched. He needed her body. He was far from disappointed with the recent turn of events, though he didn't dwell too much on the details that had reduced his wife to this state of affairs.

Fleetingly, he did wonder who had seduced her. Some poor drunken oaf at Max's dinner party no doubt. He felt the familiar press in his groin, momentarily thinking about his prim little wife flailing wildly, impaled beneath some faceless stranger. He owed the chap his thanks. Now, thanks to her sense of guilt, he had her exactly where he wanted her. Helen and Annie both. What a delightful thought.

He rolled onto his side to look onto the floor. Perhaps later, when she had truly learnt her lesson and what he wanted from her, he would let her back into his bed. Meanwhile, the idea of her sleeping beside him on the floor, subdued and submissive, waiting to service his every need, was something that excited him.

'Helen,' he said softly to the jumble of blankets and pillows. She didn't move; he imagined her waking to the sound of his voice and knowing that she would have to obey him. His groin ached.

'Helen?' Still nothing. He would make her pay for that. He slid across the bed and poked the blankets with his foot, then angrily bent over and whipped them back. The makeshift bed was empty. She had gone. He sat up, stunned and furious. She would have to pay for this – wherever she was.

He leapt out of bed and rang the bell that was connected to the kitchen. Within seconds, he heard Annie's footsteps on the stairs.

She opened the door when he called her in. 'Have you seen my wife this morning?' he snapped, looking past the girl into the hall, in case Helen was already up.

Annie was still half asleep. Charles noticed that the buttons on her uniform weren't all fastened. Between the uneven gaps he could see her pale flesh.

She peered at Charles uneasily, as if she hadn't quite understood what he'd said. While his face remained impassive, inside he was beginning to feel his excitement rekindle, his anger abating in the face of his pressing desire. 'My wife,' he said again more slowly, 'have you seen her this morning?'

The girl shook her head. 'No, Mr Garrison,' she said quietly.

He stepped closer to her. She smelt warm and sleepy. He lifted his hands to the buttons on her dress. 'In that case, Annie,' he murmured, 'you will just have to take her place.'

The girl's eyes widened. He slid the buttons undone, exposing her heavy rounded breasts and pressed his lips to one of her puckered nipples. Beneath his fingers he felt Annie tremble.

He smiled. Helen could wait until later. When he found her he would make sure she knew just how angry she had made him. Annie whimpered as Charles pulled up her full skirt and pushed her back onto the bed.

* * *

The journey seemed endless to Helen as the little boat meandered through the narrow Fenland waterways. Nip whistled cheerfully, producing tea and sandwiches for her when the sun was high in the wintry sky. Helen thanked him but really didn't feel like eating or like talking to her guide.

She had to make longterm plans, but now she wondered what Jack would say when she turned up at his cottage uninvited. What if he was still away and the cottage was deserted? This trip could be the most dreadful mistake. She huddled down miserably under the blanket Nip had given her and cradled the steaming mug of tea. It wouldn't be long now before she found out.

Charles' face flashed through her mind. What would he say when he discovered she was gone? She blinked away tears and stared instead at the grey cold water lapping at the little boat's sides.

'Helen's gone.'

Max, sitting behind his desk in his study, looked up at his younger brother with surprise. 'What do you mean "gone", Charles?'

Charles snorted, moving closer to the fire, 'What the hell do you think I mean? When I woke up this morning she wasn't there.'

Max shrugged. 'She likes to walk in the park, maybe she's gone out for an early morning stroll.'

'It was barely light. No, I know she's gone.' Charles' voice became lower and more aggressive. 'And I think you might have a damned good idea where's she's gone – and why.'

'Me? Why, for God's sake? She's your wife. Have you had some sort of disagreement with her?'

Charles shifted his weight and looked his elder brother straight in the eye, 'No, but she's been acting very strangely over the last few days. Tell me, I need to know. Did she pair up with one of the chaps at your dinner party the other night?'

Max shook his head thoughtfully, his mind full of the images of Helen tied naked in the upper room, her slim body writhing under the kiss of his whip and afterwards her desperate need for satisfaction as she had moved eagerly beneath him. 'No,' he said evenly, 'she was with me most of the night.'

Charles slumped into an armchair, his face pale and angry, 'I'm sick of this, something's happened to her. She's changed. I just don't understand, if it wasn't here at your party . . .' his voice trailed off.

Max poured them both a drink, hoping to hide the knowledge in his eyes, 'What exactly do you mean, old chap?'

Charles pulled a face, nodding his thanks as he took the proffered tumbler of scotch. 'It's very difficult to talk about, but trust me, since that damned fair—' he hesitated as if something had just occurred to him. 'That bloody tinker—' he looked up at Max. 'My God, that's it, it was that bloody tinker.'

Max sipped his drink thoughtfully, relieved that Charles had come to another conclusion and not pressed him further on the events after Liddy's dinner party.

'Are you telling me she's left you for a tinker?'

Charles shook his head, 'No, but she's been different since then.'

Max thought about Helen in the shadows of the laundry room, moving against the man's caresses and her little moans of pleasure as he'd lapped at her naked body. He suspected that if Helen wasn't at the Hall, the chances were she had gone to find her tinker and – although it surprised him – he could almost see why.

He looked at his younger brother levelly, trying to hide the contempt in his eyes. 'It might be a good thing to find him first, before you get on to her family or anyone else. Just to see if he knows anything,' he said.

Charles looked up at him in astonishment, 'You're not serious, are you?'

Max shrugged. 'Best to look close to home first. It shouldn't take a lot to track him down. I mean, you don't want to cause a lot of fuss.'

Charles stared into the flames in the hearth, 'I think you're mistaken. I'm not sure I can remember the chap's name.'

Even as he said it, the man's name came back to him: Jack Hartman. He remembered now the way his wife had stepped boldly towards the dark man, her eyes alight and eager. She hadn't protested or fought but just stepped away from her husband to take the man's arm. Charles shuddered, perhaps Max was right. He stood his glass down on the hearth.

'I'm going to take a drive into the village,' he said slowly.

* * *

Helen could see distant lights twinkling amongst the reeds; around them the daylight was fading fast. She looked back at Nip Hunter.

'Is that where Jack lives?' she asked, pointing towards the light. She had had no idea that it would take so long, or that Jack lived so far away from Ferrybridge. Fear bubbled up inside her. What if he refused to let her stay with him? She must be sure Nip would take her back if Jack turned her away.

The little man nodded. 'Aye, not far now, ma'am,' he said. He grinned, 'Is he expecting visitors?'

Helen looked away. 'I hope so,' she murmured and fixed her eyes on the approaching lights.

As they rounded the next bend, a dog began to bark furiously, joined a split second later by another. The frantic excited noises sounded eerie and haunting in the still evening air.

Nip stood up in the boat. On the far side of the river bank, Helen spotted the dark outline of a cottage. An instant later a door opened revealing a rectangle of light and a figure framed within it. 'Who's there?'

Helen felt her stomach leap as she heard Jack's familiar voice echoing out across the dark water.

Nip shouted. 'Evening, Jack, it's only me, Nip Hunter from Ferrybridge.'

Jack laughed, 'And what brings you out on the Fen this late in the day, Nip? Got a gamekeeper on your tail, have ya?'

'No, I've brought you a visitor,' replied Nip, guiding the little boat towards a makeshift jetty.

Helen shivered. The only sound now was the dip

and splash of the boat and the wind in the reeds. Above her, on the jetty, Jack stood holding a storm lantern. Nip threw him a line and Jack pulled the boat closer. As he did so the circle of light fell onto Helen's upturned face.

Jack smiled in the gloom and extended his arm to her. 'Good evening, lady,' he said softly, his eyes reflecting the bright glow of the lamp. Helen reached out towards him, her heart beating furiously. As she felt his strong fingers close around her arm she let out a sigh of relief and stepped up onto the slippery boards. Nip slid her little case alongside her.

Jack slipped his arm round Helen's waist. She shivered, relishing the sensation of his body against hers and the sense of relief that his approving touch gave her.

Jack looked back down at Nip. 'Would you care to join us for a glass of beer? It's cold on the river tonight.'

The little man shook his head. 'Thanks but no, I'll be heading back.'

Jack lifted an eyebrow. 'It'll take you most of the night.'

Nip Hunter grinned, letting his eyes travel up over Helen's body. 'Maybe you're right, Jack, but I'm sure you've no great need of my company tonight.' He touched his cap and held out his hand towards Helen.

She slipped her hand into her coat pocket and pulled out a five-pound note, still as carefully folded as when she'd found it beside her pillow. 'Thank you,' she whispered, pressing it into his hand.

She and Jack stood side by side in the darkness until Nip's boat had rounded the first bend, then he turned towards her, his eyes glistening. She trembled. He tipped her face towards him and his lips brushed hers. Instantly she felt a plume of desire glisten in her belly. He pulled her closer, crushing her to him, his lips hard and needy.

'I'm pleased that you made the trip, lady,' he whispered.

She moaned, opening her mouth to him, letting him drink her in. When she felt his fingers fumbling with the fastenings of her coat she moved to help him, slipping it off her shoulders so that he could have free rein over her eager aching body.

It seemed as if they were in a world apart. Around them the snow lay on the cold hard ground, but in Jack's arms Helen could only feel his heat and the hard press of his cock against her belly. She moaned, desperately fighting to free him from his clothes. As her hands found his thick leather belt he bit her tongue, his fingers ripping away her thin blouse. His lips dropped to her nipples, which hardened under his caresses. Below, his fingers fought to drag up her skirt. She slid his belt undone, fighting now to free his cock.

He stepped back for an instant, his eyes fiery with desire. 'I have thought of little else but you, Helen Garrison,' he muttered. 'You haunt me, woman.' He grabbed her blouse and ripped it off her shoulders as she freed his engorged phallus. It sprang towards her like a beast unleashed, crying for attention.

She took it gratefully between her hands, relishing

its strength and beauty. Slowly she sank to her knees in front of him, to take it into her mouth. Above her, she heard Jack moan as she drew the head between her lips. Her fingers lifted to cup the heavy bulk of his balls, drawing her fingers over the sensitive puckered skin. She could taste him; the rugged hypnotic taste of the wild Fen man. As she let her tongue trail across it, he caught hold of the back of her head and pulled her closer. She gasped with pleasure, working her fingers back and forth along his shaft.

Between her legs she could feel her excitement growing, forming into a wild spiral of desire. Oblivious to the cold night around them she worked on, lapping and kissing his sex, worshipping his strong muscular body. Her fingers snaked over his buttocks, kneading and stroking the firm tight orbs, while her lips closed on him again and again. She drew him deeper, gasping at the sensations that rose within her. She felt his excitement growing, felt him begin to shiver, sensing the first electric moments when he began to lose control, thrusting himself towards her.

At the instant when she was convinced that she had brought him to the point of no return, he pulled away, and looked down at her. Wordlessly he knelt in front of her and laid her back onto the wooden jetty. He lifted her skirts, fingers seeking out the wetness of her quim. Gently he parted her legs, his fingers delving and stroking, seeking the hard throbbing bud that glowed within the fragrant folds.

She almost wept when he touched it, opening her legs to allow him whatever pleasures he wanted –

knowing that he would willingly share his delight with her, giving her body every satisfaction it demanded. She felt the thick bulk of his cock brushing against her thighs, hidden by the folds of her skirt. Slipping her fingers between her legs she guided him into her. He groaned with delight as he slid home and at once she felt her body tightening gratefully around him.

As he began to move she lifted her hips up to meet his, matching him stroke for stroke, relishing the sensation of his cock filling her up and the weight of his body on hers. She gave her whole consciousness over to their bodies' needs, drinking in the heat and the power of their mutual excitement. She relished the glow building within them both, almost as if every sense was shared and doubled as they moved together.

Sobbing with pleasure, she felt him begin the hypnotic electric dance of his orgasm. As he pressed deeper the pleasures were mirrored within her. Suddenly, almost before she had time to think, she was there with him, riding out into the darkness, feeling her body contracting rhythmically around him. Every thought, every sensation was centred on the junction of their two bodies. She gave herself totally and let the heat drown out all thoughts except the pleasure and the power of the desire between them.

It seemed strange when she finally lay still, feeling the cold boards of the jetty beneath her bare back and hearing below that the dark wet sounds of the river. Jack held her so close that she could feel the thundering beat of his heart through her torn clothes. The awareness of where they were crept slowly over her and she felt the cold night air on her face and the chill of the melted snow against her body.

He kissed her gently. 'I'm glad you found me, Helen Garrison,' he said softly and slid away from her. She shivered as the wind nipped her exposed body, ripping the last of their heat away. He helped her to her feet. Unsteadily she walked towards the cottage, leaning against Jack, relishing the smell of his body, relieved that he had not turned her away.

Charles passed his glass back across the bar for a refill. The inn-keeper at The Dog looked at him with interest and took the note he was offered, pocketing the change. 'Aye, she came in here yesterday morning,' he said, sliding Charles' glass under the beer tap. 'I told her she needed to speak to Nip Hunter. He's a boatman, lives over the far side of the river.'

Charles nodded, still unable to quite believe that Helen could possibly have gone off with Jack Hartman. 'And where is this Nip Hunter now?'

The barman shrugged, lifting his eyes to glance round the almost empty bar, 'Not seen him tonight, which is odd. He comes in most nights.' He looked back at Charles. 'He may have taken her there already.'

Charles took a pull on his beer, 'I need to speak to him. If you see him, will you let me know?'

'Not if it's likely to bring Nip any trouble, Mr Garrison. He's not a bad sort of chap,' he said.

Charles slipped another banknote across the bar. 'There'll be no trouble. All I want to know is whether he took my wife to Jack Hartman and, if he did, if he'll take me, too. I need to speak to him as soon as I can, whatever time of night he shows his face. Is that clear?'

The inn-keeper nodded.

Helen sat by the fire inside Jack's cottage, wrapped in her coat, sipping a mug of tea. Jack moved silently around the warm dimly lit room. She watched him, feeling safe and happy for the first time in days.

As she finished her tea, he looked at her. 'This won't be easy, lady,' he said softly, stooping to throw more wood onto the fire.

Helen shivered. 'I don't mean to bring you any trouble but I didn't know where else to go.'

Jack settled down on his haunches on the hearth. 'I didn't mean trouble for me. What do you think your husband'll do when he discovers you've gone away to sleep with a Fen-man out in his cottage?'

Helen blanched, thinking about the way Charles had treated her, remembering his cold, unfeeling eyes devouring her body. 'I don't know what he will do when he finds out,' she said flatly.

'Nip won't be slow to tell him for the price of a pint or two.'

'He may not guess that I've come here.'

Jack laughed dryly and unfolded himself so that he lay alongside her, before the roaring logs. 'You may be right. As I said to you before, men like your husband don't often notice the likes of me.'

As he spoke the dogs began to bark, their desperate howling and snapping echoing through the cottage. Jack sprung to his feet like a cat. 'It seems as if we may have another visitor, lady,' he said, moving towards the door.

Helen froze, wondering how Charles could have found her so quickly.

Chapter 6

Anya

Helen looked around the cottage, wondering frantically whether she could find somewhere to hide. It was useless. If Charles had gone to the inn in Ferrybridge the landlord would know exactly where she had gone. There was no chance of escape.

Through the open door she could make out the shadow of Jack Hartman moving stealthily towards the river, his body dark and fluid against the grey night. The dogs barked furiously. Suddenly she heard him call out in surprise and felt the hairs on the back of her neck rising. She pulled her coat closer around her and crept towards the open door.

From outside came the sound of Jack's voice – and another – it didn't sound like Charles but she couldn't be sure. She peered out from under the porch, straining to catch the words. A second or two later she heard Jack laugh and the tension in her gut began to recede. She hurried back to the fire with relief.

Jack reappeared in the doorway, grinning. 'It's all right. I'd like you to meet a friend of mine,' he said, stepping to one side. As he and his companion moved into the lamplight Helen felt the tension return.

Close behind him, with her arm linked through his, stood a tiny woman. She was stunning, her exotic golden skin and foreign features revealing her gypsy origins. Her waist-length black hair was caught up at the sides into ornate clips and her clothes – a faded crimson cloak and long black leather boots – did nothing to soften her alien appearance. She peered suspiciously at Helen with her cat-black eyes.

Jack grinned and licked his lips, 'This is Anya, Helen – my very good friend, Anya.' As he spoke the girl crept closer to him. Standing up on tiptoe she pressed her lips to his rough cheek. Helen flinched. The two women murmured a greeting, each watching the other with undisguised interest.

Anya moved with a fluid grace that was breathtaking and at the same time compellingly erotic. Helen blushed. She knew, without having to be told, that Anya was Jack's lover. She felt foolish and vulnerable. It had been ridiculous to assume a man like Jack would live alone. Helen sat back in the chair, wondering what she should do next.

Across the room, Anya put a heavy bundle down by the back door and began to drag off her long boots. Throwing them carelessly onto the floor, she wriggled her toes, hauling up her cloak to reveal her long shapely legs.

'It's so cold out there tonight,' she said, rubbing her calves. 'I'm frozen through to the very bone.' Her low rich voice had the slightest trace of a foreign accent.

'Come by the fire and warm yourself,' Jack said, pushing the kettle back over the fire.

Anya grinned. 'Wait. No tea tonight, Jack,' she purred, springing to her feet. 'I have brought something better to warm us up.' She looked at them both with her dark sparkling eyes and then, like a fairground magician, produced two bottles from the folds of her cloak. She peered at the labels and handed them to Jack. 'What do they say?'

Jack grinned, pulling a penknife from his back pocket. 'They say stolen and very expensive.'

Anya looked at him for a second and then roared with laughter. 'They say it right then.' She glanced at Helen, 'I like Jack, don't you? He makes me laugh.' She paused and stretched like some exotic animal, slipping her cloak off her slim shoulders. 'And he makes me sing,' she whispered mischievously. 'Does he make you sing too?'

Helen blushed. Anya clapped her hands with delight. 'I see that he does,' she said, stepping up onto the hearth. The little woman was so close that Helen could smell her perfume, a strange blend of citrus and musk. Helen shivered. She looked at Helen evenly, waiting for Jack to prise the corks from the wine bottles. 'Don't be afraid of what he makes you feel,' she said, as if somehow she could see inside Helen's mind.

Helen looked up at her. 'Are you his wife?'

Anya laughed and shook her head. 'No, no one owns me. I come and go as I please. What do you say, Jack?'

Jack had gone to rummage through the dresser and had found three odd glasses.

'That's right, we're all free out here on the Fen,' he said, pouring the wine. He turned and handed the two women a drink. As he did he lifted his own glass. 'To the bright and wild night,' he said with feeling.

Anya laughed and lifted her glass. 'And to the bird that sings.'

They both looked at Helen, who smiled. 'To freedom,' she said quietly, raising her glass, and then downing the wine in one long fragrant swallow. The alcohol glowed in the pit of her stomach.

Jack pulled up a bench in front of the fire and they shared the two bottles of wine between them. Jack was right; it was expensive and tasted like the heady fruit of summer.

Helen, who had eaten nothing all day but the sandwiches Nip Hunter had given her, soon felt tipsy. Anya, crouched on her haunches, looked like a strange kind of magical creature trapped in the hearth. Beneath the cloak she was wearing a thin white blouse and full skirt. In the firelight Helen could make out the tight curve of Anya's full breasts through the sheer material. Cut off the shoulder, the white fabric was in startling contrast to her golden skin. Jack poured them more wine and then, when the bottles were empty, brought beer from a jug in the pantry. Helen let the drink carry her away, realising how tired and aching her body felt.

As the night drew closer, Jack blew out all the lamps and they sat in comfortable silence around the fire's glow. Outside the wind had risen, whipping and crying around the cottage chimneys. Helen could feel a growing sense of anticipation between them all. Anya padded across towards the sink to find more beer. Jack was lying full length on the bench, his dark features relaxed and open, feral eyes alight and glistening from the warmth and the effects of the alcohol.

Anya suddenly turned around. 'I want you, Jack,' she whispered, her voice carrying through the shadows. Helen swallowed hard, curling up into her chair. She could suddenly sense the need in the small dark woman; raw and expectant.

'I know why you came, Anya. Come to me, let me make you sing, little one,' Jack said softly, without moving. His tone was even but something about it made Helen shiver. His voice held the promise of his power; a sensual command that warmed and excited her. Cradling her glass, she watched them, feeling as if she had stepped inside a dream.

The dark woman, moaning softly, dropped to her hands and knees. Like a sleek cat she crept across the room, towards Jack, her eyes glittering.

Jack watched her progress with idle curiosity. As Anya approached he dropped his hand and stroked her hair, petting her as if she were indeed a cat. She rubbed against him, almost purring, then sat up slowly. 'Take off your clothes,' he whispered. 'Let me see what else you've brought to warm me.'

The gypsy girl, her eyes fixed on Jack's face, slipped the white blouse over her head, freeing her breasts, their heavy curves highlighted in the fire's glow. Helen was stunned, both by Anya's body and her boldness. She was breathtaking. Jack ran his hands over the uptilted plump orbs, stroking her engorged nipples.

Anya trembled with anticipation under his caress.

'Come closer,' he whispered. She moved towards him, lowering her eyes in a gesture of submission. Pulling the clips from her hair she shook her head and the rich blue-black tendrils fell forward in a broad curling cape, gathering into glinting pools on Jack's chest. Between the soft curls, Anya's nipples jutted forward, hard and dark. She crept closer, undoing the buttons on his shirt and pulling it down over his muscular shoulders. She pressed her lips to his nipples, to the tight dark curls of hair that grew between them, down onto his belly – while below, her long fingers sought out his belt buckle.

Jack slid his hands over her compliant frame, drinking in the feel of her, as the lithe woman worshipped his body. Helen could already see the hard outline of his erection pressing against his trousers as Anya's fingers struggled with the buckle and the buttons. Slowly she slipped her hand inside the fabric. As she gently pulled his cock out, her expression – at odds with her downcast eyes – was triumphant. She knelt over him and slipped his cock between her wide sensual lips, tugging his trousers down over his hips as she sucked him deeper. Jack arched his back and moaned with delight, lifting his hips to allow her to slip them off. Anya whimpered as his hands toyed with her magnificent hair, pulling her lips closer around his shaft.

Helen gasped, knowing that not three hours earlier it had been her own mouth that had closed around him and, later, it had been she who had moaned as he had driven his cock home into her waiting desperate body.

She shivered, imagining the woman tasting the salty remnants of her excitement on Jack's hard arched phallus. Anya worked him slowly as if she were oblivious of Helen watching them. Her long tongue glistened in the firelight as she played it along his shaft, her subtle fingers echoing her mouth's caresses on his muscular body.

Helen could feel the excitement rekindling in her belly, sensing every touch and caress. She swallowed hard and looked at Jack. To her surprise and embarrassment he was already watching her face with interest. She looked away, feeling the colour rising in her cheeks.

Anya, without missing a stroke, slipped off her skirt. She was naked beneath and, even more surprising to Helen, the outer lips of her sex were shaved. She stood up slowly while Jack's eyes moved across her exposed body with pride. She turned round slowly in the firelight, letting his fingers trail across her curves. Her body was a perfect hourglass, her waist thinning below her heavy breasts then swelling again into rounded hips. Her golden sun-kissed skin seemed to glow from within.

'Do you want me?' she said, her exotic voice thick with emotion. It was almost as if she feared he would deny her.

Jack smiled lazily and nodded. 'Come closer,' he whispered. 'Let me show you just how much I want you.'

Eagerly Anya stepped towards him, cupping his sex in her hands, bending to press her lips to it again and again, her tongue lapping down over the heavy bulk of his balls.

Helen found it impossible to tear her eyes away as Anya stepped across the bench, straddling Jack with her athletic golden body. The gypsy woman held herself above him, the lips of her naked sex parting, crystal drops of moisture glistening on her labia.

Jack's hands lifted to her hips. 'Come to me,' he purred.

Anya's eyes were alight, her whole body flushed and crying out for satisfaction. She lowered herself slowly, as if it were a game they had played a thousand times before. Finally she was fractions of an inch above the engorged head of his cock.

Helen swallowed hard, imagining the heat between them. She nearly cried out as Anya guided Jack's phallus inside her. He closed his eyes for a second. Helen could read the pleasure in their faces. The erotic image of Jack's sex gliding between Anya's slick hairless lips made her shiver. Her naked sex seemed to swallow up his shaft, sealing him deep inside her.

Helen felt hot. Her own body ached to be touched, to be loved and possessed but she was rooted to the spot, her hands tightening around the glass, her body stiffening with expectation.

Anya ran her fingers through her hair, stretching herself up into an electrifying arc, easing herself down onto Jack again and again. Her fingers moved over her breasts, toying with her flushed nipples, her face glowing with ecstasy. Slowly she drew a circling spiralling line down over her belly and then dipped between the plump golden lips of her quim. Her fingers sought out the bud that peeked provocatively between them. Helen swallowed hard as the dark woman circled the little pink tip, eyes closed, her head thrown back as she revelled in the sensations. As Anya moaned softly, she and Jack began to move like a single wild creature, sinking into a throbbing engulfing rhythm.

Helen held her breath, sensing every blissful thrust, feeling everything, as if it was her body impaled on Jack's thick phallus. As their breath quickened, Helen felt her own sex contract, her breasts flush, her mouth fall open in expectation.

On the bench Anya let out a desperate throaty groan and ground her pelvis against Jack's body, her fingers trapped between the two of them. Jack bucked instinctively and struggled to press deeper inside his lover.

Helen, her mind following every tiny sensation, let out a long low sob of pleasure. At the very peak of their excitement Jack looked across into Helen's eyes and she felt herself being drawn into his feverish excited mind, as surely as he was being drawn deep inside Anya's hot, wet body. He held her gaze, willing her to join them. She shivered, her mouth wet with hunger, her body aching. She grabbed hold of the chair and tore her eyes away from his. When she looked back he was holding Anya's waist, rearing up to meet her impulsive thrusts, caught in the final ecstasies of their climax.

At last the lovers lay still, panting, satisfied, their bodies glistening with sweat. Helen gasped and slumped exhausted back into the chair as if the climax had been her own.

Sleepily, Anya crept off Jack's body, her quim leaving wet fragrant kisses on his naked belly. She pressed her lips to his flaccid sex, a final act of worship to her lover. He smiled lazily, stroking her hair. She took hold of his hand, pressing his fingertips to her open mouth. His eyes moved from Anya to Helen and back. Anya yawned, creeping closer to him, and he did not resist when she twined her fingers between his and led him towards the stairs.

At the bottom of the stairs Jack looked back at Helen, still sitting close to the fire. His eyes held an invitation that Helen found hard to resist. As Anya stepped up into the shadows, Helen shook her head slowly and, a second later, Jack's face was hidden in the gloom.

She peered into the firelight, feeling strangely elated and yet at ease. Here, with Jack and Anya, there were no lies – no pretence of hiding their needs behind a veneer of respectability. She sat for a long time, watching the fire fade from gold to red thinking about the two lovers and Max and Charles. Her mind refused to be still. She drank the last of the beer and then realised she needed to find somewhere to sleep. Her body cried out for rest, her eyes suddenly heavy. Pulling her coat around her, she slowly climbed the stairs into the roof of the cottage.

As her eyes adjusted to the gloom she could see the stairs opened onto a small landing. On one side, through an open door, she could see Anya and Jack asleep, curled around each other in bed. Their exhausted bodies were kissed silver by moonlight. Helen smiled.

Through another door she saw a smaller bed, tucked beneath the window in the other bedroom. She stepped inside and pulled off her clothes before gratefully slipping between the cool coarse sheets. The bed linen smelt of wind and sunshine. Closing her eyes, she was happy to let sleep claim her.

It was in the early hours of the morning when Charles Garrison was woken by the sound of knocking. He sat up, blinking in the moonlight that streamed in through his bedroom window. Who could be knocking at this time of the morning?

He stretched, perhaps it was Helen. For an instant he imagined her cowering in the porch, damp, cold and dishevelled, full of fear and remorse. Any sense of outrage and pain he felt at her betrayal was more than compensated for by the power it gave him over her. There was another flurry of knocking from downstairs.

He got out of bed stiffly and slipped on his dressing-gown. From the hall, he heard the sound of voices. Damn, he thought to himself, listening to try and pick out the words. Annie must have heard her coming home too.

In his mind, in the seconds between hearing the noises and climbing out of bed, he had imagined going down and letting his wife in. She would, of course, be beside herself with guilt and regret. Her blue eyes would be bright with fear and expectation. He smiled; he would have had her there on the hall floor, making her pay for this ridiculous hysterical flight. She would have given him anything, begging for his forgiveness – her body, his to use as he wanted. He shivered thinking of her soft rounded hips as she crouched, naked before him, her sex open and wet. He shivered, feeling annoyed and cheated now that Annie had got to her first.

He put on his slippers just as he heard Annie's familiar footsteps climbing the stairs.

'Mr Garrison,' she whispered through the door, 'Are you awake, sir?'

Charles threw the door open, 'Yes, is that Helen downstairs?'

Annie, wrapped in her dressing-gown, clutching an oil lamp, shook her head, 'No, no it's not, Mr Garrison. It's some man. He says you told the landlord down at The Dog that he ought to come and see you when he got back.'

Charles snorted, 'Nip Hunter?'

Annie nodded slowly, 'Yes, I did tell him you were in bed.'

Charles hurried across the landing. 'You didn't send him away, did you?'

'Oh no. No, he said it was important,' Annie said, scurrying behind him. 'I told him to wait downstairs in the sitting-room.'

Nip Hunter was standing beside the empty hearth clutching his cap against his belly. In the lamplight the little boatman looked exhausted, his eyes heavy and dark-ringed. When Charles came in he looked up nervously. 'Sorry to disturb you so late, Mr Garrison, but the landlord said it was urgent.'

Charles nodded, 'No need to apologise. I'm glad you came.' He glanced back over his shoulder where Annie was standing, still clutching the oil lamp. 'Go upstairs and get my wallet, Annie.'

He gestured for Nip to take a seat. The Fen-man shifted nervously and sat down. He perched on the very edge of the armchair, his fingers still ringing the life from his cap.

Charles looked down at him, 'I don't think we need to beat about the bush, do we, Mr Hunter? Have you taken my wife to meet Jack Hartman?' he said slowly.

The colour drained from Nip Hunter's weatherbeaten face.

'No need to spare me,' snapped Charles. 'I want the truth, man.'

Nip nodded slowly. 'Aye, I've just got back. She arranged to meet me at the bridge this morning first thing.'

Charles nodded. 'And was she expected by Hartman?'

Nip hesitated, 'I don't know, sir. She didn't say very much but I got the impression that he wasn't expecting her.'

Charles took a deep breath, stroking his chin thoughtfully. 'Can you take me there tonight?'

The little man got to his feet and began to protest, 'I want no trouble, sir, I've no wish to come between man and wife. Besides it's a long way. I'm tired—'

Charles glared at him, 'Will you take me?' he snapped.

Nip looked at him with rheumy eyes. 'Aye, but I'll have to take my lad with us. It's bitter cold out on the river tonight, it's dangerous to be too tired out on the water.'

Charles had all the answers he needed. 'Stay here, while I get dressed. We'll take my car to Ferrybridge and pick up your boy on the way.' Annie reappeared in the doorway holding Charles' wallet. Charles snatched it from her. 'Tell me what my wife paid and I'll give you double.'

Nip's eyes brightened. 'She gave me five pounds, sir,' he said.

Charles opened his wallet. He looked at Annie. 'Get Mr Hunter a glass of brandy while he's waiting and see what food is left in the pantry for us to take with us. Mr Hunter assures me it's cold out on the river tonight.'

Pressing two notes into Nip Hunter's hand, Charles hurried upstairs. He was going to enjoy running Helen to earth. He would make her pay for all this nonsense – and he would make her pay for a very, very long time.

Safe in Jack's cottage, Helen tossed and turned, her dreams hot and feverish. In her imagination she saw Max stepping towards her clutching a whip but this time it was Anya, not she, who was blindfolded and tied to the hook in the upper room of Garrison Hall.

The dark gypsy girl writhed against her bonds, her naked sex glistening in the lamplight, her breasts flushed and swollen. Max swung his whip back, his eyes holding Helen's as the tasselled end hissed through the air. Helen could see that the girl sensed the blow was coming. Her golden body tensed and, a split second later, the whip head caught her full across her buttocks. Anya screamed, struggling, trying to pull her body away. Max turned towards Helen and handed her the whip.

Helen protested, stepping back – as she did so, she felt strong arms closing around her waist. Glancing over her shoulder, she looked straight into Jack Hartman's dangerous glistening eyes. Against her naked back she felt the hard press of his cock. She whimpered, 'Please, no – I can't, I can't.'

Max smiled thinly. 'We know all about you, Helen, we know. Bend down. We need you—'

Helen stumbled forward onto her hands and knees. Instantly she felt Jack's cock sliding between the cheeks of her bottom and his fingers seeking out the wet opening between her legs. She moaned and instinctively dropped her belly to let him into her, gasping as she felt him slide home. His fingers moved to seek out the hard sensitive bud of her clitoris.

In front of her, Max slipped off his trousers. His cock jutted forward, glistening with excitement. He sank to his knees and locked his fingers in her hair. 'Take me in your mouth,' he whispered, 'I want to feel your lips around me.'

Helen strained forward, trying to control the rising tide of excitement she felt as Jack pressed down expertly on her swollen clitoris. She closed her fingers around Max's phallus, pulling it eagerly between her lips. Behind Max she could still see Anya, straining against her bonds, a livid weal rising on her buttocks.

Jack leant close to her, whispering in her ear, 'I want

you to use your lips on Anya. Wouldn't you like to taste her? Feel her slim body writhing under you, little one? You could make her sing too.'

Helen shivered, gasping as his thumb brushed again over the hood of her clitoris.

'We want you to make her sing, make her wet for us,' Max said, pulling her closer. 'If not, I'll tell Charles all about you – and then what would he do? What would he do?'

Helen groaned, the sound trickling out around Max's phallus.

Max's mention of her husband conjured him into Helen's dream. From the shadows Charles, dressed in his outdoor clothes, stepped forward. He looked furious, his face white, his jaw set. Helen stiffened.

He looked across at the three of them and then smiled angrily. 'She has no idea how to behave, she's no better than a common whore. Not like Liddy. You can use her any way you want. I know just how to treat whores. I'll take her home when you've done—'

As he spoke he spotted Anya hanging from the ceiling. His eyes fell on the whip which Max had discarded on the floor. He picked it up, testing its weight by passing it from hand to hand. The tied gypsy girl seemed to sense that something had changed and began to struggle desperately.

Charles drew back the whip and cracked it down across her naked body. The tasselled head caught Anya low across the lips of her open sex. Her scream was terrifying, her wide sensual mouth breaking into a frenzied sob.

'No!' Helen screamed, pushing Max away, feeling Jack slide from her as she leapt to her feet to protect the beautiful gypsy girl. Her hand closed on the whip's handle as she tried to wrestle it away from Charles.

Charles' face was contorted with fury and lust. He swung towards Helen, throwing her onto the floor. His fingers struggled with his flies as she collapsed onto the floor in front of him.

'I know how to treat whores,' he hissed, stepping towards her. His shadow fell across her like an ice-cold breath. She turned over, scuttling back across the room away from him, her breath coming in short desperate gasps.

Charles lunged forward again and grabbed her by the shoulders, a trickle of saliva spilling down onto his chin. She wrenched herself away from him, seizing the whip he was still holding and leapt to her feet. He moved closer, his eyes dark and menacing. Helen pressed herself back against the wall, coiled and ready to take him on.

As he took one step closer, she screamed, 'NO! No, Charles, you don't understand. It's supposed to be a game.' As she screamed the words she was awake, struggling for breath, gasping, sweating, her heart crashing furiously against her ribs.

The little cottage bedroom was empty and silent, the tangled sheets knotted up around her waist. She shivered, trying to control the overwhelming sense of fear and anger in her gut.

Moonlight still shone through the cottage windows and from close by she could hear the soft untroubled breathing of Anya and Jack sleeping. Miserably she crept back under the blankets, trying to suppress the emotions that fluttered in her belly. She would have to leave – she couldn't risk Charles coming to find her with Jack.

Slowly her breathing settled and her heart stopped pounding in her chest. She would ask Jack to take her back to Ferrybridge. She had to find a way to get away from the Garrison family for good.

'How long will this trip take?' Charles stepped down unsteadily into Nip Hunter's boat. Above them the night was still dark, stars glistening in the wintry sky.

'A fair few hours, Mr Garrison. We should be there afore mid-morning. It would be best if you make yourself comfortable, sir. Get a few hours' sleep.' Nip glanced at his teenage son, hunkered down in the stern, 'My lad will take us the first half of the way, while I grab a few hours meself.'

Charles grimaced. 'Is there no quicker way?'

Nip shrugged. 'Not that I know of, Mr Garrison.' He passed Charles a blanket. 'Best if you wrap yourself up, it's damned cold out here. The damp'll make yer bones ache.'

Charles took it without word and sat himself down in the prow. He was looking forward to finding Helen holed up with her filthy little tinker.

Jack Hartman slipped out of bed at first light. He had traps and lines to check out on the banks. He glanced down at the sleeping woman in his bed. Anya turned over drowsily and then curled up in the warm spot Jack had left behind. He pulled on his trousers and shirt.

Across the landing, through the open door, he could see Helen Garrison, tossing and turning restlessly in her sleep. He watched her thoughtfully for a few seconds and then leant back over the bed. 'I'm going out now, Anya,' he said softly. 'I'll be back for breakfast. Do you hear me?'

The gypsy girl murmured something and then rolled onto her back, eyes opening slowly. 'You're going out now?' she said sleepily.

Jack nodded, 'Aye, I've things to do, but I'll not be gone long. Will you take care of Helen for me?'

The girl stretched, her eyes now focused and glistening. 'Take care of her?' she said steadily, glancing past him into the room where Helen was sleeping.

'That's right,' he said softly. He leant across the bed and pressed his lips to hers, his hands fondling her naked, sleep-warm breasts.

She giggled and rubbed against him. 'Don't be too long, will you, Jack?' she whispered provocatively.

Jack winked. 'I'll be as quick as I can,' he said, picking up his cap from the dressing-table before slipping out of the door.

Anya pulled herself up onto her elbows to watch him go and then looked thoughtfully at the sleeping woman.

Helen's feverish dreams crowded in on her; she felt as if she were running and running through the woodland around the Garrison estate. Up ahead, between the trees, she could see the gun cottage. With every breath ripping red-hot in her lungs, she hurried through the trees and out onto the main path, head down, haring towards its shelter. She glanced anxiously over her shoulder. The woodland seemed alive and menacing behind her. She knew she was being followed, though it was impossible to see who her pursuers were. She had to get away, she had to. She stumbled and cried out in terror . . .

Warm arms folded around her, strong knowing arms that offered her sanctuary. She sobbed, knowing that her unseen saviour could sense the unfulfilled need in her aching tired body. Her rescuer would take away her fear. She surrendered, not resisting, as her unseen companion pulled her down amongst a tangle of bushes and trees.

Safe, hidden amongst the thick undergrowth of the copse, the warmth of her lover's body was comforting. Helen breathed in the delicate smell of their body, relished the soft sleek touch of their warm flesh pressing against her. Their embrace filled her with relief. She sighed with pleasure, all thought of her pursuers receding. For a few seconds the arms simply held her, holding her close. Helen let out a long shuddering sigh and snuggled closer still, drinking in the feeling of security.

As she began to relax, knowing fingers stroked at the tight pink peaks of her nipples, teasing them into hardness. At once she felt a little flutter of excitement in her belly. Pulling her unseen lover to her, she lifted her face to seek out their lips. Soft lips pressed against hers in a gentle inquiring kiss. Helen shivered, opening her mouth as she felt a tongue press for admission. The kiss was sweet and warm, while the fingers continued their soft exploration of her breasts.

She let out a low throaty moan as she felt her lover's lips moving to her throat, nibbling and lapping at her pulse, trailing wet heady kisses down to the glowing swollen orbs of her breasts. She gasped as they drew her nipple between waiting lips. The tension and fear in her belly had vanished, replaced by a raw aching need. Eagerly she rolled over on the soft ground to give her lover greater access to her body.

The mysterious tongue lapped and teased around her breasts. Helen shivered with delight as she felt the fingers moving lower, seeking out the swell of her sex. Her body longed for their intimate attentions. She opened her legs, lifting her hips up in invitation. The fingers dipped, circling, stroking apart the heavy lips. Her sex cried out to be caressed. Instinctively she lifted herself again, moaning as she felt a long slim finger slide into the secret recesses of her body. The fingers teased the soft fragrant folds apart—

'Please,' she whimpered, thrusting herself up onto her lover's fingers, 'please.'

The hot wet lips pressed against her ribs, drinking in the salty taste of her sleepy warm body. Sliding down, they lit intense circles of sensation as they lapped at the sensitive skin in the bowl beneath her hip bones. She moaned and writhed, feeling the heat building inside her, anticipating the intimate kisses she felt sure would follow.

'Hold yourself open for me,' purred a familiar low

voice, filtering in through her sleeping mind. Helen let
her fingers slide down over her body and pushed them
between the heavy outer lips of her sex. She held them
apart, exposing the soft inner lips and her pleasure-
bud for her lover's knowing tongue.

'Good, good,' whispered a voice, full of excitement
and expectation. Lips closed over her open mound,
tongue teasing at the sensitive wet places, lapping at
Helen's fingers. Her lover's kisses were featherlight,
almost no more than teasing breaths. Helen began to
tremble, sparks igniting and lighting up her mind as
the lips moved back and forth.

Helen shuddered. She could feel the moisture
growing between her legs; slick fragrant offerings for
her lover's pleasure.

'Sing,' said the voice. 'Let me make you sing.'

Helen gasped and suddenly knew, without any
doubt, exactly who her lover was. The realisation ripped
her from sleep. Instantly her eyes snapped open. She
was safe in Jack's cottage. Between her open legs,
beneath the coarse cotton sheets, Anya lapped with
enthusiasm at Helen's throbbing quim. Helen stiffened,
trying to stifle a little cry of horror. It was all she could
do to stop herself from leaping off the bed.

Anya looked up at her sleepily from beneath coal-
black lashes, her hands resting on Helen's open thighs.
'It's all right,' she purred. 'Let me teach you, little one,
don't fight it.'

Helen's fingers tightened over the soft folds that she
had been holding open, so willingly, for her dream lover.
While every fibre of her body ached for fulfilment her

mind fought back, revulsion and shock threatening to drive away the heady spiralling sensations that were building in her belly.

Anya seemed to sense her mixed feelings and smiled lazily. 'Lie back and close your eyes,' she whispered. 'Don't fight what your body tells you. If you cannot see me I can be anyone. You like the way it feels—'

'No—' Helen snorted, knowing that even as she denied it, her eyes betrayed her growing excitement.

Anya shrugged. 'That's not what your body tells me,' she murmured.

Helen couldn't help but notice the slick trail of juices on Anya's full lips – her own juices. She shivered as the woman's pink tongue appeared between them. She watched with a horrible fascination as Anya dipped down again and drew it lightly over her clitoris. The woman's caress sent a bolt of pleasure through her sweating excited body.

The gypsy girl looked up at her again. 'Tell me you don't like the way it feels when I kiss you,' she purred, 'and I will stop.'

Helen knew she couldn't say the words. She let out a hungry sob and closed her eyes. She felt the brush of the girl's hair against her thighs and shuddered, wishing that she could slip back into the dream where the caresses and the hot kisses had belonged to an unknown lover.

The girl sucked her clitoris, milking it, her tongue flicking back and forth between her pouting lips. Helen gasped and, as the pleasure intensified, called out in delight and horror. She couldn't believe this was happening and yet it was blissful, all-encompassing.

She closed her mind to Anya's bright eyes and, in that second, surrendered herself entirely to the electric sensations the gypsy girl was lighting inside her. The act of surrender pushed away every shred of control. As the waves came closer and closer together she tangled her fingers in the girl's hair, pulling her closer, absorbing every last flicker of delight. As the first ripples of her orgasm rolled through her, she screamed out with bliss, pressing her sex up against the girl's face, while between her legs Anya purred with pleasure.

When it was over and the glistening roar of sensations had abated, Helen collapsed amongst the pillows gasping and shaking with pleasure. Anya crept up Helen's body, rubbing her soft warm body against hers. Without thinking, Helen encircled Anya with her arms. The woman kissed her softly and Helen was stunned to taste her own musky scent on the woman's open mouth.

Anya wriggled and took hold of Helen's hands. 'I want you to touch me now,' the girl whispered. Helen stiffened, opening her eyes to look into the dark cat-like eyes of her companion. 'It's all right,' Anya purred. 'Don't be afraid, I will show you, let me teach you how to share the pleasure—'

She guided Helen's hands to her heavy breasts. Helen was stunned at how soft and fluid Anya's body felt beneath her fingertips, her curiosity and surprise at odds with her repulsion.

'Close your eyes,' said Anya softly. 'Let your body feel the way. You know what I want.'

Helen shivered and obeyed. It almost felt as if she was exploring her own body or, at least, one like hers. It was strangely familiar but subtly different; the rise of the breasts, the narrowing waist. She knew then, as she felt the gypsy girl's pulse quickening beneath her fingertips, that Anya was right. Some part of her knew exactly what the other woman wanted, it was only her mind that fought her. She tried to still its insistent shocked voice, letting her fingertips drink in the soft delicate curves of the woman lying in her arms. She could almost feel the sensations echoed in her own body – it was blissful – so soft, so warm and unthreatening. It made her understand why men desired women so much.

Anya started to moan softly. Helen pushed aside her doubts and closed her lips around one of Anya's pert swollen nipples, sucking it deep into her mouth.

The gypsy girl hissed. 'Oh yes,' she murmured, 'make me sing, Helen, make me sing.'

Helen held her breath and slipped her fingers down over the hot naked lips of Anya's sex and tentatively slipped a finger between them. She gasped as she felt the heat and wetness there and then the hard swollen ridge of her clitoris. Slowly she began to stroke her finger back and forth. Anya moaned contentedly and opened her legs wider, her hands joining Helen's to push her fingers home. The muscles inside Anya contracted sharply around Helen's forefinger, drawing her further inside.

'My God,' Helen whispered, astounded at the invitation and the sheer sensual delights of Anya's

body. She had an overwhelming compulsion to give
Anya the pleasure she so much desired and slowly,
slowly began to run her tongue down over the gypsy
woman's ribcage. Anya tasted salty, still smelling of
Jack's hard rugged body, but beneath it Helen could
detect the sweet musk of Anya's own fragrance. On
her fingers she could smell Anya's excited sexual musk
and froze – realising with horror that the scent was
making her mouth water.

Anya stroked her face gently. 'Take it slowly, little
one. Let your body guide you. We can give each other
so much pleasure.'

Helen shuddered, sliding lower in the bed. She ran
her tongue speculatively across the place where the
golden woman's outer lips met, planting a tentative
kiss on the junction.

Anya lifted her hips. 'Make me sing,' she whispered
and Helen pushed away all reluctance and closed her
mouth over Anya's jutting swollen clitoris, sucking it
gently between her lips.

It was like a strange dark feast. Helen relinquished
all of the controls that held her back, sliding her fingers
into Anya, smearing her juices out over her thighs,
dipping into her with her tongue and her fingers. The
gypsy girl bucked, opening her legs wider, still pressing
Helen's head down into her groin. Meanwhile Anya
curled around so that she could touch Helen. Helen
gasped as the girl's fingers found her, splaying her sex
open, her thumb seeking out Helen's pleasure-bud.

Locked together in a dance of excitement, it felt as if
every movement Helen made with her tongue on Anya

was echoed, an instant later, by the girl's fingers. It was an enticing engulfing magic that drove Helen to the very edge of sanity. It felt as if she were making love to herself, driving on and on until Helen thought she would die. Suddenly she knew she couldn't hold back the well of excitement that boiled and rolled inside her. Beneath her, Anya's body seemed to explode with delight. Roaring tumbling waves coursed through Helen's body, echoed and mirrored in the body of the woman beside her. For an instant, the whole world was centred on the two of them.

When Anya drew Helen into her arms, she was still trembling uncontrollably.

'Rest now,' whispered Anya. 'It's all right . . .'

Laying her head against Anya's shoulder, Helen closed her eyes and within seconds was asleep.

When she opened her eyes again, morning light filled the room and Anya had gone. Helen reddened as she thought about the delight they had given one another. She could still taste the other woman on her lips. Her thoughts were interrupted by the sound of Anya's singing and her footsteps on the stairs. The gypsy girl's face appeared around the door. She was smiling.

'I've lit the fire, would you like to bathe?'

Helen nodded dumbly.

'Good, I've put lots of water on for us,' she paused. 'You won't mind sharing a bath with me, will you?'

Helen shook her head, feeling the flush of colour return to her cheeks. Anya seemed oblivious to her embarrassment, 'Good, it won't be long before it's hot enough. Why don't you come down and we'll have some tea while we wait.'

Helen climbed unsteadily out of bed and wrapped a blanket around her. It wasn't until she turned around that she realised Anya was still standing by the doorway. She clutched the blanket tighter.

Anya laughed, stepping into the little bedroom. She was naked except for an open shirt that looked as if it might be one of Jack's. 'I can see why Jack likes you,' she said, moving towards Helen. 'You are very beautiful, you shouldn't be ashamed of your body.' She caught hold of the blanket and Helen didn't resist as Anya peeled it off her. The gypsy woman's eyes moved appreciatively over Helen. She smiled broadly, 'You look as beautiful as you feel. Come, let me find you something to wear.'

Charles had shivered himself awake. There was a mist out over the river, the reeds and bushes were heavy with new frost. He rubbed his eyes. The sun was hanging low in the morning sky, touching the icy ground with a soft red-gold glow. He stretched, his body stiff with the cold and the damp. The little boat barely seemed to be moving through the sluggish grey waters. At the stern, Nip's son was hunched over the tiller, his face grey with cold and fatigue. Charles licked his lips and swallowed down the bitter taste of sleep.

'Will it be much longer?' he said to the boy.

Nip's son didn't move, as if he was asleep, even though his eyes were open. Charles' voice disturbed Nip, who stirred himself from under a pile of blankets.

The little boatman blinked uncomfortably in the raw daylight and then looked left and right to get his bearings before glancing back at the silent boy.

'Slept longer than I meant to,' he muttered, coughing to clear his throat. 'I'll get a brew on. We could all do with warming up. Are you all right, lad?'

The boy lifted his eyes and nodded stiffly.

Charles rubbed his hands to drive out the chill of the frost, 'How long before we get there?'

Nip shook his head. 'Not too long now, Mr Garrison, not too long at all.'

When Jack pushed open the cottage door he was met by squeals of protest. He shut it quickly behind him and looked up in astonishment.

In front of a roaring fire, Helen and Anya were sitting either end of a huge tin bath. Both women turned towards him. Clouds of steam hung in the air around them. He could only see their heads clearly, their bodies were partially obscured by a clothes-horse hung with sheets and towels that they'd arranged to keep out the draughts. The little room smelt of soap and echoed to the sounds of giggles and splashing. He looked back and forth between the two of them and shook his head.

Helen's hair was dressed like Anya's, with glittering combs and a single feather plaited into it. Her bright blue eyes were ringed with a line of kohl.

Jack grinned, pulling off his heavy jacket, 'Seems I've found two free spirits on my hearth this morning. I thought it looked quiet when I came across the yard.'

Anya laughed, flicking water at him, but Helen

seemed more uncertain. She looked up nervously. 'Do you like it?'

He nodded, 'Aye, but I liked you well enough before that little minx painted your face.'

Anya stood up, catching hold of Helen's hand. 'Stand up,' she said, giggling. 'Let him see if he likes the rest too.'

Helen stood up slowly as Jack moved towards them. The two women were glistening with moisture, trickles of soapy water clinging to their breasts and bellies. Jack smiled and nodded, reaching out to run his hands over Helen's naked body. She shivered under his fingertips. 'When I told you to take care of her, Anya, I'd not expected you to take a razor to her.' His fingers stroked the slick naked mound of Helen's sex. 'You look very beautiful,' he whispered, holding her gaze.

Beside her, Anya crowed triumphantly. 'I told her you would like it,' she said, then she reached out and caught hold of Jack. 'You look so cold. Why don't you take your clothes off and get in the bath with us? The water is lovely and I've got more on the stove.'

Jack nodded, his eyes not leaving Helen as he undid his shirt buttons.

Chapter 7

Charles' Wife

'I think you're misleading me. I'm not such a fool as you take me for,' snapped Charles as he watched Nip Hunter brewing tea. 'We've been out on this damned river all night.'

Nip shrugged, 'I did say it was a fair way, sir. It'll be midmorning before we get there, but it ain't that far now.'

Charles hissed. His breath rolled in great dragon plumes before him.

'Maybe my lad's been taking it a big more cautious than I would've done, but I was all in. We've not made bad time considering.'

Charles sat down heavily and dragged the blanket up over his frozen legs. Helen would pay for this.

Helen soaped Jack's back, relishing the feel of his tight strong muscles beneath her fingers. Anya curled like a tiny cat, crouched over his feet, dipping her fingers teasingly below the water. Bubbles and foam spilt in hot glistening puddles over the cottage floor.

185

'My turn now.' Anya held out her hands to take the soap. Helen sat down, feeling Jack's slick body against her own. He lifted her legs so that they circled his waist. She could feel his swollen cock pressing against her knees. Water lapped over the sides as they moved.

Anya soaped her hands and began to lather it over her own shapely body, giving it an erotic glistening sheen. Jack reached out to cup the weight of her breasts. She giggled as his fingers stroked her dark nipples into hard peaks and then turned her attentions to him, streaking tight soapy lines over his chest hair. He lay back contentedly against Helen's body, closing his eyes, resting his head between her breasts.

Anya's hands worked lower, soaping the dark hair on his belly, sliding his swollen cock between her slippery fingers. He moaned and lifted himself clear of the water. She placed a single soapy kiss on the swollen engorged head and then looked up.

She glanced across at the stove and pulled a face. 'No more water, it'll get colder now.'

Jack grinned. 'You'll wash yourself away. I'm done outside for a while. We'll stay indoors, it's too damned cold out there to work.'

Anya lifted her eyebrow, her fingers still stroking idly along his shaft. 'And what shall we find to pass the time until my friends come for me?' Her voice suggested that she already had the solution. She wriggled closer, pulling herself up onto her knees so that she was almost close enough to take Jack inside her. She stroked herself along his body, her mouth pouting in a provocative teasing bow.

Jack lifted his hands to caress her soapy breasts. 'I'm sure we can find something to occupy us,' he purred throatily, circling her nipples with his palms.

Helen pressed herself closer against his back. The night before she had been too afraid to join them in front of the fire, in spite of the excitement she had felt. Now the fear had evaporated and her body ached for the pleasure she could share with them.

Anya slipped from the bath and threw more logs onto the fire before wrapping herself in a sheet. She turned towards Jack and Helen and lifted her arms above her head. Humming a strange eastern tune she began to roll her hips around, swaying from side to side.

Jack turned towards Helen and grinned. 'Take no notice of her, she's a show-off.'

Anya slipped out the combs that held up her hair and shook her head. The thick lustrous curls fell in a dark damp curtain over her slim body. She ground out the beat of her tune, swaying provocatively from side to side. 'He's only jealous, I'm a dancer and no man I know can resist this.' She flipped her head back, revealing her sparkling excited eyes. 'What do you say, Jack?'

He leapt from the bath and grabbed hold of her. Anya squealed with delight, rubbing her lithe body up against his. He kissed her on the lips as he encircled her waist with his strong arms, lifting her off the ground. Her shriek turned to a low whimper of pleasure as he pulled her closer.

'I say,' he whispered, 'that you are a teasing wicked woman.'

Anya laughed, wriggling away from him. Helen watched them, their affection and mutual desire was a delight. She felt ridiculously privileged to see them together. Jack snatched a towel off the clothes-horse and wrapped it around his waist, covering the impressive arc of his erection. They both turned to look at Helen.

She slithered down so that she was lying full length in the tub and smiled. They both looked surprised. She rolled over slowly onto her belly, resting her chin on her arms on the bath side. Taking the lead from their intimate teasing banter, she grinned. 'Finally,' she sighed closing her eyes, 'I've got enough room to soak myself.'

Anya laughed and picked up another sheet, 'Come out, you'll get all wrinkled if you stay in there much longer.'

Helen pouted mischievously and then climbed to her feet. Anya stepped forward and wrapped the sheet around her. 'You look very lovely,' she whispered. 'All soft and pink. Here.' She picked up a flannel and wiped Helen's face gently. 'The kohl is starting to run; if you're going to look like a gypsy we can't have you all smudged.'

Helen looked into the little mirror balanced on a shelf above the mantelpiece. Her strange exotically dressed eyes gave her the same cat-like expression that Anya had. Behind her Jack and Anya had begun to clear away the remains of their bath. She turned to help them.

When they'd done, Jack hurried upstairs. Anya

followed and then Helen, afraid that she might miss whatever they had planned. Upstairs Jack was rolling the mattress off the bed and Anya was making a pile of pillows and bed linen.

'What on earth are you doing?'

Anya grinned and threw her a pillow. 'It's too cold to go outside, and there's a lovely fire downstairs,' she said, raising her eyebrows.

Jack dragged the mattress past her. 'We might as well be comfortable as well as warm.'

Downstairs Anya built a nest of blankets and pillows on the mattress which Jack had unrolled in front of the hearth. They looked like three strange survivors from a shipwreck, naked except for their sheets and towels. Jack was the first to climb into the mattress raft.

Helen shivered. Stepping into the bed in front of the fire would commit her to whatever followed. It was an act of total acceptance. Anya slithered artfully out of her damp sheet, like a golden snake sloughing its skin. There was just the merest, fleeting glimpse of her beautiful body before she vanished beneath the heavy counterpane.

Two bright pairs of eyes watched Helen from beneath the blankets, two bright pairs of eyes that both revealed their desire for her and each other. Helen dropped her sheet onto the cottage floor and slipped quickly beneath the warm covers.

'Where?' snapped Charles, peering through the spyglass that Nip had given him. The Fen-man had pulled the boat into the bank so Charles could scramble up the grass to look out into the Fen beyond.

Out in front of him the flat land was white and bleak. Dykes and rivers, their banks higher than the surrounding land, were the only real features. In the very far distance was a darker contour marking the far edge of the Fen.

'I can't see a damned thing.' Charles dropped the lens from his eyes and peered accusingly at the Fenman.

Nip sucked his teeth and then spat thickly onto the frozen grass. Behind him, amongst a fan of white tangled bushes, a plume of steam rose up around Nip's son as he relieved himself. Both of them looked steadily at Charles.

'Over that way,' said Nip slowly, looking at Charles with utter contempt.

Damned cheating bastard, thought Charles, looking him straight in the eye. Through the last remaining strands of mist he could still see nothing.

Nip climbed slowly up onto the bank and pointed, 'Over there, between that clump of trees.'

Charles put the glass back to his eyes, feeling a momentary flicker of fear as he felt Nip Hunter step closer.

'Can yer see it now?' he hissed, almost in Charles' ear.

Amongst the grey misty outcrop of scrubby trees, Charles could see a little squat shape. As his eyes sharpened to what he was seeing, he could make out a narrow plume of smoke from the chimney. 'Yes,' he whispered quietly. 'Yes, I can see it now.' He swung round to look at Nip, 'Is that where she is?'

Nip shrugged. 'That's where I took her yesterday. I've no way of knowing if she's still there.'

Charles stood very still, it hadn't occurred to him that Helen might not have stayed with Jack. He coughed uneasily. 'Fair enough,' he said, handing Nip the spy glass. 'How long before we get there?'

Nit spat again. 'I keep telling you, mid-morning, not too long now. If we stop looking and get going we'll get there all the sooner.'

Charles stuffed his hands back into his pockets, 'Well, best we get on then.'

Nip's boy climbed stiffly back into the stern. He looked at Charles with barely concealed annoyance. Nip slithered quickly back down the bank and started to undo the lines. For one awful moment Charles considered the possibility that they might leave without him. He rushed down the bank, staggering and almost falling over the uneven slippery ground as he hurried back to the boat.

Jack kissed Helen with a soft intensity. His tongue teased an entry between her lips. Anya, watching intently, moaned and crept closer, rubbing her body against Jack's arm. Her fingers stroked across both their faces, linking them with an electric caress. Jack turned his head and kissed her too. Helen watched now, as the gypsy girl's eyes closed, sooty lashes fluttering on her tanned cheeks. The air between the three of them was crackling with sensual possibilities.

Jack rolled over onto his back so that he lay between the two women, his eyes glistening with excitement. Anya turned towards Helen and brushed her lips against her cheek, seeking out her mouth. Helen shivered, fighting the contradictions of her desire and fear.

The gypsy girl slipped her arms around Helen and pulled her closer, her cat-like tongue lapping at Helen's full lips. 'Sing,' she murmured, pressing her tongue into the sensitive depths of Helen's open mouth.

Helen moaned and surrendered to Anya's kisses. As their lips met she felt Jack's lips close around one of her nipples, his tongue curling around its tight peak. Her stomach leapt with the intensity of the sensations and she gave herself up entirely to her body's desperate aching call.

Their love-making was slow and intense, like a carefully orchestrated ballet. Helen felt as if every cell of her body was alight. Slipping his arms around her Jack guided her down carefully onto his already throbbing cock. She could feel his hardness nuzzling between the full swollen inner lips and lifted herself up to allow him to slide deep inside her. Her body tightened around him, drawing him further in. She knew she was wet. She could feel the warm slick juices already bubbling up from deep inside her, trickling down over Jack's phallus.

Anya, lithe and subtle, straddled Jack's head, facing Helen so that she could turn her attentions to Helen's breasts and her mouth. The other woman's fingers teased and stroked, drawing electric patterns of pleasure on her body. Helen found it impossible to hold back – her own fingers began to mimic the girl's caresses. Anya smiled sleepily and stretched herself under Helen's tentative touch, murmuring soft words of encouragement and pleasure.

Jack began to move slowly in and out of her aching eager sex. She whimpered. As they began to move to a slow intense rhythm Helen felt Anya's fingers flickering down over her hot tingling belly. Searching lower, rubbing her hips, circling her navel, seeking out the junction where her naked sex sucked and folded around Jack's thick cock. Anya sighed as she found the swollen ridge of Helen's clitoris. Helen gasped and lifted herself up to let the girl explore her further, revelling in the attentions of the girl's knowing fingers. As she moved upwards against Anya's fingertips, Jack plunged deeper, making her whole body contract and thrill with sheer delight. She revelled in their possession of her body.

It felt as if she could never want for anything more. Her lips sought out Anya's swollen nipples. As she closed her mouth around the firm peaks she glanced down to see Jack's tongue darting in and out of Anya's open, expectant sex.

Anya began to move in time with Jack's eager lapping tongue, rolling her hips back so that he caught her clitoris with every upward stroke. Helen felt herself being drawn down into a spiral of excitement that seemed to echo every thrust, every kiss, every scintillating caress. Everything they did registered somewhere deep inside her.

She gasped at the sensations her two lovers created

in her. Between the gasps and little animal noises of pleasure, she could hear a desperate baying call of delight and was shocked to realise it was her own voice calling out for more and more—

Jack lifted his hips, trapping Anya's fingers tight between Helen's outer lips. The split second of pressure was enough to drive Helen over the brink. She screamed out, pulling Anya towards her, grinding her hips down onto Jack. The glowing, arcing roar of her orgasm swept through them all.

Helen opened her eyes, stunned at the expression of ecstasy on Anya's face as the gypsy dancer breathlessly completed her circle of pleasure. Beneath them both, hot and slick with sweat, Jack writhed and jerked, signalling his own desperate climax.

Slowly they slipped down amongst the tangle of sheets and curled into a hot tangle of legs, arms and bodies.

Anya was the first to stir. Helen stroked the other woman's shoulders, drinking in the softness of her skin. The gypsy girl smelt of soap and sweat and the scents of their bodies mingled – a heady erotic perfume. She slipped silently out of Helen's arms and slid the kettle back over the fire to boil. Helen closed her eyes and let the warmth of Jack's arms and the lingering perfume of Anya's body soothe her into the silky grey space between sleeping and waking.

It seemed like only a second or two later when Anya shook her awake. 'Tea,' she whispered.

Helen grinned sleepily and pulled herself onto one elbow. 'You are wonderful.'

Anya stood the mug down on the hearth and stretched. 'I know,' she giggled. 'Let me back into that bed, I'm frozen.'

Jack peeled the bedclothes back. 'Come here,' he murmured throatily. 'We'll soon warm you up.' He glanced at Helen, 'Won't we?'

Helen nodded, realising that what they had just had was a prelude. She and Jack closed Anya into the space between them. The girl's body was cold. Helen could feel the chill drawing out her warmth and shivered. Instantly Anya pulled Helen into her arms. She didn't resist, instead she linked her arms round Anya's waist and held her close, feeling the heartbeat of her new lover echoing through her own body.

Charles stood up in the prow of the boat, looking like some kind of bizarre figurehead as he peered through the eyeglass. Not that he could see a great deal, he thought angrily, the banks cut off the view on either side. His impatience was growing with every passing minute.

He glanced over his shoulder. Behind him, Nip Hunter and his son were silent, watching him with barely concealed disdain. He wanted to ask how much longer it would take, but the last time he had asked Nip, the man had spat furiously over the side of the boat and said nothing, answering his enquiry with an angry stare.

Helen slid her tongue between the lips of Anya's open sex. Between the golden outer lips a pink wet flower blossomed in the soft light of the cottage. Kneeling on all fours, while the girl lay beneath her, Helen slipped a tentative finger inside her. The heat of her quim took Helen's breath away. Anya tightened her muscles around her. Helen looked up in surprise. Anya grinned.

'Kiss me,' she murmured. 'Use your tongue on me.'

Helen dipped again, moving her tongue along the ridges and folds, tasting Anya's salty excitement as she lapped again and again. She brushed the engorged ridge of her clitoris and Anya moaned, lifting her hips up, offering herself to Helen.

Behind her, Helen felt Jack's hands stroking her buttocks and waist, felt his body heat as he crept closer. A single finger stroked the sensitive bridge between her wet open sex and the tight closure behind. She shivered, astounded that her body responded at once, dropping instinctively to give him greater access.

Under the attentions of her tongue and lips, Anya was starting to writhe, opening her legs wider, lifting herself to take every advantage of Helen's wet offering to her naked body.

Jack brushed his cock against Helen's swollen quim with a teasing delicate caress. Helen tried to wriggle back to draw him into her. He slipped away from her easily. She moaned between her lips, closed tight, still sucking at the little pink bud of Anya's clitoris.

Slowly, slowly he moved over her again, pressing his lips to her spine. He held her hips, moving her slowly, back and forth against Anya's body. His fingers moved to caress her breasts, rolling their hard sensitive nipples between his thumb and forefinger.

The sensations he was igniting in her glowed like an intense fiery pit in her belly, the heat moving out through her body, making every last cell quiver with expectation.

As he brushed against the open naked lips again, Helen suddenly got the most vivid picture of Charles in her mind. She saw him hunched over her, sweating and furious. She froze, thinking about Annie, thinking about the way her husband had treated them both.

In her mind, Charles' face, contorted with lust and fury, leered over her nakedness. 'I know how to treat whores,' he hissed, his voice cold and controlled as he forced himself into her body. Each brutal thrust stole her pleasure, snatching away her love and desire.

She stiffened as she felt Jack's first tentative exploration. Suddenly she was cold and afraid. She gasped for breath, wrenching herself away from Anya and Jack, and practically leapt off the mattress.

'I can't,' she whispered, 'I can't.'

She hurried across to the window and looked outside. The little cottage garden was empty except for Jack's dogs, resting in their kennels. The frost still whitened every branch and leaf. Beyond the rough square of grass, the river, mist still rising from its dark water, rolled slowly by the low banks. She swallowed hard, her heart beating wildly against her ribs, as she tried to control the growing sense of panic that threatened to overwhelm her. The cold and apprehension made her shiver. She felt foolish as a hard sharp knot of pain rose in her throat and tears stung her eyes.

She glanced back at Jack and Anya, still lying, as

she had left them, on the mattress in front of the fire. Both of them watched her with tenderness and concern. Fighting back tears, she whispered, 'Charles.'

Anya, raising her head, pulled a face, her expression holding a question.

Jack shook his head at the prone girl and got up. 'Come back here,' he whispered to Helen, extending his hand. 'He isn't here yet. There is only Anya and I, lady. You know we won't hurt you.'

A single tear rolled down Helen's cheek. 'But he will come, won't he?'

Jack nodded, 'Aye, but now we have just ourselves. Come back to be with us.'

Helen bit her lip and crept back towards them. As she approached Jack he closed his arms around her, pulling her close. She felt his strength and protection enveloping her. She let out a long sad sigh and did not resist as he guided her back onto the mattress. He rolled her slowly onto her hands and knees and she shuddered as he slipped easily inside her.

'Whatever it is,' he whispered as his hands moved knowingly to caress her sex, 'it's not here, it's not now. Give yourself to me. I'll not treat you wrong.'

Helen groaned, relishing the sensation of his cock filling her. He was right; he wasn't Charles and what his body promised her was a different thing to the cruel unfeeling treatment that Charles dealt out. She pushed the thoughts away and eased herself back against the hard muscular curve of his thighs. Jack gave her only pleasure. Anya crept closer, her eyes glittering, and uncurled herself beneath Helen like some exotic orchid.

Helen caught the hint of her perfume and pulled the dark woman closer. She opened her mouth over the hard bud of her clitoris and drew it between her lips, surrendering herself to the woman's smell and the hypnotic magic of her golden body.

Jack pressed home into her, fingers stroking down over the hood of her clitoris. She whimpered, all thoughts of Charles rapidly receding as her excitement rekindled and her body took control. She shuddered and gave herself over to its eager desperate demands.

'*There!*' snapped Nip Hunter to Charles, 'around that next bend. Can yer see the smoke from the chimney?'

Charles pulled his coat up round his throat and pushed himself back to his feet, 'Indeed I can. Now we shall see an end to this nonsense,' he said quietly. He puffed out his cheeks. Now he would see what Helen had to say for herself.

Dogs began to bark furiously. Charles looked back at Nip, 'His dogs?'

Nip nodded. 'Aye, if you'd hoped to creep up on them, they've put paid to your plans.'

Charles shook his head, 'Oh no,' he said briskly, 'I want my wife to know that I'm coming for her.'

Anya was rolling back and forth, her fingers tangled in Helen's hair as her orgasm pressed up behind Helen's lips. Helen could feel it mirrored in her own body. Jack had brought her so close to the edge that she didn't know if she'd be able to hold back the tide of sensations long enough to drive Anya over into the deep well of pleasure that yawned beneath them.

The gypsy girl's body tightened around her fingers and she screamed out in triumph. Behind her Jack snorted. Helen could feel his sweat dripping onto her back and thrust back against him one last time. He gave a dark throaty groan and at the same instant brilliant lights exploded inside her head. A tide of ecstasy broke over her exhausted throbbing body.

As they collapsed forward in a hot breathless heap, Helen heard the dogs. She stiffened, glancing at Jack with bright fearful eyes.

'Stay there,' Jack whispered, slipping out of her and springing to his feet. He dragged on his trousers and shirt.

'Where are your clothes?' whispered Anya to Helen.

'Upstairs.'

Anya pulled a sheet up over her slick naked body. 'Jack will keep them talking while we get dressed.' She hurried across the room and picked up her pack and the bundle of clothes she had taken off the night before. 'Here,' she said quickly, throwing Helen the pack, 'there are some things of mine in there, put them on.'

Jack was pulling on his boots. He looked at Helen.

'Charles?' she whispered unsteadily.

Jack shrugged. 'We'll soon see,' he said and hurried towards the door. He opened and closed it in a split second. Helen tipped the pack up and dragged out the clothes whilst, beside her, Anya dressed quickly.

Nip's son, carrying the bowline, leapt from the boat onto the jetty. He slipped the rope around a ring set into the side and hauled the boat closer. Charles clambered stiffly up onto the icy planks and surveyed Jack Hartman's estate.

Two mongrel dogs barked furiously, straining madly against the chains that tied them to their kennels. Beside the makeshift jetty two other small boats were moored.

Charles stretched and tidied his clothes. The door of the cottage opened and Jack Hartman stepped out into the cold morning air.

The two men weighed each other up from a distance.

Charles stepped onto the river bank. The tinker was taller than he remembered, with bright dark eyes. Hartman looked dishevelled, dressed in an open-neck shirt and faded worn trousers. Charles noticed that he hadn't even bothered to tie his boot laces. He coughed and took a step closer. 'I believe,' he said very slowly, watching the tinker's face with interest, 'that you have something here that belongs to me.'

Jack rested his forearm against the porch and lifted his eyebrow. 'Belongs to you, does she?'

Charles nodded. 'You heard me. She is my wife and I want her back.'

Jack pursed his lips and let out a silent whistle. 'The lady in question comes and goes as she pleases,' he said flatly. 'I've no say whether your wife stays or goes. The choice is surely hers to make.'

Charles could feel the anger building in the pit of his belly. 'Enough of this damned nonsense. Send her out to me, Hartman, and it's the last you'll hear of the matter.'

Jack didn't move but his eyes darkened. 'As I said sir, the choice isn't mine to make. The lady comes and goes as she pleases.'

Charles glanced behind him. Nip Hunter and his son were standing in the stern of the boat, their expressions blank and closed. Charles straightened himself up. 'Am I to take it that you'll not bring her out to me?' he said stiffly.

Jack shrugged.

Charles leapt forward, white hot fury boiling up in his belly. 'You filthy little bastard, hand over my wife to me or I'll set the law on you. I'll have you hauled through every court in the land for kidnapping, for rape, for theft. I'll run you off this paltry filthy little acre, straight into the poor house and ensure you never work nor eat again. Do I make myself clear?'

Still Jack didn't move.

'Do you know who I am?' Charles growled malevolently.

Jack nodded. 'Oh, I know exactly who you are, Mr Garrison.'

The door to the cottage opened and Charles watched as a small woman stepped alongside Jack. She slipped under his arm and leant against him. Charles blinked unsteadily; it wasn't Helen.

She lay provocatively against the curve of the tinker's body. 'Is this Charles?' she purred, regarding Charles with idle curiosity.

Jack nodded, his dark eyes still focused on Charles' face. The woman pulled a face. 'Helen's husband?'

Jack nodded again. 'It would seem so.'

The dark woman grimaced as, from the shadows, Helen stepped up alongside the tinker.

Charles gasped. His wife was dressed in some sort of costume: a white blouse and a full brightly coloured skirt that barely covered her knees. Her feet were bare. She crept close to Jack Hartman, her eyes glistening. The gypsy girl moved closer to Helen. Charles noticed the way she slid her arm protectively around Helen's waist. He felt his colour rising. Helen glanced up at him. He could sense her fear and was disconcerted to feel a familiar stirring in his groin. He coughed to cover his embarrassment.

'Get your things together and get in the boat,' he said as evenly as he could manage. Helen didn't move, though her eyes flashed with an intense mixture of emotions.

'I do not intend to repeat myself.' He held her gaze, 'If you don't get your things and come with me now, I will ruin your little tinker, Helen. And be sure that I mean it.'

He saw her flinch. The gypsy woman's arm tightened around her, while Jack, who had not moved until then, laid his hand gently on Helen's shoulder. 'Don't let him bully you,' he said in a low even voice. 'It wouldn't be the first time I've come up against the likes of him.'

But Charles could see that Helen was rattled. He pressed home his advantage. Ignoring Jack, he looked directly at Helen. She had begun to tremble. 'I'll see him driven off this land, out of his filthy little cottage.' He paused, looking evenly at the gypsy girl who stood so close to his wife. 'He'll not be left with the clothes on his back. Him and his little whore with him.'

The gypsy girl's eyes flashed black with fury. She took a step forward as if to pounce – only Jack's hand on her shoulder prevented her from leaping at Charles. 'Leave him, Anya,' murmured Jack, 'he's not worth the candle.'

The girl shook Jack's hand off furiously and crouched like a wild cat ready to spring.

Helen let out a long juddering sigh. 'I'll get my things,' she said softly, her voice tight with emotion.

'Don't go with him,' Anya hissed.

Helen looked at them. 'I have to,' she said softly. 'If I stay, there will be nothing but trouble for you both.'

Charles smiled triumphantly. 'A wise move,' he said in an undertone. Helen stepped back inside the cottage.

She looked around the warm interior of the cottage. Her stomach fluttered with panic and fear and, worse still, a great well of pain that threatened to engulf her. On the cottage floor were the ruins of the makeshift bed, puddles of soapy water still lay amongst the tiles. She shivered and glanced back out of the open door. Charles stood on the bank, his face pale, eyes dark and angry.

Under the porch Jack and Anya stood side by side. As she thought Jack's name he turned to look at her, his face full of concern. 'You have no need to go,' he said in an undertone.

Helen bit her lip. 'I have to go back with him and sort this out, or I'll never be free of him.'

Jack nodded. 'I said you were a brave woman, Helen

Garrison. Don't let him break you, he has the face for it.'

Helen nodded and then hurried upstairs to find the remains of her clothes.

She lay Anya's beautiful exotic clothes on the bed where she had spent the night and pulled on the clothes she had brought with her from the Hall. Even though it had been only a few hours since she had last worn them they seemed strange, alien. They even smelt unfamiliar. When she got downstairs Charles was sitting in the boat waiting for her.

Anya stepped into the cottage and caught hold of Helen's arm. 'You can't go with that man,' she hissed. 'He will destroy you.'

Helen shook her head. 'He won't. I won't let him.'

'You could stay,' said Anya, glancing back at Jack. 'Jack wants you to be with him, I can tell.'

Helen embraced the little gypsy woman. 'I know, but Charles wouldn't rest until he has hurt Jack.'

'And what about you? What will he do to you?'

Helen blinked back the tears and shook her head. 'There isn't just me to think about.' She thought about Annie. 'His family's reputation means everything to him. As far as he's concerned, I'm not just betraying him but his family too. If I don't go I don't know what he might do, or what he is capable of.'

Anya's face contorted with anger. 'He's a wicked man.'

Helen shook her head. 'No, not wicked,' she said sadly. 'Just unhappy and lost.' She looked back at the tangle of sheets on the mattress in front of the fire. 'He

doesn't know how to sing. I don't think he's ever been
free.'

Anya sighed. 'And he will never let you be free
either.'

Helen picked up the little case she had brought with
her. 'Don't be so sure,' she whispered, almost to herself,
and then stepped back out into the cottage garden.

Jack turned towards her, his eyes held a thousand
questions. He reached out to her with both hands. 'You
don't have to go with him,' he said.

'I know.'

'There is nothing that he can do that others haven't
tried.'

Helen nodded. 'I have to sort this out, Jack. I can't
stand by and wait for him to do something. I have got
to go back.'

Jack sighed and pulled her to him. As his lips closed
on hers she glanced at the boat. Charles was sitting
rigidly in the stern, his eyes fixed firmly on the river.
She slipped from Jack's arms, wishing that there was
some way she could stay. She lifted her hand to his
cheek; she had so much she wanted to say to him. Instead
she let her hand fall away and picked up her case.

The dogs whined, straining at the end of their chains,
as Helen walked slowly down the path towards the
river. At the jetty, Nip Hunter took hold of her hand
and helped her down into the boat. His small darting
eyes held an unspoken apology. Helen bit her lips and
looked down at the water. She stepped stiffly into the
little cabin, not looking back, her mind crowded and
spinning with thoughts.

As the cottage vanished around the first bend, Charles handed her his handkerchief, 'Wipe that muck off your face,' he said coldly.

Helen's fingers closed round the little piece of cloth. She shivered and sank lower into her seat. Even though she knew she had to face returning to the Lodge with Charles she wondered if she truly had the courage to do what she had planned.

The journey home was painfully silent. Every time Helen looked at Charles he was staring blankly at the river or the banks. The tension hung between them like a tight shiny wire. Nip and his son seemed to be almost invisible. Helen kept the tears she felt in check. She was determined that Charles wouldn't see her cry.

It was very late when they finally drew under the dark shadow of the bridge over the river at Ferrybridge. Parked under the shelter of the bank was Charles' car. Helen sat still whilst Charles stepped out, unsteadily, onto the wooden jetty.

As she got up to climb out, Nip hurried to take her arm. Even in the dark his little eyes were bright, reflecting the winter moonlight. 'If I'd known what sort of man he was I'd have left you be,' he whispered.

Helen nodded, clutching his arm. 'It doesn't matter, Nip. If he hadn't hired you he'd have found someone else to take him.'

Nip sighed. Helen stepped up beside her husband and did not resist when Charles grabbed hold of her wrist and led her to the car.

The Lodge looked dark and deserted in the headlights

as they drew into the Hall road. Charles drove up to the front and switched off the engine.

'Go inside and wait for me in the sitting-room,' he said flatly.

Helen, without a word, slipped from the car and let herself in. A single lamp was burning on the hall table. As she closed the door, Annie stepped out from the corridor, her face pale, her eyes dark ringed. 'Are you all right, ma'am?' the girl whispered, her voice betraying her anxiety.

Helen nodded, suddenly feeling completely exhausted, 'Yes, I'm fine, thank you, Annie.' She looked their maid up and down. As their eyes met a flicker of mutual understanding passed between the two of them, 'How are you?'

Annie's eyes filled with tears. 'I'm frightened, Mrs Garrison.'

Helen gently folded her arms around the girl's shoulders. 'It'll be all right, don't worry. I promise you. It will be all right.'

The front door opened. 'What a very touching scene,' said Charles thickly. He threw his hat onto the stand and looked at their maid. 'Annie, get back to your room. I want to talk to my wife alone.' Annie slipped out of Helen's arms and scurried away.

Charles slowly removed his coat and hung it up. He walked straight past Helen and into the sitting-room. Helen swallowed hard and then followed him.

Inside Charles had lit the lamp and was pouring himself a whisky from the tray on the sideboard. 'Sit down,' he said over his shoulder. When he turned back his eyes were dark unfathomable pools. 'So,' he whispered, 'how was your night with the little tinker? Did you enjoy yourself out there on the Fen?'

His voice was almost unnaturally cold and free from emotion. Helen shivered.

Charles poured a little water into his glass, 'I think it would be better for all concerned if we didn't mention this little incident again outside these four walls. It's a private affair. I've paid Nip Hunter to keep his mouth shut.' He looked her up and down. 'Well?'

Helen nodded. Her mouth was dry, she could feel the pulse throbbing in her ears.

Charles stared into the empty grate, 'I hadn't expected his little whore to be there with him. Did you sleep with her too?' He stepped closer, closing his fingers tightly around her chin, wrenching her head up to face him. 'I could see from the way she rubbed up against you that you did.'

Helen swallowed, trying to keep some kind of control over the fear that was wrenching at her gut.

'You have betrayed everything my family stands for,' he said, staring at her, 'and you're going to pay for it, every single day of your life. Do you understand me?'

Helen bit her lip. Charles let go of her and swallowed his drink in one mouthful. 'Go upstairs, and wait for me in the bathroom. You're not fit to sleep under this roof.'

Unsteadily Helen got to her feet, feeling as if she were losing control. She tried to keep sight of her plan, holding onto its bright shining light in her mind. In the face of Charles' cold brittle fury, the light flickered.

She swallowed hard, there was nothing Charles could do to her that would take away her plan for escape. She held onto the image of a little slip of paper tucked safe inside her skirt pocket in the wardrobe upstairs.

Charles got hold of her wrist and pulled her to her feet. 'I said wait upstairs for me in the bathroom.'

Upstairs she stood by the empty bath tub, dreading the sound of Charles' footsteps approaching on the stairs.

He crossed the landing and slipped off his jacket. She stood very still, watching him. He put the plug into the bath and turned on the cold tap. The water roared and foamed against the cast iron. He turned to look at her, eyes gleaming in the lamplight. 'Take off your clothes, I'm going to scrub the stink of those two off you.'

Helen fumbled with the buttons of her coat, the breath catching raggedly in her chest. As she slowly removed each garment he threw it out into the hall. Left in her slip she began to shiver.

'Get the rest off or I'll rip them off you,' he snorted thickly.

Helen slowly lifted the silky petticoat over her head. As she did Charles lunged forwards and ripped at her panties. His teeth closed around her breast, biting down on the tender flesh. She could feel his hot moist breath on her bare skin and shivered. 'You filthy little whore,' he snorted, grabbing hold of her sex through her drawers. 'How dare you give yourself to anyone else? You are my wife. Do you hear me?' He looked up and grabbed her chin, his eyes glinting on the verge of madness. She flinched.

He ripped away the thin fabric of her drawers and then gasped as he saw the naked open lips of her shaved sex. 'What in God's name is this?' he gasped. Helen felt herself flush scarlet. He drew his fingers down over the heavy outer lips, parting them roughly. 'My God,' he whispered with disgust, 'you're still full of his bloody seed.' He looked up at her again. 'Or was it that whore's tongue that got you so wet?'

Helen whimpered.

He got hold of her elbows and pushed her backwards. 'Get in the bath and let me get the stench off you.'

Helen stepped unsteadily into the icy water, it snatched away her heat and her breath in an instant. She shivered as Charles rolled up his shirt sleeves and took a scrubbing brush from the sink. His eyes narrowed to thin slits. 'When I've finished with you,' he hissed, 'you'll wish you never set eyes on Jack Hartman or his little painted bedmate.'

Helen let out a thin high-pitched squeal as the bristles bit into her tender skin. She closed her eyes tight and tried to concentrate on the folded slip of paper.

When he was done, Charles guided Helen, shaking, her skin scrubbed pink, into their bedroom. Her eyes were blank and unseeing as if she were asleep. He looked at her reflection in the bedroom mirror. There was still a single blue feather plaited into her hair.

He smiled thinly. Helen was his now, there was absolutely no question; she had chosen him over the tinker, she had chosen to come home. Now he would teach her what whores and wives were for. He ran his hands over her naked frame, feeling her tremble beneath his fingertips. Between her legs the open swollen lips of her sex glittered invitingly. He ran a finger speculatively over the naked slit; its exposure and vulnerability gave him a little shiver of pleasure.

He bent her forwards over the dressing-table, enjoying the way her scrubbed pink breasts hung forward. He spat into his hand and parted her legs, rolling his saliva up over her sex. She would give him anything he wanted now – and would be grateful for the chance.

He pushed a finger deeper, her silken inner sheath still felt slick from the tinker's touch. He shuddered; soon it would be wet for him. He pressed her hips down so that her backside splayed a little. Her sex opened, revealing the folds and creases, and behind, the tight pink bud of her anus.

He fumbled with his fly. There had been a little whore in Paris before the war who had understood him perfectly. He'd walked Helen along the street where the girl lived on their honeymoon. Not that he'd mentioned it then of course. The Helen who had walked arm in arm with him then had been a different woman to the woman who was bent naked over the dressing-table. The Helen from his honeymoon would have been shocked by his preferences, she would probably have fainted away. But his new Helen, this desperate guilty Helen, wouldn't turn a hair – she had no choice.

He picked up a jar of hair oil from the dressing-table

and smeared it over his fingers. Slowly he stroked it around the gaping lips of Helen's sex and then back towards the little tight closure that he truly preferred – the one that the little whore had opened so obligingly for him, as he'd pressed her down amongst her perfumed sheets.

He felt Helen stiffen and let out a gasp as he sought entry. Her muscles resisted him. He smiled, pressing her hips down harder onto the dressing-table. As she moved, the secret place gave a little and he slipped a finger inside. Her body closed deliciously around him.

'Good,' he whispered to himself on an outward breath and pressed a little deeper. Helen's shoulders shuddered spasmodically as if she were crying. He slid deeper still, trickling the oil over his fingers to ease his entry. He didn't mind her tears, in fact he thought she deserved them.

He stood the oil beside her and ran a hand over her belly, pulling her back against him. He dipped lower, rubbing his palm over her naked lips, then between them into the pit of her sex. He could feel the progress of his finger through the delicate connecting wall of her sex and the secret passage that lay behind.

Slowly he eased his finger out and rubbed the hair oil over the dark swell of his cock. She was after all, he thought, no better than a whore, even if she was his wife. Hadn't he taken her from that dreadful little provincial family and married her? Hadn't he taken her back in, even after she had so clearly betrayed him with Jack Hartman? She had been paid very well to give him what he wanted.

He felt Helen tense as he rubbed his phallus over the rosebud of her backside. He leant closer. 'Don't fight me,' he whispered, just as he had whispered to the whore in the Paris brothel. 'It won't hurt if you don't fight me.' As he spoke he tried to press his cock home. Helen's body closed instinctively against him. He stroked more oil over her. 'This is what I want,' he hissed, 'and this is what you will give me.'

Helen shuddered and let out a miserable sob as he pressed her down harder against the dressing-table. He gritted his teeth as the crown of his cock breached the tight pucker. He trickled more oil over his shaft, 'There,' he whispered, feeling the mesmerising tightness swallow him. 'That wasn't so bad, was it?'

Below him, Helen gasped and began to sob.

Chapter 8

Prisoner

The next morning Max Garrison heard a car pulling up outside the Hall. He glanced at his watch. Damned inconsiderate of his unseen visitor to arrive just before lunch. His stomach rumbled. Sitting behind the desk in his study he looked up, expecting the butler to knock and announce the arrival. Instead the door of his study opened slowly and Charles walked in.

Max smiled. 'Morning, old chap,' he said with forced heartiness. 'You've arrived just in time for a spot of lunch.'

Charles' expression did not suggest he was in the best of humours. 'No thank you, I'm on my way to High Hatters Farm.'

'Well, how about joining me for a drink then?'

Charles nodded, pacing the floor with his gloves clutched tightly between his fingers.

Max moved across to the sideboard. 'Have you sorted out all that nonsense with Helen?' he said, taking the lid from the decanter.

Charles nodded. 'That's what I came over to tell you. I've found her.'

Max looked away as he framed his next question. 'And was she with the Hartman chap?'

Charles said nothing.

Max held out a drink to him; his younger brother's cold expression gave him the answer he needed. 'Ah, well,' he said evenly, unable to think of anything else to say. 'Where is she now?'

Charles reddened. 'At home, where she damned well should be. I've locked her in the bedroom.'

Max snorted. 'Don't you think that's a rather melodramatic solution, old man? It's totally ridiculous. Have you tried talking to her?'

Charles' expression didn't change.

'For goodness' sake, Charlie,' Max continued, 'what do you hope to achieve by locking her up? She's your wife, not some errant dog that slipped the leash.'

Charles took a hefty swig from his glass. 'That's rather a matter of opinion, I'd have said,' he snapped. 'I'm teaching her a lesson she won't forget.'

Max found it hard to take his brother seriously. 'This is some sort of joke, isn't it?'

Charles' expression hardened. 'No, of course it isn't a joke. She could have made us all a laughing-stock. Have you any idea what people would say if this got out? She deserves to be punished.'

Max sat down slowly; it was perhaps time that he confided in Liddy. It was preposterous for Charles to keep Helen caged like some wild animal. He looked at his younger brother, who was standing by the window surveying the park, and wondered what on earth was going through the other man's mind.

Helen sat at her dressing-table looking coolly at her reflection. In repose, her face looked unchanged, nothing was different. She picked up the single blue feather that Anya had plaited into her hair at Jack's cottage, stroking it between her fingers until all the little fibres and fronds were joined together. The bedroom seemed very still, the only sound the soft tick, tick, tick of the bedside clock.

On a side table under the window stood her breakfast tray. Annie had carried it up, accompanied by Charles, in his role as jailer. She was a prisoner in her own bedroom. Helen looked into the mirror again – and had the most overwhelming compulsion to giggle.

She went to the wardrobe and found the piece of paper she'd slipped into her skirt pocket days before. She settled down by the dressing-table again and found her writing case; the letter she wrote didn't take very long to finish. She had been thinking about what she wanted to say for days.

In their sitting-room at Garrison Hall, Liddy lay back in the armchair and blew a plume of silvery grey smoke into the air above her. She looked back at Max and shook her head. 'I did rather suspect that you weren't telling me the whole truth,' she said flatly. 'But I'd never have guessed you were with Helen.'

She took another long pull on her cigarette-holder. 'It seems so out of character, no wonder you were interested in her. As for Charles? I personally think it might be better to leave them to sort it out for themselves. It can be dreadfully messy to come between husband and wife.'

Max sighed. 'I think I've already done that. Besides, he can't lock her up. It's bloody ridiculous. It's like something out of a penny dreadful.'

'She *is* his wife.'

Max snorted. 'Oh, so you'd take kindly to being locked away in penance for your little sexual adventures, would you? I'll bear that in mind.'

Liddy grinned. 'It might add a certain something to our passion. A prisoner of love – there is something in that.' She stretched. 'But, then again, you did know what sort of woman you were marrying, didn't you, darling? Whereas I get the distinct impression Charles was totally in the dark about Helen.' She shook her head slowly. 'In fact, we all were. Fancy Helen turning out to be a painted lady of the night,' she giggled. 'Running off with some wild little tinker! I'm really astounded.'

'I don't think that Helen knew what it was she wanted until she met Jack Hartman.' Max hesitated. 'And then me,' he added in a voice barely above a whisper. 'I got the impression she was pretty inexperienced before she got married and even afterwards.'

For a moment he thought about Helen pleading with him not to send her back to the Lodge after the dinner party. She had practically begged him to make love to her and give her the satisfaction her body craved.

'And Charles? Do you think he was experienced?' Liddy watched him with interest.

Max lifted his hands in mock surrender. 'No idea, really. It's not the sort of thing we ever talked about. He was in the army, he must have seen a little action along the way.'

Liddy licked her lips. 'Charles strikes me as the kind of man who would keep all that sort of thing fairly buttoned down. One set of rules for the barracks and another for the wedding bed. It seems that may have been a mistake.'

'Will you talk to him about Helen?'

Liddy sighed. 'You really do feel responsible for all this, don't you?'

Max shrugged. 'To some extent.'

'I can't promise any results. Charles isn't the easiest chap to talk to.'

'Just try, I can't bear to think of Helen locked up in her room.'

Liddy nodded, with a look of resignation on her face. 'All right, if you insist, but don't blame me if it all goes horribly wrong.'

Helen heard the sound of Charles' voice downstairs in the hallway. It made her stomach contract sharply. All day, as she sat in their bedroom, she had convinced herself that everything would be all right.

In the back of the wardrobe amongst her dresses she had hidden the letter. To get what she wanted she would have to play along with Charles. It was her only chance. She stood up when she heard his footsteps outside the bedroom door. The key rattled unnervingly in the lock.

She looked down quickly as he stepped into the room. It was the gesture of submission she had seen Anya make when she had made love to Jack. She would have to be convincing. From beneath her lowered eyelids she could see Charles' boots as he stood a few feet in front of her. A heavy, ominous silence hung between them. She bit her lip; it would have to begin now or she would never be free. 'I'm sorry, Charles,' she whispered.

He said nothing.

'I *am* no better than a whore,' she said slowly, trying to control the tremor in her voice.

The air between them crackled.

'And . . .' She swallowed hard. 'And I understand that I deserve to be punished for what I've done.'

She glanced up at him. His expression was set and cold but his eyes flashed with triumph. The look was so unexpected that she almost forgot to drop her eyes. He was enjoying this; the realisation struck her like a punch. She could feel her colour rising. Her submission excited him; her guilt, her fear – he was revelling in it. Even amongst the feelings of shock and anger she realised Charles' reaction would make it far easier to put her plan into action. She took a step closer to him and sank slowly to her knees. 'I'll do whatever you want,' she murmured. 'Anything to please you.'

Charles smiled as his wife collapsed at his feet, her head bowed, shoulders hunched. He had won. He could feel the pulse throbbing in his temple. Now she would be what he wanted, he could do what he liked with her. He felt the anger abate in the face of his triumph.

'Get up,' he murmured thickly, 'it's time for dinner.'

Helen got to her feet, her eyes lowered. Charles trembled. He stepped towards the wardrobe and opened it.

'I'd like you to wear that dress Liddy gave you. The blue one you wore for the dinner party.' Helen nodded dumbly. He slipped his finger under her chin, tipping her face towards his, 'and keep yourself shaved, I rather like you like that.' He pulled the blue dress off its hanger and threw it on the bed. 'Wear this,' he said slowly, 'Nothing else, except perhaps for your stockings and shoes.'

Helen reddened and he smiled. She was his now.

Helen sat beside him at dinner, rather than at the far end, which was her customary place. The showy little party dress looked strange and out of place in the dour dining-room.

Annie, as she served their meal, seemed unable to take her eyes off Helen. The girl looked so nervous and unhappy that it was all Helen could do to stop herself from saying something to reassure her. As Annie left after serving the soup, Charles slid his hand over Helen's thigh, stroking higher to reach the exposed mound of her sex.

He closed his eyes. 'Good,' he murmured, letting his fingers move across the naked folds, 'now open your legs.'

Helen bit her lips and did as he asked, bracing herself against his invasive fingers.

He smiled narrowly and pulled his hand away. 'I want you like this all the time,' he said slowly, stroking her trembling thigh with proprietorial casualness. 'From now on, you will do as I say. Do you understand?'

Helen nodded and picked up her soup spoon.

Liddy pulled off her gloves and looked around for Max in the shadows of the entrance hall. 'It's no use hiding. I know you're there,' she snapped crossly.

Max, cradling a large drink, stepped out from his hiding place under the stairs. He had a broad grin on his face. 'So how was church?' he said teasingly.

Liddy pulled a face. 'I thought I might be able to talk to Charles on the way home.' She stamped her feet. 'Get me a drink will you? God, it's so cold out there. I've walked miles. To top it all, the church was like an oven. I'll probably catch pneumonia.'

Max walked across to the sitting-room as the footman took Liddy's coat.

'And,' he called over his shoulder, 'what did you say to him?'

Liddy followed, 'Absolutely nothing. Helen was there, looking like a little church mouse, tight on his arm, eyes downcast. The very image of the dutiful wife.'

Max handed her a gin and tonic, 'Perhaps all this hoo-hah has done the pair of them some good, then? Sorted things out.'

Liddy grimaced. 'I don't think so. Helen looks absolutely dreadful and Charles looks like the cat who got the cream.' She paused thoughtfully. 'He looks so cruel, I'd never noticed that about your brother before.'

Max glanced out of the window. The avenue stretched out along the edge of the park and, in the far distance, he could see the smoke from the Lodge chimneys curling above the trees. He had no doubt his younger brother could be very cruel. He turned back to Liddy, 'Would you mind awfully if I invited them up for Sunday tea today?'

Liddy groaned, 'How much longer have we all to suffer because of your guilty conscience? Meddling might make matters worse.'

Max shrugged. 'I don't know,' he said, watching the distant plume of smoke thoughtfully. 'I feel I've got to try and do something.'

They had Sunday tea in the breakfast room overlooking the Hall's gardens. It was a smaller, much less formal, room than the main dining-room and Max hoped it might encourage a more relaxed atmosphere. Helen and Charles arrived just before four. Max was shocked at how gaunt Helen looked. He needed to talk to her alone. Charles, meanwhile, looked as sleek and self-satisfied as Max had ever seen him – almost jovial.

Over tea, Charles chatted about the farms and the spring lambs, due anytime at the Home Farm, while Helen sat in silence. Charles even flirted outrageously with Liddy, who – as ever – simpered and preened under the attention.

As Max passed a plate of cakes to his subdued

sister-in-law, he looked pointedly at Liddy. 'How about you taking Charlie off to the music room and playing him those ghastly new records you bought last time you were in London?'

Liddy rolled her eyes heavenwards in annoyance.

'You'd like to hear them, wouldn't you, Charlie?' Max continued.

Charles glanced across at Liddy who had now, obligingly, painted on her most teasing expression. 'Well, er . . .' he blustered.

'Please say yes,' Liddy purred theatrically, leaning towards him, resting her hand on his arm. 'Max really doesn't appreciate good music.'

Max chuckled. 'That's the point entirely; I do appreciate good music and that racket isn't good.' He looked at Helen. 'Perhaps you'd like to join me for a game of gin rummy?'

Instead of replying Helen looked across at Charles, who was still watching Liddy with undisguised interest. He nodded, 'I can't see why not.'

Liddy smiled at Max and Helen, playing Max's game, 'Well, perhaps you two could stay in here? It'll be quieter for you.' She glanced back at Charles and fluttered her eyelashes provocatively. 'Meanwhile Charlie and I can have a little dance. Do you like to dance, Charlie? I simply adore it.'

When the others had gone into Liddy's music room, Max had the footman set up a card table in front of the fire.

'So, are you going to tell me what's the matter?' Max said as he dealt the cards.

Helen shook her head. 'I don't want to talk about it.'

Max snorted. 'How very convenient. I've conned poor Liddy into dancing the night away with your boorish husband and you won't talk to me. For God's sake, you won't even look at me.'

Helen looked up slowly. He could see the hurt and uncertainty in her eyes. The impression was so strong that he flinched. 'What in hell is Charles doing to you? You can't carry on like this.'

Helen scooped up her hand from the table. 'You don't want to know, it's not very pretty.'

Max caught hold of her wrist. 'Did you tell him about what went on here after the dinner party?'

Helen smiled as she arranged her cards. 'No, your little secrets are safe with me, Max. Wasn't that part of our deal?'

'That isn't how I meant it at all. For goodness' sake . . . Look, is there anything I can do to help you?'

Helen shook her head. 'No, I'm afraid not.' She looked at him again. 'You know, you're very different to how I'd always thought of you.'

'What do you mean?'

She laughed dryly. 'I always thought you were self-indulgent, lazy – totally self-centred.'

Max held up his hands in mock defence. 'Ouch, ouch—'

Helen grinned. 'But you're a lot more decent than I gave you credit for.'

'Not really.'

She tucked two cards in behind the others. 'I might need your help later, but not now.'

Max looked at her levelly. 'What are you planning to do?'

Helen laid her first card. 'I'd rather not talk about it.'

Max shrugged and looked at his own cards, hoping Liddy was having more success with Charles.

Despite Liddy's protestations, encouraged by Max, Helen and Charles left early. At the front door of the Lodge neither Helen nor Charles spoke but walked wordlessly upstairs. Helen knew what was to follow – Charles had told her in explicit detail as they had driven up to the Hall. Now it was only a matter of getting through it. She glanced across at Charles and slipped off her dress.

Charles slid the belt from his trousers. Helen was standing beside him – waiting for his command. Her eyes were bright. He smiled as she looked down. He had never anticipated that married life could be so fulfilling. He leant across the dressing-table and took a lipstick from the jar. Slowly he rubbed the slick scarlet gloss onto Helen's nipples. They hardened under his attentions.

He handed her the kohl stick he'd bought in town. 'Put the lines around your eyes,' he said softly, stroking the curve of her firm little breasts with his fingertips. 'I want you to look like what you are.'

Helen shivered.

'What are you?' he whispered darkly.

'A whore,' she muttered.

'Say it more clearly,' he snapped, pressing the pencil into her limp fingers.

'A whore,' she said flatly.

'And what do you do with whores?'

Helen peered into the mirror, outlining her eyes with trembling hands. She stopped and looked into his eyes in the mirror. 'Anything you want,' she whispered.

He stood back and watched her finish her task. She looked a little like the gypsy woman at Jack Hartman's cottage. It was a great shame that he hadn't been able to find a way to persuade the gypsy to come home with them too. He would have enjoyed that.

Helen stood up slowly. She looked superb in the soft lamplight with her dark cat-like eyes and reddened nipples.

'Get on your hands and knees,' he said thickly.

She bent down without a second's hesitation. Her thighs were slightly apart, revealing her open sex. Her rounded buttocks framed the delicate secret places that fascinated him so much. He let the belt trail across her naked back. She stiffened as she felt its coolness on her exposed skin.

He wrapped the buckle around into his palm and drew the leather strap back. She tensed as he brought it down with a dark hollow crack against her pink backside. He heard her sob and drew the belt back again as a red hot glow spread across her pale skin. The strap struck again and again, lifting welts across her back and buttocks. With each blow, Helen sobbed.

Finally he dropped the belt to the floor and stood behind her, shaking, his breath coming in tight little gasps. He could feel the dark angry press of his cock against his trousers. Helen was shivering. He smiled and dropped to his knees, letting his fingers invade the soft delicate places between her legs. She shuddered as one finger found its way into the slick tight opening of her sex. She was wet, hot and inviting to the touch. He reached across and got the hair oil.

'Turn around,' he whispered. Helen moved slowly. Her face was red and tear-streaked.

'You know what I want,' he said. She nodded and began to undo his flies. Feeling his cock between her fingers he stretched with pleasure, not flinching as she closed her lips around the bulbous end.

She worked well, though without enthusiasm, sliding her lips back and forth along his shaft. He noticed how wet she left him and smiled; she was thinking about what was to follow. He relished her firm hands and lips on him, bringing him closer with every gesture to the point of no return. He pulled her head closer; she did not resist him. He could feel the knot tightening in the pit of his belly. Her lips closed again and again as her fingers stroked his foreskin back and forth. He gasped as he felt the low throb that told him that his climax was closing fast.

'Stop. That's enough,' he snorted. She looked up. The kohl around her eyes was smudged now into softer dark shadows. Her expression was still obedient but did he detect something else there, something glittering in her eyes? Something subversive? She looked away quickly, her face reddening. He must have been wrong.

'Turn around,' he said, regaining his composure and

taking control of the excitement that moments before had threatened to engulf him.

Her backside was reddened, angry welts lifted against the pink flesh. He ran one cool finger across a tender livid stripe and Helen flinched. For an instant he almost regretted that he had had to hurt her – but she did have to learn her lesson. Simple words of apology were not enough.

He lifted the hair oil and trickled it over the sensitive crack between her buttocks, letting it run down between the cheeks of her bottom. She shivered as he smoothed it over the tight, reddened close of her backside. The little bud twitched invitingly. He let out a soft throaty groan. Sensing her anxiety he laid his other hand on her back.

'You know what I want,' he whispered. 'Don't fight me.'

Helen let out a thin high-pitched gasp as he slid his finger home.

'There,' he purred, 'It won't be long now.' He crept closer, guiding his cock inside her.

The following morning, Jack Hartman watched Charles' car pull away from the front door of Garrison Lodge. Hidden by the trees he had watched the house since the first lamp had been lit before the day was born. He was frozen. Even winter clothes offered no protection against the bitter frost that crept up over his bones.

He'd seen the maid open the curtains and the fires stoked after being banked down for the night. Just after it was light he'd seen a large bustling woman arriving – the cook, he assumed – and Charles leaving to get the car, but no Helen.

He stepped into the driveway and watched the car vanish around the corner into the roadway beyond. He needed to see her, whatever the risks.

The front door of the Lodge opened and the maid stepped out, face pinched, eyes unseeing. She shook the front doormat, looking up vacantly. As she spotted Jack, her expression changed.

'Who are you?' she said suspiciously. 'If you want Mr Garrison he's just left. If you've business at the Hall it's up there a way.' She pointed along the drive.

Jack stepped closer. 'I've no business with either man nor place. I've come to see Mrs Garrison.'

The girl sniffed. 'She's indisposed at the moment. She isn't seeing anybody.' But her face said something else, something that rang alarm bells in Jack's head.

'Besides,' the girl continued huffily, 'I don't think she'd have much to say to the likes of you.'

Jack was almost on the front doorstep by now. 'You'd be surprised. Will you tell her I'm here?'

The girl looked uncomfortable. 'She ain't supposed to see no one, nor get any messages.'

Jack grinned, trying to hide his growing sense of unease. 'How about you nip inside and tell her anyway?'

The girl considered it for a moment or two, then shook her head. 'She's in her room and I can't go in to see her,' she said flatly.

'Is she ill?'

The girl snorted. 'No, Mr Garrison's locked her in

and gone away with the key.' As she spoke she took a
step back into the Lodge and went to close the door but
Jack was too quick for her. Before Annie could stop
him Jack was in the hall and bounding up the stairs.

The girl's mouth fell open. 'You can't come pushing
into someone's house like that. I'll get the police after
you.'

Jack turned on the stairs. 'I wouldn't if I were you. I
don't think Mr Garrison would be too pleased if the
local sergeant heard that he'd locked his wife in his
bedroom to keep her from straying.'

The girl considered it for a few seconds. 'It ain't right,'
she said huffily

Jack was unsure whether she meant him being in
the house or Helen being locked up in her bedroom.
Whichever it was, the girl didn't move, looking
strangely bizarre standing in the hall, still clutching
the doormat to her chest.

Helen was still in bed, stiff and sore from Charles'
attentions. She glanced at the wardrobe which held
the letter she so desperately needed to send. It was
taking far longer than she had planned. If only she
could persuade Charles to trust her enough to let her
go out. It felt as if she had spent weeks in her room,
reading, dozing fitfully, waiting for Charles to come
home for lunch, waiting for him to come home for
dinner. She had grown to dread the sound of his car
crunching on the gravel. She shivered; worse still was
the sound of his steps, slowly climbing the stairs.

'Helen?'

The voice was so unexpected she sat up. 'Jack?'

She heard him laugh.

'What on earth are you doing here?' she hissed, clambering off the bed, dragging her dressing-gown on. Her body protested at every movement. 'If Charles finds you here he'll—' she paused. What would he do? He wouldn't confront Jack but what would he do to her? She shuddered. What was there left to do to her?

'You have to leave,' she whispered unhappily through the locked door. 'You can't stay.'

'Seems like you have to, though. Wait on.'

She heard his footsteps recede and the sound of muffled voices. He was back a minute or two later. 'I've sent your maid for some wire, we'll have this damned lock undone in no time.'

'No, please, Jack.' Helen snapped to the closed door. 'He'll be furious. Please go away.' She knew her voice held no conviction.

A few minutes later she heard the scrabble of something in the lock and the door of her prison swung open. Jack stepped into the room followed closely by Annie. Before Jack had a chance to speak, Annie said, 'I told him he couldn't come in, Mrs Garrison, I did tell him.'

Helen nodded. 'It's all right, Annie.' She looked at the girl, holding her eyes. 'But you're not to breathe a word of this to Charles. Do you understand?'

The girl screwed up her face. 'But Mrs Garrison . . .'

'Do you understand?'

The girl nodded unhappily.

'Right, now go and make Mr Hartman and me a pot of tea.'

Annie backed out of the room, her eyes firmly on Jack Hartman and the piece of wire he held in his hand.

Jack looked her up and down. 'You look dreadful, lady. What's going on here?' He sounded desperately concerned.

Helen made an effort to smile. 'Not very complimentary this morning, are you, Jack? What brings you this far from your cottage?'

He looked at her steadily with his dark glittering eyes. 'You.'

Helen bit her lip, glancing at the curl of wire he had between his fingers. 'I hope you can lock the door as easily as you undid it.'

Jack nodded. 'Aye, no problem. So will you tell me, what's with you?'

Helen shook her head, there was no way she could begin to tell him. Jack took a step closer and instinctively she flinched. His eyes flashed. 'What in God's name is going on, Helen?' he whispered.

Helen backed away from him. 'Haven't you heard how the gentry keep their wives in order, Jack?' she said softly.

'By locking you away in your room like some sick thing?'

Helen felt her eyes fill up with tears. 'Yes, Fen-man, along with other things.' She smiled thinly. 'You really have to go, Jack. You may not think all is well here, but it will change.' As she said it, she suddenly thought about her letter hidden in the wardrobe. 'Will you do something for me?'

Jack nodded. 'Say the word. Anything.'

Helen opened the wardrobe door and pushed the clothes to one side. The letter was in her coat pocket. 'Here, this is very important. Will you take it to the post office at Ferrybridge for me?'

Jack turned the letter over in his fingers and then slid it into his pocket. 'No problem,' he stepped closer and slid his arm round her waist, 'but what about you?'

Helen bit her lip, stiffening under his touch.

'What is it?' he hissed. 'Tell me.'

Helen swallowed hard. 'Oh Jack . . .' She felt the tears bubble up.

His arms closed gently around her; every touch, every movement made her body hurt. He brushed his lips against hers. He smelt of the outdoors, of wind and wood smoke. Her body ached for his caress but every gentle pressure on her skin reminded her of Charles. She let out a thin strangled sob and curled close into Jack's strong arms. He slipped her dressing-gown back over her shoulders, pressing his lips eagerly to her cool skin.

'What the hell is this?'

Helen stiffened, hearing the anger in Jack's voice. He pushed the robe back off her shoulders, letting it drop to the floor.

His fingers traced a pattern across her shoulder. 'Take your nightdress off,' he said softly.

Helen looked at him, still trying to hold back the

tears. 'No, Jack,' she muttered, 'I can't, Annie might come in. I really can't.'

'Take it off.'

Helen slipped the shoulder straps down and let the thin cotton shift drop to the floor. She couldn't hold the tears in check any longer. In the dressing-table mirror she caught sight of her reflection. Bruises and angry red weals stretched from the back of her thighs to her shoulders.

She heard Jack curse under his breath. Before she could cover herself Annie appeared in the bedroom doorway carrying a tea tray. Helen snatched up her dressing-gown but not before the girl saw the marks on her back.

Annie gasped, standing the tea tray on the bed and then walking towards Helen as though she were mesmerised.

'Did he do that t'you?' she hissed incredulously. 'Mr Garrison?' Her fingers lifted automatically to an angry blue-black bruise on Helen's shoulder as if she couldn't believe her eyes.

Helen nodded. 'Yes, he did. But he won't do it for much longer.' She looked squarely at Annie. 'He'll not do it to either of us.'

The maid flushed scarlet. 'He's never hit me,' Annie blustered.

Helen pulled the robe around her, tying the belt tight, 'You've been lucky then, haven't you?'

The girl backed away, her eyes wide. She looked first at Helen and then at Jack and then scurried out of the room as if the devil himself was after her.

Jack was still beside her, his eyes narrowed to sharp angry points. 'That man of yours is mad.'

'No,' said Helen. 'Not mad. I've not complained, I've been nothing but obedient since he came to get me from your cottage. This is my punishment for straying.'

Jack snorted furiously. 'There must be something I can do to help,' he said thickly. 'I'd gladly kill him for you—'

Helen stepped towards him, lifting a finger to her lips. 'You can hold me in your arms and love me, Jack Hartman. I need to feel your body against me. I need to feel your tender gentle touch, your fingers and tongue taking me to the special places only lovers share.'

He closed his arms around her, drawing her near to him. She shivered, drinking in the smell of his body. Her fingers fought with his buttons pulling his coat open so that she could creep closer to him and absorb his warmth. He kissed her again and again, his tongue searching her mouth, his lips working against hers.

In spite of her pain she could feel the delight and excitement beginning to build inside her. She groaned with expectation. Jack guided her gently back towards the bed. He pushed the door shut with his foot, closing them off from the rest of the house and the rest of the world.

As they stood beside the bed, he looked down at her. 'Are you sure you want this? I don't want to hurt you more than that man of yours already has.'

Helen nodded. 'I have dreamt of nothing else, Jack. I've had the pain, now show me the pleasure.'

Jack knelt down slowly, lifting the hem of her nightgown. His tongue and lips pressed against her feet, her calves, the soft delicate skin behind her knees. All the time his fingers lifted her hem higher. She trembled in expectation as his tongue lapped at her thighs. His fingers traced over his kisses, stroking, awakening the desire that she feared Charles might have crushed forever.

His tongue brushed the soft outer lips of her sex, the kiss like a fleeting, delicate breath. She caught hold of the hem of her nightdress, dragging it over her head so that she was naked for his caress. He moved closer, gently teasing the sensitive folds apart, seeking out her pleasure bud with knowing artful kisses.

The caresses seemed like a revelation to her aching body – the kiss of spring amongst the cold bitter wind of winter. She whimpered and opened her legs, thrusting herself onto his tongue as his fingers followed, opening her gently, seeking out the warm wet places that her body offered him.

She lay back slowly on the edge of the bed. His tongue didn't break contact with her body for an instant. She revelled in his touch, abandoning all control so that he could take her whole body and light her excitement as he pleased.

This was the kind of complicit surrender she longed for; given as a gift to a knowing gentle lover, not snatched away from her as a right. She lifted her legs, opening herself wider and wider. She heard him groan with delight as she felt her body flood with juices. She lifted her hips so that every part of her was exposed to his fingers and tongue. He dipped his finger into her wet slick quim, smearing her excitement onto her thighs.

Inside her mind, she felt the tight wild dance of excitement building. The spiral grew brighter, spinning, glowing, spreading through her like a forest fire.

'Please, Jack,' she whispered. 'I want to feel you inside me, please—'

He moved away from her. His eyes glittered with excitement. 'My pleasure, lady,' he murmured.

He stood beside the bed, looking down at her. His eyes travelled across her naked body. She moaned. It was almost as if she could feel his eyes caressing her – explicit, tender, visual kisses, looks that registered in her excited mind like his breath on her skin or the touch of his tongue. She could feel the low electric hum of his excitement as he shed his clothes. He dropped them where he stood, oblivious to everything except her and the desire their bodies had kindled.

Slowly, slowly he crept towards her. His cock, swollen and magnificent, brushed against her. She shivered, her whole body aching. She reached up towards him and folded her arms around his muscular neck. Between her thighs she felt the brush of his cock and opened her legs. It was almost as if her body reached up and drew him into her. He let out a thick shuddering moan as she pulled him deeper. Her muscles and wet lips closed round him. For a split second they lay still, closed in each other's warmth.

Helen had the most peculiar sensation that they were

two halves of the same creature. He seemed to melt into her, as if there was no division between their skin. She pressed herself to him, afraid that she would lose the electric one-ness of the moment. The feelings were so intense that she thought she would cry. Just as she felt the hot tears of delight rising in her eyes, Jack began to move slowly, with the softest of brushing strokes.

She hissed, feeling the glowing pulse, alive and white-hot between her legs. She looked up into Jack's face. His eyes were impossibly dark, drawing her in, pulling her deep inside his mind. She gasped and pressed up to meet him. He brushed against her again and again, plunging deep into her desperate body. She lifted her legs around his waist, holding him tight inside her. He set a soft entrancing rhythm as she moved with him, all pain, all sense of hurt being eased away by Jack's loving, mesmerising body.

His excitement rippled through her, complementing and echoing her own feelings. He dipped again, stroking his whole body against hers. The glow grew, the excitement rolled through her, swallowing them both up as it spun out like a great light from the junction of their two bodies. She felt as if she would die under him. She clawed at his back and buttocks, spurring him on for one last engulfing wave of pleasure. As the wave roared through them both she screamed out his name again and again, pulling him close.

When they were finally still, he moved across her. He pressed gentle kisses to her eyes and lips, her shoulders, her breasts, her poor aching back; kisses of compassion and care, kisses of tenderness and love. She lay back on the bed, relishing the healing that his attentions ignited in her. She *would* be free and Jack Hartman's desire and love would help her.

At last they lay together in each other's arms, exhausted, satisfied, at peace.

'Will you come away with me, lady?' he whispered, from the edge of sleep.

She shook her head. 'No, if we went Charles would never give us a moment's peace. He would set out to ruin us both.'

Jack propped himself up on one elbow. 'We could find a place where he'd not find us. I've friends up north . . .'

Helen sighed. 'I don't think there is such a place. No, I have to finish what I've started.' She looked at him; naked and so desirable, still warm from their exertions. It would be so easy to fall under his spell and promise him anything.

'I need to be safe, Jack. Free of him. I have to stay and finish this, once and for all. Don't ask me to go with you, the temptation is too great.'

'If there is anything I can do . . .'

Helen smiled lazily. 'Come and surprise me once in a while. I'll make sure you know when my plan is complete.' She glanced at the bedside clock. 'You ought to go now. Charles will be home soon for lunch.'

Jack pulled a face. 'I'd better him in a straight fight. You know that, don't you?'

Helen nodded. 'Yes, I know that. But at the moment, the best way you can help me is by posting the letter I gave you and keeping an eye out for me when you're this way on your travels.'

Jack slipped reluctantly from the bed. 'If that's what you want, lady.'

Helen nodded. 'It is.'

He dressed slowly, almost as if he hoped she would change her mind. Finally he slipped on his heavy coat and stood by the bed looking down at her. 'You haunt me, woman,' he said slowly.

She nodded, lifting her fingers to touch him. Smiling affectionately she said, 'I know.'

He bent down and pressed his lips to hers, his fingers lifting to caress her naked breasts. 'It breaks my heart to leave you like this, knowing that you'll be with him.'

Helen pulled the bed cover up around her. 'Please,' she whispered, 'it's time to leave. Don't make it any harder.'

Jack walked reluctantly to the bedroom door, slipping the piece of wire from his pocket. 'Are you sure you want me to lock you in again?'

Helen nodded dumbly, afraid to speak in case she lost the battle raging inside her that encouraged her to leave with him before Charles came home. She slipped off the bed and threw her arms around his neck. 'Thank you, Jack,' she murmured as his lips found hers. 'Thank you.'

The door closed quietly behind him with a soft unhappy click. She heard the wire rattling in the lock and stood there for a minute or two until she was sure that Jack had gone. When she heard the front door close she threw herself onto the bed and broke into floods of hot miserable tears.

When Charles came home at lunchtime his wife seemed even more subdued than when he'd left her that morning. He said nothing as she joined him in the dining-room. After all, what was there to say? She would learn. She wasn't dressed, which he thought a trifle slovenly, but then again it gave her the look of the girl in the Paris brothel. The French whore had never been dressed. Every time he visited her she had been wrapped in a silky cream gown.

He remembered vividly how she had leant against the door of her room, her hips thrust forward in a provocative invitation. Charles swallowed hard and tried to turn his attentions to his lunch. It was an impossible task; the whore, her ripe body ready for him beneath the thinnest of silky dressing-gowns, pressed up in his imagination. He could see her wide red painted lips and her dark flashing eyes. The smell of her perfume on the still air ... In his mind she leant back further so the dressing-gown fell open and as he looked up at her painted face, her tongue peeped between her lips, goading him into action.

He glanced across the dining-table to where Helen was sitting, to see if she could sense his arousal. She was hunched unhappily over her plate, her eyes distant and unfocused. It struck him that she would look wonderful in cream silk. In the cold dining-room her nipples had hardened and were pressing against her dressing-gown.

He laid his napkin down carefully beside his plate. The memories of the whore in Paris and Helen fused together. He leant forward and his fingers traced the delicate swirl of her hardened areola through the fabric. She shivered. He couldn't tell whether it was with cold or fear. Whichever, he really didn't mind. Beneath the table he pushed her legs apart with his foot and let his hand drop to her lap. She sat very still, her eyes widening as he dragged up the material to expose her quim.

He stroked the split between the lips and thought about the whore. She had never flinched, she would be pressing his fingers into her, wriggling against him. He looked at Helen – perhaps he could teach her that too. If Helen had been the whore she would be leaning back now, opening herself gratefully for him. He looked at his wife's clouded, unhappy expression and pressed his fingers home. He saw the pain on her face but inside she was wet.

An interesting thought crossed his mind. One night, in Paris, he had been to a show where two women had been pitted against each other. One, a great blonde peasant girl with a quim like some voluptuous sea creature, had stroked herself into a frenzy. Her thick fingers had dipped again and again between her huge hairy lips, sliding into her own slithery slit, spreading the juices over her saucer-sized nipples so that her partner could lap it off.

It had been the first time he had realised that women could pleasure themselves and he wondered if perhaps Helen had been indulging herself. He couldn't really imagine she would. Even given her newfound compliance she still retained an air of prudish disapproval.

Annie appeared in the dining-room doorway, holding a tray. Charles looked up at the maid with a small tight smile on his face, trying to disguise his arousal. 'I think,' he said evenly, before the girl had had chance to cross the room, 'that we will leave dessert today, Annie. You may clear the table after we've left.'

Annie stood very still.

Charles glared. 'Are you deaf or stupid?' he snapped.

Annie glanced anxiously at Helen's stricken expression then turned on her heel and closed the door quietly behind her.

Charles let the sensation of Helen's body engulf his fingers. He glanced at the door thoughtfully.

It had been some time since he had taken Annie into his study. At least she understood her place. Perhaps he would take Annie in there after tea. He glanced back at Helen, wondering what she would think of their plump little maid writhing beneath him. He sighed; it was better if she never found out. That way he would have her exactly where he wanted her – at his beck and call.

He used his other hand to pull open the front of Helen's wrap. Her breasts were far smaller than Annie's. He pulled his chair closer so that he could close his lips around Helen's pert swollen nipples.

He would have their maid downstairs on the hearth rug whilst his wife waited upstairs for him, locked in her room. But in the meanwhile he had to go out to Vanton's farm within the hour.

He stood up slowly, drinking in the details of his wife's undress. 'Bend over the table,' he said thickly. Helen got up as if she were waking from sleep. She moved slowly, almost fluidly. He lifted her robe and shivered. It was a great shame the hair oil was upstairs but there was always the more usual route to pleasure. He slipped his fingers into her sex; it was slick and hot. Her juices trickled out onto her thighs in a fragrant warm pool.

He grunted as he pressed up inside her, enjoying the heat of her body closing around his engorged shaft. As he pushed deeper he thought about Annie with her heavy swaying breasts and the little Paris whore. He caught hold of Helen's hips. 'Move with me,' he snorted angrily. 'I'll not have you lying under me like a slab of meat. Whores are meant to pleasure their clients, not endure them.'

Helen began to thrust half-heartedly back against him. 'That's better,' he muttered.

He didn't doubt, in his own mind, she had been more enthusiastic when she had been with that bloody tinker. He leant over so that his mouth was level with her ear. 'I want you to move like you did beneath your little tinker.' He felt Helen stiffen and jerked her roughly onto him. 'Or perhaps it was his dark little whore you preferred, was it?'

As he said it, he imagined Helen with the great blonde peasant woman he'd seen in Paris. As the thought grew in his mind he felt a throb of unstoppable excitement in his groin and knew all was lost.

Chapter 9

London

'This is totally ridiculous, Max.' Liddy threw her suitcase down onto the bed and waved her maid away. 'I've danced with your damned brother. I've trailed behind him to and from church. He *won't* talk to me.'

Max stuffed his hands in his pockets. 'One last little favour.'

Liddy snorted. 'Stop it. I'm off to London at the weekend and I really do want to get packed.'

Max pulled a face. 'Give my love to your darling little Aretha. Are you sure you wouldn't like me to come along?' He grinned, 'You two always put on such a spectacular show.'

Liddy shook her head. 'No, we're going dancing with Fifi and her crowd. You'll only be bored, you hate modern music.'

'I'll sulk,' said Max, with a tone of mock hurt. 'I'll be all on my own in this great big house, rattling around . . .'

'Stop it, stop it, stop it,' snapped Liddy, 'I can't cope

with your wounded tragic hero act. All right, what is this favour?'

'Talk to Helen, find out what's going on.'

Liddy rolled her eyes. 'And how am I going to do that? Charles has got her secreted away in the Lodge under lock and key.'

'I'll ring him up and say you need Helen to give you a hand with . . . oh, I don't know – your packing – that's it. He's always keen for Helen to help you.'

Liddy pouted. 'He's always keen on me. He looks at me like a lovesick spaniel. Really, Max.'

He looked hurt.

'All right, all right. Run along and ring him, if it'll make you happy.'

Helen was watching the birds from her bedroom window when she heard the phone ring. Charles had said he would be working in his study until lunchtime and she was certain the call wasn't for her. It was odd, she thought, but she was beginning to get quite used to her strange imprisonment. Not happy, not content, but familiar. Even the livid bruises had begun to fade. She stretched. At least her compliance meant that Charles no longer felt he had to lay the belt on quite so hard. His attentions with the belt were rapidly becoming a ritual to symbolise his dominance.

She got dressed and read for a while. Inactivity wasn't good for her, she knew that. Her mind constantly wandered towards possible futures and the strange, complicated developments of the recent past.

It was so strange; the man she believed loved her

had become her jailer and those who she thought despised her – Max and Liddy – had become her allies. Perhaps allies wasn't really the right word, she thought. She wasn't certain how far they would go to help her but the fact they would even consider it had come as a complete surprise.

From outside in the drive came the sound of whistling. She glanced at the clock; it had to be the postman. She leant towards the window and opened it a little.

'Morning, Mrs Garrison. Nippy again this morning.'

Helen smiled pleasantly. 'It certainly is. Have you anything for me?' She tried to keep her voice low. She didn't want Charles to hear her.

The postman shuffled the letters through his fingers. 'No, afraid not, ma'am. They're all for your husband or the Hall. Are you expecting something?'

Helen nodded. 'Yes, but I'm sure it will turn up in good time. Good morning.'

She waved and pulled the window closed.

Days had passed since she had seen Jack Hartman. She was sure he'd post the letter for her but, with too much time to think, she imagined all sorts of other darker possibilities. He could have dropped it, lost it – he could have met Charles and fought, he could have . . . Helen bit her lip.

'No,' she said aloud, clenching her fist. 'Jack would have posted it. I know he would.'

'Liddy would like you to go and help her at the Hall this afternoon.' Charles peered at Helen across the dining-table. 'I've said you will be there around two. I'll take you over after lunch.' He paused as Annie came in with their lunch. 'I have several things here that need to be seen to this afternoon. Pressing business,' he said archly.

Helen nodded, careful to show nothing on her face. She glanced across at Annie. The girl was gnawing at her lip as she laid the meal in front of them. Helen had no doubt whatsoever that Annie was amongst the items that Charles considered pressing.

Charles shook out his napkin and placed it across his lap, ignoring Annie and looking steadily at Helen. 'It's high time you learnt the lessons I've taught you.'

Helen nodded, wondering what was going to follow. Charles coughed. 'I really have no great desire to see you spend the rest of your life locked in your bedroom. The day-to-day running of the household is your responsibility after all.'

Still Helen didn't speak, lowering her eyes in case they betrayed her. Free from her room, she could ensure her plans came together.

'So, we'll try it. But I warn you, Helen, if you step out of line you'll be back in your room.'

'Thank you, Charles,' Helen said softly. She glanced up from behind her lashes. Charles looked pleased with himself. 'Shall I walk back from the Hall?' she said very quietly.

Charles shook his head firmly. 'No, I'll call for you when I've finished here.'

Helen noticed the way that Annie's hands trembled as she stood the vegetable tureens on the table.

* * *

Next door to Liddy's luxurious bedroom was a pretty sunlit dayroom. As Helen went through to find Liddy she couldn't help noticing the huge mirror that overlooked Liddy's bed. She touched the glass out of curiosity.

'I do know what's behind it.' Liddy's cultured voice came from the dayroom door.

Helen jumped. 'I didn't see you there.'

Liddy smiled. 'The whole house is full of places for Max to watch the odd goings-on. It's his little hobby.' She paused. 'But I forgot, you know all about that, don't you?'

Helen flushed scarlet. 'I . . .' she began.

Liddy lifted her hand. 'Don't say anything silly. You're only here because Max feels so damned awful. He thinks he got you into this mess.'

Helen shivered. 'He told you that?'

Liddy nodded. 'More or less. Come through and we'll have a drink.'

Helen fell into step behind her. Liddy indicated she should sit down. 'I thought I'd come to help you pack,' Helen nodded.

Liddy laughed. 'That's all done. I've been told by Max that I have to talk to you.'

Helen glanced around the room, wondering if somewhere Max was watching them and listening to every word.

'Is Charles really keeping you locked in your room?'

Helen nodded. 'I come down for meals and church.'

Liddy snorted. 'How very civilised.' She poured two

large gin and tonics and handed Helen a glass. 'And what about your tempting little friend?'

Helen stiffened. 'Who?'

Liddy tutted. 'Oh please, there's really no need to be so coy. Your wild dark Fen-man.'

Helen felt herself flush scarlet. 'You know about him?' she said uncomfortably.

Liddy nodded. 'Max told me all about it,' she looked steadily at Helen. 'It's a very dangerous game you've been playing.'

Helen sipped the drink. 'I have to get away from here,' she said very softly.

Liddy nodded. 'I think you're probably right. What are you going to do?'

Helen shook her head. 'I can't tell you.'

Liddy sighed and folded herself into her chair. 'Don't be so damned ridiculous. I'm trying my best to help you. You can't stay locked up in the Lodge for the rest of your life. Charles is going to be watching every move you make from now on. What on earth possessed you to take off like that?'

Helen thought about discovering Charles in the study with Annie. The girl's unhappy face filled her mind. She had no doubt that Annie was in the study now, silently accepting what the master of Garrison Lodge had to offer her. She looked up at Liddy. 'Would you mind if I used your phone?'

Liddy grimaced. 'For goodness? sake – I'm supposed to be talking to you.'

'You did say you would help me.'

'Oh, all right then, if you must, but hurry back. Max

won't be satisfied with half a dozen things he already knows.'

Helen glanced back at her, wondering exactly what it was that Max did want.

Helen waited impatiently for the operator to put her through. A soft cultured voice answered as Helen introduced herself.

'Ah yes, Mrs Garrison,' said the disembodied voice. 'I have your letter here. I'd intended to write to you this week.'

Helen clenched her fists, trying to control the anxiety building in her stomach. 'I rang to enquire whether you thought I'd make a suitable candidate,' she said nervously.

The woman on the far end of the line laughed. 'Yes, actually I was going to write and ask if you could come down to London to see us.'

Helen took a deep breath, thinking about Liddy's luggage stacked neatly in the day-room. It was now or never. 'I'd be delighted,' she said evenly. 'Actually I'm coming down for a visit this weekend.'

The woman paused. 'Wonderful, could you perhaps come in to see us on Monday, then? I see from your address that you do live quite some way away.'

'That would be perfect,' Helen said, controlling the tremor in her voice. 'Shall we say about ten on Monday morning?'

'Absolutely, now perhaps you'd like to tell me a little more about yourself . . .'

* * *

As Helen laid the phone back in its cradle her heart was beating wildly. She hurried upstairs to Liddy who was still folded in her armchair, sipping her gin.

Liddy looked up as she came in. 'God, what on earth happened to you? You look totally different. Who did you ring? Your friend, Jack?'

Helen shook her head. 'No, I . . .' she stopped and felt a great wave of uncertainty about what she was about to ask.

'Out with it then,' snapped Liddy waspishly.

Helen glanced at the pile of luggage under the dayroom window. It really was now or never.

'Liddy, would you ask Charles if I can come with you to London this weekend? Please.'

Liddy looked stunned. 'What?'

'I wouldn't be in the way. I promise. I have to go somewhere on Monday morning in London.'

'Are you sure that's wise? Charles will probably say no anyway.'

'Not if you ask,' Helen said slowly, thinking about the way Charles held Liddy up to her as an icon of how good wives should behave. If only he knew, she thought ruefully. She looked at Liddy. 'He thinks you're a perfect wife. He's always telling me so.'

Liddy threw back her head and laughed. 'My God, what a complete fool that man is. And I don't suppose you've found fit to disillusion him about me, have you?'

Helen shook her head. 'No. No, I haven't.'

Liddy clambered slowly to her feet. 'Then best I go and ring the man and see what we can arrange.' She looked Helen up and down. 'I'll get my maid to pack some of my clothes for you. We can't have you trotting around behind me looking like Cinderella, now can we?'

Helen waited in tense silence for Liddy to return. Her fingers were clenched around her glass. If she failed this time there might be other chances but she so much needed this to work. She took a long pull of gin. She wasn't sure how much longer she could carry on playing the dutiful, subservient wife.

Liddy returned wearing a broad smile. 'Well, my dear, it appears you're going to London with me this weekend. I told Charles that you'd be more or less coming along as my maid. He seemed very taken with the idea.'

Helen shuddered. 'Thank you,' she said softly, while her mind was flooded with the images of their maid. No wonder Charles had agreed so readily.

Liddy looked at her thoughtfully. 'You do realise of course, Helen, what sort of weekend this is likely to be?'

Helen looked up from her thoughts.

Liddy held her gaze. 'I'm going to stay with Aretha Blackmore.'

'The woman who came to your dinner party.'

Liddy poured herself another drink and looked at Helen, holding her gaze. 'That's right, but I thought you might remember her more clearly from the gun cottage.'

Helen licked her lips and blushed. 'Yes,' she said, unsteadily.

Liddy nodded. 'I just wanted to make you understand what you're letting yourself in for.'

* * *

It was very timely, thought Charles as he replaced the phone in its cradle, that Helen should spend some time with Liddy. At least, in London, Helen wouldn't be tempted to find that bounder, Jack Hartman. Liddy had said she intended to spend the weekend with her friend, Aretha. Charles conjured with the name. A face appeared from his memory, the face of a dark, striking aristocratic woman he'd met at Max's on numerous occasions. She'd seemed like a thoroughly decent sort of woman. Well out of Helen's class of course. Spending time with real ladies would show Helen just how fortunate she was to have married into such a fine family. It would show her how grateful she ought to be.

On the hearth rug beside the fire, Annie was waiting for him. She was shivering but she hadn't moved. He smiled narrowly. She would be in the house all weekend anyway, so he wouldn't be alone. He looked at the thick dark thatch that trimmed the pink, moist lips of her sex. Perhaps he would shave her so she looked more like Helen. He rather liked the way it rendered Helen's body so exposed and open. How delicious it was to see his thick cock slide right between those moist slick lips.

On the mantel shelf, above the fire, was a bottle of Brownings patent hair oil. He hadn't used it on Annie yet; he was too afraid to have her cry out when she realised what he had in mind. But this weekend he might try introducing her to his special pleasure. He rebuttoned his fly. Annie looked up at him in relief.

Charles shook his head. 'Stay there,' he said in a

low voice. 'I'll be back in a few minutes. My wife is going to be away this weekend. I'm just going to go and tell the cook we won't be needing her.' He smiled. 'After all, you'll be here and you can provide me with what I want, can't you, Annie?'

The girl's eyes were bright, threatening tears. 'Yes, Mr Garrison,' she mumbled, flushing scarlet.

He closed the door silently and headed towards the kitchen.

Helen sat very quietly in the taxi that would take her, Liddy and the maid, to Aretha's Kensington home. She found it hard to believe that they were actually away from Garrison Hall. It had been months since she had left the estate – except of course to go out onto the Fen to find Jack. Jack. Her mind whispered his name as they drove through the busy streets.

Liddy looked wonderful in the most glorious and extravagant spring outfit. 'Are you all right?' she said, watching Helen's face with concern.

'Yes, I'm fine. I was just thinking how long it has been since I left the Hall.'

Liddy groaned. 'Oh, for heaven's sake! Don't get all maudlin or I shall send you home to Charles on the first train. This weekend is supposed to be fun. When we get to Aretha's you can change out of that awful parish-meeting frock. We've packed hundreds of dresses.' She waved her hands expansively, 'And while I'm here I intend to order a few more if I get the chance.'

As she spoke, the taxi turned a corner and pulled up outside a huge and very elegant Victorian mansion.

Helen felt nervous. 'Does your friend know I'm coming?'

Liddy looked skywards, 'Of course she does. I don't make a habit of springing country mice on unsuspecting friends. You'll be fine.'

Inside the elegant hallway there was much kissing and embracing between Aretha and Liddy. Helen hung back, feeling self-conscious, whilst the servants made short work of hurrying Liddy's luggage upstairs. Aretha turned to Helen, her arm still wrapped around Liddy's narrow waist.

'Liddy has told me *all* about you,' she purred mischievously.

Helen blushed.

Aretha laughed. 'Don't be nervous. I can't promise you any interesting rough labourers here but I'm sure you'll find something to your taste.'

Before Helen could answer, Aretha continued, 'I've put you in the Blue Room.' She looked at a tall uniformed footman standing by the stairs, 'Oliver will show you up to your room.'

Helen nodded.

Liddy called after her, 'And I've asked my maid to lay something out for you to wear.'

As Helen began to climb the stairs she looked down in time to see the two women kiss lightly and then walk, arm in arm, into the room beyond the hall. She swallowed hard. Perhaps this hadn't been such a good idea after all.

A few steps ahead of her the footman waited. She couldn't help noticing that his eyes glittered mischievously. As he opened the door to the Blue Room, he said, 'Are you one of those?' he nodded towards the stairwell. Helen blushed.

He grinned. 'I see you're not. You'll have to watch yourself here. Nothing in this house is quite the way it seems.'

The Blue Room was in fact a small suite, with a sitting-room overlooking the street, a small bathroom and a large luxurious bedroom. Helen looked around in amazement; it certainly wasn't what she expected. Everything was decorated in rich Chinese blue, which contrasted beautifully with the delicate satinwood furniture.

Across the bed, the maid had laid an elegant cream silk suit, complete with shoes, cloche hat, even stockings. Helen was touched. As she stroked the delicate material the maid reappeared, carrying a small jewel box and a large silk bag.

'Mrs Garrison said I was to bring you these and help you dress. Now and then later for dinner.'

Helen nodded.

By the time the maid left her, Helen was transformed. She peered at her reflection in the large mirror, wondering fleetingly if it was like the one at Garrison Hall. Set against the wall it could well disguise a secret observation room. She shook her head; did it matter? She wasn't planning on doing anything worth watching.

The maid, from her glorious silk bag of tricks, had produced powder and eyeliner, lipstick and rouge. The Helen that looked back from the mirror seemed the epitome of sophisticated London society. To complement the outfit, Liddy had loaned her a long string of amber beads that brought out the colour of the suit and a small matching brooch. The soft kid-leather shoes and hat had been dyed to match the beads exactly. Helen did a slow turn and then picked up the matching clutch bag from the bed. She felt wonderful.

Downstairs, Liddy and Aretha were taking tea in front of a large fire. They both turned as Helen came in. Liddy sat in a great leather armchair with her legs tucked under her, her shoes abandoned in the hearth. She grinned. 'My God, country mouse to town mouse in one easy lesson.'

Helen flushed. 'Does it look all right?'

Aretha patted the sofa beside her. 'It looks wonderful. Have you ever seen *Pygmalion*?'

Helen laughed with genuine amusement. 'Yes.'

Liddy clapped her hands and roared with laughter. 'I'd never seen myself as a Professor Higgins but I take the point. Come and sit down and have some tea before Aretha hogs it all.'

The two women were so at ease with each other that, as Helen joined them, it almost felt like the days when she had been nursing. Aretha was sharp-witted and funny, Liddy a willing stooge and great gossip. Both women giggled furiously at each other's jokes and confidences.

Although Helen barely knew any of the people they were talking about it was impossible not to be amused. A footman brought in more tea, toast and potted shrimps and Helen tucked in, feeling more relaxed than she had in weeks.

After a while, Aretha glanced up at the clock and then at Helen. 'Tonight we're having a little soirée here. Just a few close friends for dinner, dancing and conversation. Very relaxed.'

Helen nodded. Aretha looked pointedly at Liddy, before looking at Helen. 'And I must point out to you that it may not be quite what you expect.'

Images of Max's wild menagerie filled Helen's mind.

Liddy leant closer. 'You know what we're saying, don't you, Helen? Max understands me. I don't need you to but I do need you to be discreet.'

Helen sighed. 'I don't think it will be any problem.' She looked at the two women; so at ease, such good friends – as well as lovers – and for a few seconds felt desperately envious. 'I've got too many secrets of my own to risk compromising yours.'

Aretha smiled. 'Good, well in that case I shall ring for the tray of cakes and then perhaps you'd like to rest until dinner?'

Helen was aware of the little flurry of excitement that passed between the two women and dropped her eyes. She had promised to be discreet. When she'd eaten her fill of pastries she left the two friends to their gossip.

It wasn't until she got to her room that she realised she'd left her clutch bag beside her seat. She hesitated, wondering whether to leave it until later. It did seem a little off-hand to leave Liddy's beautiful things around so casually. She turned and went back down.

The double doors of the sitting-room were open. As she was about to walk in, some sixth sense made her stop. The timbre of the voices from within had changed since the raucous laughter of the tea party. She stepped silently into the room, hidden from the two women by the door. On the long sofa Liddy and Aretha lay in a passionate embrace, murmuring soft words of love and encouragement.

Liddy's fingers were gently sliding Aretha's dress higher. Helen could see the tops of her stockings and the dark triangle of her sex. Aretha moaned appreciatively as Liddy pushed a finger inside her.

Helen blushed, feeling the first crackle of her own arousal, as the woman across the room began to writhe deliciously beneath Liddy's caress. Their lips were locked in deep heady kisses. Helen turned away quickly and hurried back upstairs; the clutch bag could wait. Between her thighs she could feel the flickering flame of her own need. Its unanswered call made her feel desperately alone.

She went back upstairs to sit in the blue sitting-room and watch the traffic below. Images of the two women in the room below her tangled with the heady memories of Anya and Jack in the cottage. She could almost feel the gypsy woman's tongue on her lips, parting the delicate folds of her sex and bringing her to the edge of heaven while Jack caressed her breasts.

She swallowed hard. She would have to be careful; her body ached for satisfaction. Getting up slowly, she went to the bathroom and turned on the bath taps. If only it was as easy to wash away her need. She stepped into the bath and let her mind wander free. The erotic memories refused to be stilled and when she finally climbed, pink and slick from the foaming water, the ache in her body was stronger than ever.

Despite the suggestion by Aretha that dinner was going to be an informal affair between friends, the maid laid a full-length evening-dress out for Helen when she returned to the bedroom. Helen looked at the delicate silky confection and sighed. 'Poor country mouse,' she whispered, slipping the sheer silk over her shoulders.

When Helen reappeared at the top of the staircase at the stroke of eight, the hall below was full of sounds of voices.

Amongst the elegant surroundings couples were engaged in the social niceties, laughing, drinking, chatting. She couldn't spot Liddy anywhere, although Aretha was standing by the salon door deep in conversation with a tall elegantly dressed man. As soon as she spotted Helen, she raised a glass in salute.

'Ah, country mouse, there you are. Let me introduce you to people.' She turned to her companion. 'This is my friend, Bon Fielding. Bon, this is Liddy's sister-in-law, Helen.'

The man took Helen's hand and pressed it delicately to his lips. Helen shivered; the kiss relit the feelings she was trying so hard to control. As he let go of her hand and looked up into her eyes, Helen had to suppress a little gasp of surprise. She could feel her colour rising. Bon Fielding was most certainly not a man. She looked in desperation at Aretha who smiled pleasantly. 'Bon is a poet and on the very brink of fame and fortune, aren't you, dearest?'

Bon Fielding made modest noises. Dressed in a

beautifully cut dinner suit it had been easy to mistake the handsome short-haired woman for a young man. She smiled easily at Helen. 'Aretha has told me all about you. How was your journey up to town?'

Helen stumbled uncomfortably over her reply. She glanced around the room as Bon asked Aretha about Liddy. The truth struck her like a body blow. There were no men in the room. The elegantly dressed chaps with their cigarette-holders and carefully tailored suits, squiring beautiful girls on their arms, were all women.

Helen realised it would be impolite not to make conversation but she couldn't find any words. Instead she stood in uncomfortable silence, unable to tear her eyes off Bon's handsome but obviously female face.

Aretha caught her eye and gave her a look of rebuke. 'Perhaps we ought to find you a drink before I introduce you to everyone,' she said gently. Catching hold of Helen's elbow, she steered her towards a footman bearing a tray of champagne cocktails.

'I'm so sorry,' Helen whispered unhappily. 'I just didn't think.'

Aretha handed her a glass. 'No need to apologise, you've done nothing really. Bon's a real darling and certainly won't take offence at you gawping, though I should warn you there are others here who might.' She glanced around the crowded room. 'You may find yourself rather popular this evening. New blood always is.' She stared at Helen. 'These are my friends.'

Helen nodded and took a long pull from the champagne flute.

Aretha smiled. 'Try and relax for goodness' sake. Let

me introduce you around and do try not to stare.'

As she spoke, Liddy appeared at the top of the stairs. She was dressed in the most beautiful black gentleman's evening suit. Her pale hair was slicked back and in one hand she sported a silver-topped cane. Helen swallowed hard. Liddy looked stunning, her masculine garb doing nothing to detract from her innate eroticism.

Aretha smiled broadly as she saw her partner arrive. Her dark eyes were alight with affection and arousal. 'Here's Liddy,' she said unnecessarily and Helen was abandoned as Aretha hurried across the crowded room to join her lover.

Helen looked around in desperation.

'I told you things aren't as they seem here.'

Helen looked up at Oliver, the footman, who had appeared at her elbow bearing a tray of glasses.

She smiled. 'I have to agree with you there,' she whispered in an undertone, taking another glass from his tray.

Before he had time to reply, Liddy and Aretha swept towards her, arm in arm. They made a stunning couple.

Liddy smiled and leant forward to kiss Helen on the cheek. When her lips were level with Helen's ear, she whispered, 'Don't panic, country mouse.'

Helen flushed and took another sip from her glass. She felt she needed the distance the alcohol would give her.

Aretha turned round and clapped her hands to call everyone together. 'Ladies and gentlemen,' she said without a trace of affectation. 'It's time for dinner.'

Helen downed the glass in one and then fell into step behind Liddy and Aretha.

She suppressed an involuntary shiver as Bon Fielding stepped forward to take her arm. Helen looked fleetingly into the other woman's eyes. There was a look of interest and amusement there. Bon leant closer. 'I don't bite,' she whispered. 'Relax.'

Helen nodded dumbly and let Bon lead her into the dining-room.

In spite of Helen's deep sense of foreboding, dinner was a most jovial and pleasant meal. Most of the guests were from the world of the theatre or the arts. All had more than enough to say for themselves. If anyone noticed that Helen was being quiet nobody said anything; they were grateful, no doubt, to have a willing audience. Helen felt herself relaxing, despite Bon's presence on her left.

The wine flowed and Helen, for once, didn't resist the temptation to drink it. She was very aware that Liddy and Aretha had their eyes on her.

After dinner everyone retired to the music room for cocktails and coffee. One of the 'gentlemen' played the piano whilst a beautiful Eurasian chantress sang a selection of popular ballads. Groups gathered in conversation. Helen noticed, now the wine had taken effect, shows of affection were becoming more public. Couples held hands and kissed, others stood with their arms around each other. In one corner, against a pillar, one tall besuited woman ran her hands with familiarity over her partner. The girl quivered deliciously.

Helen slipped away from Bon and found herself a

quiet corner near the hearth.

Just a few more days and she could have her passport to freedom. She thought about the interview she had arranged for Monday. Along with that came thoughts of Jack, of Charles, of Annie, even Max . . . She shook her head, trying hard to concentrate instead on what she planned to say on Monday. The very last thing she needed now were her own erotic thoughts amongst Aretha's strange assortment of guests. The sexual tension already hung in the air like tobacco smoke.

'Penny for them?'

Helen looked up, recognising Bon's carefully modulated voice.

'I'm afraid a penny wouldn't be quite enough.'

Without waiting for an invitation, Bon sat down beside her. 'You don't look very happy.'

Helen smiled. 'No, I was just thinking about my life.'

Bon pulled her face into an exaggerated grimace. 'Is it that bad?'

Helen was stunned to realise that she could quite easily cry. She shook her head. 'I don't think I want to talk about it. Coming down to London with Liddy might give me the solution I'm looking for.'

Bon moved closer. 'You mean this?' she lifted her hand to encompass Aretha's party guests.

Helen laughed. 'No, that wasn't quite what I meant, I'm afraid. I've got an interview on Monday morning. If I'm accepted it could change my life for ever.'

Bon was so close now that Helen could smell the other woman's cologne. Bon tentatively lifted her fingers to stroke Helen's neck. She shivered, suddenly thinking about Anya, hearing the desperate pulse of her own desire. Bon's touch was so gentle, so knowing.

Helen looked steadily into the woman's dark glittering eyes. 'My life is too complicated already,' she murmured with genuine regret. 'I don't think I'm ready for any other complications.'

Bon's fingers stroked the pit of her throat. 'It doesn't have to be complicated,' she whispered. 'You don't have to tell me you need to be loved. I can see it in your eyes.'

Helen moaned unhappily. 'Please,' she said softly, on an outward breath, 'don't. I'm so muddled now.'

'Let me hold you,' whispered Bon. 'Let me take you in my arms and make it all better.'

Helen fought the temptation to surrender.

Bon's fingers caressed her shoulders then she leant forward and stealthily pressed a dry kiss to the tender flesh behind Helen's ear.

Helen shivered, feeling her nipples hardening against the thin fabric of her evening-dress. She pulled away and looked into the dilated pupils of her would-be seducer.

'I don't think I'm ready for any of this,' she mumbled. Bon pulled her close, pressing an exploratory kiss on her lips. Helen felt her body respond instantly; it longed for tenderness, longed to be held and caressed. She complained softly but did not resist as Bon's lips pressed harder; her tongue like a tiny darting arrow seeking entry into Helen's mouth.

Bon's lips tasted of brandy and cigars. Helen felt

muddled, her rational mind at odds with her body's desires.

Bon pulled her lips away. 'Why don't we go somewhere that's more private?' she whispered.

Helen sighed, knowing the battle was futile. She let Bon help her to her feet. She wished she hadn't drunk quite so much; her head was spinning.

Across the room, Liddy was sitting near the piano with Aretha perched on her lap. Her elegant hands were linked round Liddy's neck. They both smiled as Bon led Helen across the music room.

Looking back, Helen caught Liddy grinning at her companion. She knew then, with unfailing certainty, that Bon had been invited to the dinner party to seduce her. At the door, Bon pulled a bottle of champagne from a cooler and handed Helen two glasses. In silence they stepped out into the dimly lit hallway.

At Garrison Lodge, Charles was watching Annie with interest. She was lying on the cold tile floor of the bathroom. Her dark eyes were alight with sheer terror as he walked towards her with the razor. He knelt down and slipped his fingers under the heavy lips around her sex. A great white sheet of lather engulfed her quim.

'Stay very still,' he whispered darkly. 'Or I might cut you.'

Below him, the girl let out a strangled cry of fear and closed her eyes as the razor hissed through the foam. Above her, on the bathroom shelf, was a bottle of hair oil. Charles cut away another swathe of foam and

thick dark hair and smiled to himself. Perhaps Helen
should go away more often.

Bon took Helen's hand. Away from the others Helen
felt self-conscious and afraid. What on earth was she
doing? She didn't need this. She stopped at the bottom
of the staircase.

Bon turned towards her and pressed her lips to hers.
'It's all right,' she purred, 'I really won't hurt you.'

Helen shuddered. 'Bon, I don't know whether I want
to do this. Every sensible thought I have tells me it's
ridiculous.'

Bon laughed. 'It's all right, come with me. I'm not
going to force you into anything.'

They went upstairs to the Blue Room. Bon lit the
lamps in the sitting-room and poured them a glass of
champagne. She pulled two chairs up by the hearth
while Helen hovered uncertainly in the doorway.

Bon tried to tease the fire into life. 'For God's sake,
come and sit down and don't look so bloody terrified.
I'm not going to pounce on you. That's not my style at
all.'

Helen took a step or two across the room.

'Then why have you brought me up here?' she said
unsteadily, accepting the drink Bon offered her.

Bon rolled her eyes heavenwards. 'You're cramping
the style of our friends downstairs. There aren't too
many places where ladies like ourselves –' she grinned
at Helen, '– present company excluded of course, can
meet openly and enjoy each other's company.'

Helen sipped her champagne. 'So are you telling me

you're not trying to seduce me?' She already knew the answer.

'Well . . .' Bon lifted her hands and pulled a teasing face. 'Let's say if the opportunity presented itself I wouldn't refuse.'

Helen laughed dryly and sat down close to the fire. Bon poked at the fading logs. Helen felt her eyes drawn to the strange woman. Bon was quite striking, tall with a mop of unruly bobbed black hair and a sharp angular face. Bright mischievous eyes gave her a raffish appearance. The dinner suit looked good on her but didn't quite hide the feminine lines that lurked beneath.

Helen stretched, sipping the champagne. 'I told you. My life is very complicated already.'

Bon nodded sympathetically. 'Why don't you tell me about Charles and your tinker friend while our friends downstairs enjoy their revels?'

Helen snorted in indignation. 'Does everyone know the story of my life?'

'No, Liddy rang me this afternoon. She's very worried about you.' Bon crept closer to her.

'Oh, right, and in between telling you what an awful mess I've got myself into, she primed you to take me to bed? Did she think that might do me some good?'

Bon laughed huskily. 'It was mentioned.' She leant forward and stroked Helen's knees. Her long fingers strayed up between Helen thighs. 'You are very desirable.'

Helen moaned, feeling her body respond instantly to the other woman's caress. 'You're making this very difficult,' she whispered unsteadily. 'I'm trying hard to resist . . .'

'Why fight what you feel?' Bon purred.

Helen shivered, the words sounded so much like the things Anya had said to her in the cottage.

She leant into Bon's touch, feeling powerless to resist. Her body was hungry and aching for satisfaction. Bon lifted her hand and guided Helen's face closer. Their lips touched and an electric pulse trembled between them.

Helen suddenly didn't want to hold back. Her body craved Bon's gentle touch, the passion and the ecstasy that Jack and Anya had shown her. She opened her mouth and sought out the other woman's lips and tongue, making soft hungry noises as Bon opened her lips.

Bon's fingers slipped down to Helen's evening-dress, easing the shoulder straps down over her shoulders. The silky sheath slipped noiselessly down to her waist. Helen shivered as she felt the cool evening air kiss her skin. It was followed, an instant later, by Bon's fingers closing around the firm curve of her breasts. Bon's fingers stroked the hard engorged peaks of Helen's nipples and she moaned with pleasure.

Helen slid her hands under Bon's jacket and began to undo the buttons of the other woman's shirt. Bon pulled back from their embrace and smiled lazily. 'Who's seducing who here?'

Helen grinned. 'Does it worry you?'

Bon shook her head and then dipped down to take one of Helen's hard nipples between her lips. As she did so, she slipped off her jacket and began to pull off her shirt.

Helen sighed; the woman's lips sucked and nipped, lighting a silvery flame of pleasure in her belly. 'Shall we go to bed?' she said slowly.

Bon looked up at her and the remnants of the fire. She nodded. Helen stood up and let the shiny dress slip down over her hips. Bon, eyes twinkling mischievously, caught hold of her and pressed her lips to Helen's navel. Her hot daring tongue lapped at the delicate depression. 'Are you sure?'

Helen groaned and arched against Bon's tongue. 'Yes,' she whispered. 'I need to feel the things you can give me.'

Bon stood up very slowly, pressing kisses to every inch of Helen's naked belly and chest. Helen felt desperately dizzy, relishing the combination of excitement and champagne. Bon slipped her fingers through hers and led her into the bedroom.

The room was in darkness. Bon walked around and lit the lamps. 'You don't mind do you?' she said.

Helen shook her head. At the foot of the bed, she hesitated for a split second.

Bon looked across at her. 'Why don't you get into bed? It's damned cold out here.'

Helen slipped off her pants and stockings and climbed between the smooth linen sheets. She turned to watch Bon undress. It was both strange and exciting to watch a female body emerge from the dark evening suit.

Bon certainly wasn't self-conscious. Her body was a

strange contradiction. She had full breasts that had almost been disguised beneath her shirt, waistcoat and jacket. Below she had hips like a boy and a flat muscular stomach. Her breasts and the dark triangle between her legs looked at odds with her athletic boyish build.

She turned slowly in the lamplight, eyes bright with champagne and desire. 'Do you like what you see? Or would you rather go downstairs and pick another date from the palm?'

Helen laughed and shook her head, folding back the sheets for Bon to climb into bed. 'Get in and get warm,' she said softly.

Bon laid her jacket on the bed beside them and then slid beneath the covers. 'My wish is your command,' she purred.

Helen folded the tall woman into her arms, relishing the sensation of Bon's soft, warm skin against her own. As their breasts touched she felt a little bright glisten of delight. Bon pressed her lips to Helen's neck and throat, kissing her pulse, lapping at the curves and hollows with a skilled touch.

Helen instinctively lifted her hands to Bon's breasts, teasing the pink buds into hardness. She smiled to herself. Anya would be proud of how well she had learnt the lessons she'd taught her. She dipped her head and drew one of Bon's nipples between her lips, letting her tongue lap and tease at the sensitive puckering.

Bon let out a low hiss of approval. 'I think you've done this before, haven't you?' she whispered.

Helen giggled as she felt Bon skirting lower with her fingers to find her shaved quim. 'I told you my life

274

was very complicated,' she murmured, before lapping at Bon's other breast.

Bon groaned. 'I don't care, you feel wonderful,' she said and slid a finger between the naked lips, seeking out the hardened ridge of Helen's clitoris.

Helen gasped as the sensation registered. As before, when she had made love to Anya, she found the other woman's caresses tender and thrilling. As she touched Bon, she felt the sensations echoed and repeated deep inside her own body.

Without hesitation, as Bon began to stroke her, she moved her fingers down to Bon's mound. The thick shiny hair beneath her fingertips created a startling contrast with her own naked sex. She slipped a speculative finger between the lips. The tall woman shuddered and pressed herself closer. Helen felt the same electric throb between her own legs and gasped.

Slowly, with infinite tenderness, Bon pressed wet kisses down the length of Helen's body. Even as her lips brushed Helen's ribs, she could feel her sex moistening in anticipation. Bon murmured her approval. Helen realised she was unconsciously mirroring the tall woman's movements. As she felt Bon's hot damp kisses close on her flesh, between her lips she tasted the salty heat of Bon's body. Slowly the women moved around in an intricate dance. It felt as smooth and faultless as any ballet. Helen could smell the heady erotic perfume of Bon's moist slit just inches from her face.

There was a second when she felt her fear returning. Its cold fingers were driven away in an instant when she felt Bon's tongue begging entry at the lips of her quim. She gasped for breath and felt her body open to the woman's entreaty. In almost the same second she closed her lips over the gaping slit of Bon's throbbing sex and began to lap.

The taste of the woman's excitement flooded her mouth, making her sob with pleasure. Between her own legs, Bon began an eager spiral of kisses around her clitoris. Between intense kisses, the woman dipped to lap at the fragrant juice that trickled between Helen's legs.

Helen felt as if she were totally immersed in sensations. She thrust herself forward onto Bon's tongue and slipped a finger inside the tight confines of Bon's body. The other woman's sex closed and tightened around her immediately.

The combination was electrifying. Helen felt herself buck, letting the pleasure pour over her like a waterfall. She pressed her body forward again and again, lapping, kissing and sucking; milking Bon's little bud of pleasure. As she did, the sensations were almost instantly fed back to her. The heat and the wetness between Bon's legs grew and grew. She began making little convulsive jerks. Helen could feel, as much as hear, Bon's soft animal noises of pleasure, as Helen brought her closer and closer to the instant of release.

Suddenly Bon let out a low strangled sob and, at the same instant, Helen felt the floodgates of her own excitement burst. Her frenzied mind flooded with light and heat. Beneath her lips and tongue Bon bucked and tossed, pulling Helen's head tight to her.

Gasping, exhausted, the lovers finally slid apart.

Bon looked up with bright satisfied eyes. 'My God, you're good,' she purred.

Helen laughed gently and slid up the bed until she was in Bon's arms. 'You too,' she whispered.

Bon closed her lips on Helen's. Helen could taste the salty oceanic excitement of her own pleasure on the tall woman's lips.

Bon pulled away. 'Not too complicated for you, then?'

Helen snorted. 'Far too complicated but Liddy was right. You were just what I needed.'

Bon ruffled her hair and pulled her closer. 'Let's sleep,' she whispered.

Helen curled gratefully into the fragrant arms of her lover and let sleep envelop them both.

In Garrison Lodge, Charles lay awake looking at the night sky through the bedroom window. From the floor beside him he could hear the soft muffled sounds of Annie sleeping.

She had screamed when he had slid the hair oil over her naked backside and he had pulled back. A great shame, but he didn't want her running to her mother, or worse still, Helen. He'd have to wait until his wife came back for that particular pleasure. Never mind, the girl had been far from disappointing. Thinking about it woke the familiar stirring in his groin.

He rolled over and turned on the bedside lamp. He'd let her sleep a little longer and then he would invite her into his bed. He quite liked the notion that his maid could sleep with him but his wife could not.

He wondered fleetingly if Helen would contemplate the three of them sharing the bed. It struck him as unlikely. Besides, it was probably best to keep servants and wives apart.

He rolled over to the side of the bed and poked the sleeping girl. As she moved, the sheets slipped off her broad shoulders to reveal the heavy orbs of her breasts. He smiled to himself. She opened her eyes, and for a few seconds they were unfocused, then she realised where she was and shuddered.

'Get up,' Charles said thickly, feeling the hardness of his cock pressing against his belly, 'I need you.' He turned back the bedclothes and patted the space beside him.

Without a word, Annie clambered to her feet. She was far larger than Helen and there was something rather comforting about her heavy curves. Her newly shaved quim looked pink and shell-like in the yellow lamplight.

She climbed into the bed. He slid down his pyjama trousers, letting his meaty cock spring forward. Annie looked at him with bright eyes, awaiting instruction. He lifted his hand and placed it firmly on the back of her neck.

She bent forward without question. He sighed with pleasure as her lips closed around the crown of his phallus. On his ribs he could feel her heavy breasts and cold hard nipples gently brushing against him.

Chapter 10

Freedom

Helen woke in Bon's arms. Momentarily muddled, she looked around the delicate blue draperies and the elegant bedroom: Aretha's house. The answer settled in her mind along with the heavy throb of a hangover. Beside her, Bon Fielding groaned sleepily and crept closer to her.

'Morning, country mouse,' she purred thickly as she blinked in the bright morning light. 'God, what do you think Aretha put in those cocktails last night? My head is killing me.'

'I didn't think you'd still be here, not once the seduction was over and done with.'

Bon winced. 'Very cynical. There, and I was just going to ask if you'd like to come out to lunch with me. What a little vixen you turned out to be,' she snorted with mock indignation.

Helen coloured. 'I'm sorry. I just thought . . .'

Bon touched her shoulders. 'What are these marks? I didn't notice them last night.' She touched the last remains of the bruises that Charles had inflicted.

Helen defensively pulled the sheets up around her. 'My husband has very definite ideas about how women should be kept in order.'

Bon screwed up her face. 'What a bastard. Presumably it's not your idea of good fun? Liddy didn't mention anything about getting beaten.' As she spoke her fingers tracked the yellowing bruises.

Helen shivered under her touch. 'She doesn't know and it's something I'd prefer you kept to yourself.'

Bon nodded. 'Of course.' She hesitated, watching Helen's face. 'Are you leaving him?' she said quietly.

'Yes, that's why I've come to London.'

Bon wrapped her arm gently around Helen's shoulders. 'Would you like to tell me about it? I promise I won't tell Liddy.'

Helen hesitated and then realised that she needed to tell someone. 'Yes,' she said softly, her voice thick with emotion. 'I think I would. But I'm not sure where to begin.'

Bon pulled her close, her fingers caressing Helen's soft sleep-warm breasts. 'Let me seduce you again first,' she growled, 'then you call tell me all about it over a long lunch.'

Helen giggled, feeling her sadness and anxiety lift in the face of Bon's gently teasing desire. 'You're taking Liddy's suggestion very seriously.'

Bon pressed her lips to Helen's neck. 'Of course, we poets are desperately sensual beasts. Seduction first, serious stuff later. God, you feel wonderful. Why don't you come and lie down here?'

Helen crept closer to Bon, absorbing her heat. 'Yes,'

she whispered, 'I think I will.'

Bon laughed. 'You know, you're desperately difficult to seduce, country mouse,' she said, pulling Helen closer.

Helen sat quietly opposite Mrs Leven, the owner of the agency. She smiled at Helen, 'There is really no need to look so nervous, Mrs Garrison, your references are excellent. Have you thought of what sort of teaching post you would prefer or where you would like to go?'

Helen folded her hands nervously around her bag. 'I'd thought perhaps France, but I really wouldn't mind. I'm very anxious to find a position as soon as possible.'

Mrs Leven looked at her with a practised eye. 'And what about your husband?'

Helen blushed furiously.

Mrs Leven glanced at Helen's letter of application and took up her fountain pen. 'Can I take it that you're a widow?'

Helen nodded, not meeting the older woman's eye.

Mrs Leven made a note and then looked at the attractive young woman, so obviously unhappy, so obviously in need. She sighed. 'The war changed a lot of them, Mrs Garrison,' she said softly. 'Though school marms are not supposed to be the most understanding of creatures I do appreciate that life can sometimes deal us an unfortunate hand. In England, married teachers are frowned upon, but in Europe they are viewed with more sympathy. Now, let us see what we have that might be suitable for you.'

She got up and removed a pile of cards from a cabinet,

sorting through them as she pulled up her chair. 'We have several positions as governess for members of the aristocracy, all over Europe. We have some very reputable families on our books.'

Helen Garrison flinched. 'No, thank you,' she said firmly. 'I'm not seeking a position with a family, however respectable they appear.'

Mrs Leven nodded. 'Very well. Well, in that case we have three on our files at the moment that might suit you.'

She put on her glasses and read Helen the details.

When Helen clambered into Bon Fielding's sports car half an hour later, she was jubilant. Bon was dressed flamboyantly in a leather driving-coat and goggles.

'Well,' said Bon, dropping the little car into gear, 'now here's a kitty cat who's got the cream. Would you like me to ask you how it went?'

Helen couldn't resist the compulsion to throw her arms around Bon's neck. 'I've just got myself a job, teaching English in Paris,' she said with pure delight, pressing her lips to Bon's cold exposed cheek.

Bon grinned. 'Wonderful,' she shouted above the sound of the engine, 'but less canoodling when we're driving. I might hit something.' Helen's excitement was infectious, 'So where do we go from here?'

Helen's face clouded momentarily. 'Now I have to go home and confront Charles.'

Bon pursed her lips. 'That isn't going to be easy. Why don't we go somewhere and talk about it over an expensive and late breakfast, then I'll whisk you back to Aretha's in time to catch your train?'

Helen looked at her strange companion and nodded, 'That would be marvellous. I was far too nervous to eat anything this morning.'

As they drove through the London streets, Helen thought about Bon, her gentle and very unusual knight in shining armour. The weekend had been one revel after another. Liddy and Aretha were delighted to be excused from entertaining Helen – who they referred to, without fail, as the country mouse. She and Bon had been to Kew, walked in the parks and talked and talked. Now Bon knew more about her than anyone else alive. It felt so strange to have a woman companion and Bon was an easy and interested confidante. Their physical intimacy was the icing on the cake.

They found a little tea house and Bon ordered an extravagant breakfast. Helen's elation began to cool into the hard dark realisation that she would now have to go home and talk to Charles.

Bon patted her leg under the table. 'Chin up. You couldn't possibly carry on as you were.'

Helen picked unhappily at her bacon. 'You're right and it isn't just me; there's Annie.'

Bon handed her a cup of tea. 'You'll take her with you?'

Helen nodded. 'If she'll come. There's a little apartment with the position that I can use until I get myself settled.'

'And Jack?'

Helen shivered. 'I don't know,' she said softly. 'I can't really see him throwing in his hand to follow me to

Europe. I couldn't expect him to give up what he has for me.'

Bon scraped a thick curl of butter onto her toast. 'France is the wrong place to go with him anyway. The French are more class-ridden than we are. You should have thought about going further afield if you wanted to go with Jack – Canada, Australia . . .'

Helen bit her lip. 'I know,' she said. 'I did think of that, but I can't expect him to follow me. It wouldn't be fair.' Helen could feel tears in her eyes. Jack Hartman had helped set her free but realistically she knew he could have no part in her future.

Bon slapped the buttered toast onto Helen's plate. 'Come on, not so maudlin. This is meant to be a celebration of your new job and your new life, not a funeral breakfast.'

Helen looked unsteadily at Bon, so new in her life and yet so welcome. 'You're right,' she said softly.

'Good show,' said Bon. 'Besides, artists and poets are welcome in Paris. I can always come to visit you. It will be nice to have a friend in a foreign land one feels one could just drop in on. Perhaps we could rent somewhere on the coast in the summer. I've heard that it's all the rage to summer down in the Antibes. How would you fancy a visitor from Mother England?'

Helen grinned. 'That would be lovely.'

Bon's expression was suddenly as serious as Helen's had been. 'And if you need anything. In Paris or down there in the heart of the Norfolk Fen –' she smiled '– well, you know I'll do what I can.'

Helen touched her cheek. 'Thank you,' she said tenderly.

Aretha and Bon both came to the station to see them off. Bon kissed Helen chastely on the side of the cheek while Liddy and Aretha embraced flamboyantly.

'Remember, country mouse, I'm only a phone call away,' Bon whispered as she pressed her lips to Helen's face.

Helen nodded. 'It seems rather a lot to promise for one weekend of wild passion.'

Bon snorted. 'And seduction.' She became serious. 'Take care and good luck. Let me know how it turns out.'

Helen linked her arms around her and pulled her close. 'Thank you,' she murmured, feeling tears in her eyes.

Bon groaned theatrically and produced a huge handkerchief from her leather driving-coat, 'Here, mouse. I'm off, I really can't cope with sniffling.'

Aretha stepped back too. She smiled at Helen and then at Liddy. 'See you soon,' she said softly, blowing them both a kiss as she linked arms with Bon.

Liddy had, of course, booked them a first class carriage. They were barely clear of the platform when she sent the maid off to rustle up the steward to bring them some tea.

'Well,' she said. 'Now can you tell me what all this mystery was about?'

Helen shook her head. 'No, not yet. You'll find out soon enough.'

Liddy lit a cigarette and stared sightlessly at the sooty little grey houses which stretched out around the railway cutting. She pouted sulkily and flung herself onto one of the seats. 'Oh damn! And I've always thought I was rather good at cloak-and-dagger stuff. Are you sure you don't want to tell me?'

Helen shook her head.

'And why have you put that awful grey suit back on? I thought you looked quite gorgeous in the cream linen I loaned you.'

'I didn't think it would do me much good if Charles saw me looking gorgeous. He might suspect I'd been up to no good.'

Liddy giggled. 'Perhaps not. But did everything work out for you?' She hesitated. 'You seemed to make quite a hit with Bon Fielding.'

Helen blushed furiously.

Liddy rolled her eyes. 'Don't be so gauche. When we arrive home everything will be as it was.' Liddy rested her finger across her perfectly painted lips. 'Mum's the word.'

Helen shifted her weight and made herself more comfortable. Liddy was wrong; everything was no longer as it had been. She had plotted her freedom and now, when the time was right, she would seize it with both hands.

Liddy peered towards the corridor. 'Where is that dratted girl with the tea?'

Helen got to her feet. 'Would you like me to go and look for her?'

Liddy sighed theatrically. 'If you're determined to

play the role of nanny and housekeeper, off you go. See if you can rustle up some scones or tea cakes as well. I'm absolutely famished.'

At the little rural station Helen was surprised to see Max's driver waiting for them.

'I thought Max would be here to pick you up,' she said, as she opened the carriage door for Liddy.

Liddy snorted. 'Oh no, he'll be holed up in his study waiting for me to come home and tell him *everything* that happened this weekend.' She looked levelly at Helen, 'but as Aretha said, we are all very discreet. Your little dalliance with Bon will go no further than the walls of Max's study.' She stopped mid-stride. 'You know, sometimes I think Max is like a stamp collector. You and I are just exotic first day covers for his album.' She giggled at her own joke and then hurried along the platform.

Helen was dreading the journey home and as the familiar scenery rolled past the car she could feel the sense of melancholy and apprehension building up inside her.

It struck her as peculiar that she felt regret more than anything else. If only Charles could have been more understanding and tender then they would never have found themselves in the position that loomed now.

Annie opened the door for her. Helen couldn't help noticing the dark rings around the girl's eyes. She smiled with genuine pleasure when she saw Helen. 'Nice weekend, Mrs Garrison?'

'Lovely. How have things been here?' said Helen,

peeling off her gloves and coat.

Annie glanced away towards the open door of the sitting-room. 'Fine,' she said flatly. 'Would you like tea?'

Helen didn't press her to elaborate on what 'fine' might mean, her face told Helen everything she needed to know. 'Yes, please. Is Charles in the sitting-room?'

The girl nodded and hurried off towards the kitchen.

Charles was sitting beside the fire reading when she walked in. For an instant, in the soft light, he smiled and she saw the face of the man she had loved so completely and utterly when they had first met. She had barely a chance to think how wonderful and handsome he looked, when his expression darkened and closed her out. She shivered; it seemed that nothing had changed in her absence.

'Hello, Charles,' she said softly, to fill the tense silence that hung between them. 'Are you well?'

Charles nodded.

Her stomach was constricting into a tight uneasy knot. It was almost as if they were strangers.

'How was your weekend?' he said stiffly, laying his book on the side table.

'Very nice, thank you. I've asked Annie to bring us some tea.'

He looked her up and down. Helen shivered. She had considered that she ought to give him another chance. If they could only talk, begin again, then she would abandon her plan.

'Come here,' he said softly. Helen took a step towards him. 'Closer,' he snapped crossly.

She moved beside his chair. He lifted her skirt and

then snorted. 'I told you to dispense with these,' he said pawing at the front of her knickers. 'Have you forgotten so quickly?'

Helen blushed crimson, 'But—' she began.

He looked at her with dark and unfeeling eyes. 'You aren't considering disobeying me, are you?'

Helen shook her head, looking down so that he wouldn't see the flash of fury in her eyes.

His fingers dropped away. 'Take them off,' he hissed.

'But what about Annie?' Helen protested, looking at the open sitting-room door.

Charles' eyes reduced to intimidating points of light. 'Take them off,' he muttered. His voice invited no contradiction. She lifted her skirt and slipped the silky fabric down to her hips.

He nodded approvingly. 'Better,' he said and slid his hand proprietorially up between her thighs. 'Don't ever disobey me again, Helen.' Roughly he pulled his hand out from under her skirt. 'Sit down over there, I can hear Annie coming.'

Helen sat in the armchair opposite him, feeling his eyes travelling up over her legs. She couldn't look at him. For one fleeting instant she had hoped, when she'd seen his face as she stepped into the sitting-room, that they could repair what they had had. Now she was certain it was impossible.

Annie knocked and came in, standing the tea tray beside Helen. For a brief second, as Annie served tea, the two women's eyes met in mutual understanding.

Charles, oblivious, picked up his book and continued to read. Helen felt as if a great weight had settled across her shoulders and she had to fight to hold back the tears. The clock on the mantel shelf ticked out the passing silent minutes. Helen felt as if she wanted to scream. Instead she sat stiffly and watched the fire burn and flicker in the hearth, her mind racing.

Max Garrison lay back in his chair and listened to Liddy's stories with great interest, particularly the ones concerning Helen and Bon Fielding.

He grinned, handing his wife a drink. 'I told you she was astounding, didn't I? Any more about her great secret plan?'

Liddy sighed. 'You're such a gossip, Max. She wouldn't tell me anything but she looked wonderful when Bon dropped her off at Aretha's.'

Max stroked his glass thoughtfully. 'Perhaps we ought to organise another party, I'm sure Bon would be pleased to come down with Aretha. What do you think?'

'I think you're a complete rogue. In one breath you're saying you feel guilty and want to save the wretched woman from your brother and inveigle me into your plan, and the next minute you're planning to ogle her with Bon Fielding. You're totally without scruples.'

Max laughed with delight. 'Do you think Bon Fielding will come if we invite her?'

'Of course she will. She was very taken with Helen.'

'Wonderful,' said Max, picking up the phone.

'Now what are you doing?' Liddy snapped crossly.

Max grinned. 'I'm going to invite Charles and Helen

over for dinner tonight. I can't wait to see her face when I tell her about Bon.'

Liddy groaned and then shook her head with a mixture of amusement and disbelief.

In the distance Helen heard the phone ring. Charles didn't look up.

A few seconds later Annie peeped around the sitting-room door. 'Telephone, sir. It's Mr Garrison.'

Charles got up. As he left the room Helen collapsed back into her chair, letting two huge tears roll down her face.

A few minutes later, Charles reappeared, 'Max has asked us up to dinner this evening. I said we would be delighted to accept his invitation.'

Helen nodded.

Charles glanced at the mantel clock, his eyes still hard and narrow. 'We'll finish our tea,' he said, 'and then you and I shall go upstairs until it's time to dress for dinner.'

Helen shuddered as he turned to look at her. 'Yes, Charles,' she whispered unsteadily, seeing the bright cruel lights of excitement and expectation in his eyes. She saw his fingers drop to his belt.

'Please don't, Charles,' she said softly.

He looked at her coldly. 'Don't question me, Helen,' he snapped. 'Get upstairs and wait for me, I won't be very long.'

Helen bit her lip and then got to her feet. She would see this through. It wouldn't be long now.

* * *

Nothing Liddy had told him about their weekend had prepared Max for Helen's appearance. She looked ashen. During dinner Charles was jovial and pleasant, even telling Liddy that he thought she ought to take his wife away more often.

Meanwhile, across the table, Helen barely said a word. Even Max's suggestion that she might like to play cards with him while Liddy and Charles danced didn't elicit a response. He couldn't bring himself to mention Bon and all through dinner he found himself wishing that Helen's plan would come to fruition soon. It was a relief when they finally left.

He and Liddy sat side by side near the hearth. 'What in God's name is he doing to her?' Max said suddenly.

Liddy looked into the flames, 'I've got no idea but it really has to stop.'

At Garrison Lodge Charles climbed the stairs slowly. He was relieved and glad that Helen was home again. As he opened the bedroom door she was waiting for him by the dressing-table. Her eyes were black with kohl, her lips rich deep red. She shivered as he walked towards her. Across her narrow back were a series of broad angry red weals that he'd administered before dinner.

He'd thought it was important, now she was back home, that he reminded her of the lessons she had learnt. She seemed to have remembered very well. He had decided she wouldn't have to return to being locked in her room. The Lodge needed a woman's touch after all and, besides, dear Liddy had said she had been such a help. He ran his fingers over Helen's buttocks. It seemed Helen had finally learnt her place.

Helen waited in the sitting-room for the postman. Charles had already left to go to Home Farm. She moved stiffly to the window, her whole body was racked with aches and bruises; but not for much longer. Mrs Leven had promised to write and confirm the details of her position as soon as she could. Helen bit her lip. It wouldn't be much longer. She wasn't sure how much more she could take. She heard the bell and Annie hurrying to answer it and held her breath.

The girl opened the sitting-room door a few seconds later, 'Post for you, Mrs Garrison.'

Helen thanked Annie and then took the letter with its London postmark. She closed her fingers round it and then hurried upstairs. In the privacy of her own room she read the letter over and over again until she knew the details off by heart. After lunch, when she was certain that Charles would not discover her, she telephoned Mrs Leven to say that everything was in hand. When she had finished speaking to Mrs Leven she called the operator and asked to be put through to Bon Fielding's London number. It was time to arrange to leave.

On the following Sunday morning she woke up feeling sick with anxiety. Charles had finally relented and let her sleep in his bed. It felt strange to wake up beside him. As if he sensed she was awake, he opened his eyes.

She bit her lip as he slipped from bed.

'Time to get up, Helen. We'll be late for church,' he said testily.

'Would you mind,' she said unsteadily, 'if I didn't come with you this morning? I have the most dreadful headache.'

Charles peered at her thoughtfully and then nodded. 'All right, if you feel you must.'

As he hurried off to get dressed, Helen closed her eyes and prayed for him to hurry.

She had no sooner heard him close the front door than she leapt out of bed. She had packed a case and hidden it at the back of the wardrobe. It would be so easy to slip away now but she knew it wouldn't be enough. If she just left he would follow her. Quickly she dressed and hurried downstairs.

Annie looked at her in astonishment. 'Mr Garrison said you weren't feeling well, ma'am.'

Helen smiled. 'I'm feeling much better now, thank you, Annie.'

She hurried past the girl into the kitchen to dismiss the cook for the day. 'We have been invited to eat out,' she said as the elderly woman slipped her heavy coat back on.

Glancing at the clock, she picked up the telephone and called Max. He sounded very surprised to hear from her.

She bit her lip nervously. 'Max, you said you would help me if I needed it?'

Max agreed.

'Well, I wondered if you might be able to lend me some money.'

'Of course,' he said cheerfully. 'We're not talking thousands are we? How much would you like?'

'I'm not really sure.'

'Am I to gather that your master plan is in action?'

'Yes,' said Helen softly. 'Yes, it is.'

'And I presume you'd like the money this morning?'

'If that's possible.'

'I'll see what we have in the safe. Will a couple of hundred be enough?'

'That's more than I'd expected. It will take me a long time to repay you—'

Max laughed. 'Take it as a gift, on the condition you tell me all the details of your master plan.'

'Thank you,' she said with genuine gratitude.

'Don't worry about it. Oh, by the way,' he said archly, 'a friend of yours, Bon Fielding, invited herself down here yesterday.'

Helen smiled. 'Really?' she said with mock innocence. 'What a nice surprise. Please give her my regards, won't you?' She paused for a split second, 'Do you think you could give Bon the money? She might want to pop down and see me later.'

Helen could almost hear Max grinning. 'Thinking of taking her for a walk to the gun cottage are you?'

Helen laughed, 'No, not exactly.'

When Charles arrived home from church, Helen was in the sitting-room dressed in her Sunday suit. He peered at her suspiciously.

'I thought you said you were feeling unwell.'

Helen nodded. 'I was but it seems to have passed. Would you mind if I went to the late service instead? I thought a walk in the fresh air might do me good.'

Charles considered for a second.

Helen continued steadily. 'Cook's gone home.'

Charles looked up. 'Is she unwell too?'

Helen shrugged. 'I'm not sure, but Annie is still here.' She paused, letting Charles consider the possibilities. 'And I really don't mind walking, after all you hardly want to go straight out again. Would you like me to ring for Annie so she can bring you in some tea?'

Helen hesitated; she didn't want to bait the trap too heavily in case Charles was suspicious.

He nodded, 'All right.'

As Helen set out along the driveway she prayed that Charles wouldn't let her down. She had seen the way he had looked at Annie as she had come in to answer the bell.

At the top of the drive she doubled back and headed into the woods surrounding the hall. She glanced at her watch and struck off through the woodland. It was now just a matter of being patient. Slowly she walked between the trees in a broad arc that would bring her back to the Lodge.

Her hands trembled as she quietly opened the front door. The clock ticked in the hall – it seemed as if the whole house was deserted.

First she crept down to the study; the open door revealed only Charles' desk and the remnants of the week's paperwork. The sitting-room was also empty. For one awful moment she was convinced she had failed. Charles could quite easily have walked up to the Hall instead. As she stood at the bottom of the stairs all her fears surfaced. She had lost. But where was Annie?

As she considered what she should do next she heard a dark unhappy wail coming from the landing and froze for an instant. No, she hadn't failed. Charles, in this of all things, had been true to form. She climbed the stairs two at a time, her pulse banging in her ears, her heart beating out a tattoo against her ribs.

At the door of her bedroom she paused, taking a deep breath to steady her nerves. From the room beyond came the sound of Annie's voice breathing out a low strangled sob. Slowly Helen turned the door handle.

'Well,' she hissed softly, as the door swung open. 'What have we here, Charles? Is this another of your unpleasant bullying little games?'

The figures in the room froze into a sharp-edged tableau. Helen drank in every detail, fixing it in her mind as she met Charles' bright astounded eyes. Neither Charles nor Annie moved as Helen stepped into the bedroom.

Annie was bent, naked, across the dressing-table; her rounded belly resting against the cold wood. She looked up at Helen with a terrified expression. Helen shuddered, ashamed that she had felt obligated to use Annie as bait. The girl's eyes were ringed with kohl, her thick flaccid lips painted crimson red. Behind her Charles was still pressed deep inside her, his best

Sunday suit in startling contrast to the girl's naked buttocks.

Annie let out a thin whimper of pain and humiliation. Helen fixed her expression into a cold mask and looked straight at Charles. 'I think,' she said softly, 'that it would be better if you got dressed, Annie, and packed your things.'

The girl gasped. 'But Mrs Garrison . . .' she began.

Helen silenced her with a look. 'Pack you things and wait for me downstairs. My husband and I need a few words with each other.'

The girl hesitated and then suddenly wrenched herself from under Charles, picked up her clothes, and fled from the room like a scalded cat. Charles slowly rebuttoned his flies. His face was slack and red.

Helen took a deep breath. In her pocket she could feel the crisp white envelope that confirmed her ticket to freedom.

'Helen,' Charles began, taking an aggressive authoritative tone.

She didn't flinch or move. 'I think,' she said evenly, fighting to maintain her composure, 'that we have come to the end of our arrangement, Charles. I'm leaving you.'

Charles took a step forward. 'Don't be so bloody ridiculous. What will you do? Where will you go?' he said angrily. 'You can't possibly leave me. I simply won't permit it.'

Helen laughed dryly. 'You have no choice. If you try to follow me I'll make sure everyone knows what you did to Annie. It's hardly the done thing, is it? To beat and bugger your wife and seduce the servants.' She paused, 'Hardly considered good form. What would everyone say?'

Charles flushed crimson, 'You wouldn't dare . . .'

Helen nodded sadly. 'I would Charles, I would.'

Charles leant heavily against the dressing-table, his aggressive stance rapidly deflating. 'But what about the family? Liddy, Max? I'll be a complete laughing-stock.'

Helen sighed. 'You really have no idea, do you? Your precious Liddy is a sham. Did you know she prefers women to men? It's one of the main reasons your brother married her, so that he could watch her little activities.'

Charles' face was turning from red to purple. 'You're lying,' he gasped.

Helen shook her head. 'No, I'm not. The Hall is riddled with peep-holes so that Max can watch his friends making love. His desperately famous dinner parties are a front for all sorts of wild goings-on.' She paused, 'Believe me, I've seen them.'

Charles groaned.

'And the weekend I spent in London with Liddy? She went there to spend time with her lover, Aretha Blackmore.' Helen bent slowly and pulled her suitcase from out of the wardrobe. 'Annie and I are leaving you and your precious family.'

She turned in the doorway and then glanced back at Charles, who was crouched beside the dressing-table. All her anger and frustration had drained away, leaving only an overwhelming sense of sadness and loss. She had been prepared for a battle and instead the confrontation had turned into little more than a skirmish. 'You know, Charles, I've spent so much time thinking about us over the last few weeks. We had so much that could have gone so well. I truly loved you once with all my heart and soul.' She slipped her wedding ring off her finger and laid it on the dressing-table, 'But the man I loved vanished when we moved to Garrison Lodge.'

She turned and walked away without looking back.

Downstairs, in the hallway, Annie was sitting miserably by her tiny suitcase of belongings. Her eyes were still painted, lips still scarlet. Helen pulled a handkerchief from her bag, 'Here,' she said gently. 'Wipe your face.'

The girl broke into a wracking sob. 'I'm so sorry, Mrs Garrison, he made me, he made me.'

Helen nodded, making soothing noises to the terrified girl. 'I know,' she said softly. 'But we're leaving now. Will you come with me?'

Annie looked up, 'Yes,' she sniffed. 'I can't stay here with him on my own.'

Outside the Lodge, under the cover of the trees, Bon Fielding was waiting in her car. As soon as she saw Helen and Annie, she gunned the engine into life.

'All done?' she said as Helen swung her case into the back seat.

Helen nodded. 'Yes,' she said sadly. 'All done.'

Bon handed her a small folded package. 'Max said I was to give you this and told me to tell you not to forget your arrangement.'

Helen folded the bundle of banknotes into her bag and climbed into the car beside Bon.

'Can we go to the village first, please,' she said above the sound of the engine. 'There's someone I have to see.'

At The Dog in Ferrybridge Helen made her way into the smoky public bar. She spotted Nip Hunter perched on a stool talking to the landlord. The landlord spotted her first and his startled expression made Nip Hunter turn around.

The waterman grinned, 'I'd not thought to see you again, ma'am.'

Helen smiled thinly. 'You haven't seen me now.'

Nip nodded. 'Right enough.'

She slid an envelope from her handbag and a crisp five-pound note. 'I'd like you to take this to Jack Hartman as soon as you can.'

Nip nodded, palming the money and the letter into his jacket. 'Aye, I'll gladly do that for you, ma'am.' He paused thoughtfully. 'I'd not have brought that man after yer if I'd have known the sort he was.'

Helen shrugged. 'It really doesn't matter now, Nip. It's done with.'

Bon Fielding's little studio apartment felt safe and comfortable after the drive up from Norfolk. Helen, cradling a brandy balloon, sat in front of the fire, feeling the tension of the day finally easing out of her tired body. Bon, her unlikely rescuer, dressed in an oriental smoking-jacket and silk pyjamas, was trying to slip a cigarillo into a holder. Both of them were a little tipsy.

Finally Bon gave up and turned to Helen. 'So, a week with me and then the boat train away to your new brave life teaching the peasants the King's English.'

Helen nodded. 'Something like that. If you're sure you don't mind Annie and me staying here.'

Bon laconically lifted a beautifully plucked eyebrow. 'You don't have to tell me you'd rather be with your beau out on the Fens. It shows on your face. Do you think he'll come to wave you off?'

Helen taking a swig of brandy, shook her head. 'No.'

Bon sat down in the hearth at Helen's feet. 'You do fall for the strangest people, darling.'

Helen laughed and ruffled Bon's hair. She felt very strange, hardly daring to believe that her life with Charles was finally over. It seemed like a hollow victory. The elation was tinged with a sense of great loss.

She looked across at Bon. 'I keep thinking . . .' she began.

Bon looked rueful. 'Oh no, not the dreaded "if onlys". Look, you know you've done the right thing, but being right doesn't make it painless. You'll feel much better once you're in Paris.' She struck an arty pose. 'All those gay Parisian gentlemen and ladies, why, I almost envy you. It's such a shame that you had to fall in love with a ruffian. How romantic it would be to begin a new life with your sweetheart. Now, that would be poetic justice. At least the continentals are more civilised about divorce.'

Helen laughed. 'I never said I loved him, Bon. That's your poet's voice talking.'

'You don't have to tell me you love him – and it's not my voice.' Bon clutched her chest, drunkenly aping high drama. 'It's my poet's soul,' she giggled.

Helen laughed. 'Forgive me my ignorance.'

Bon looked thoughtfully into the hearth. 'There has to be a way,' she said quietly.

Helen shook her head. 'No, Jack was a key to unlock my life.' She drained the remains of the brandy. 'And it doesn't matter how much I wish things could be different, it's over.'

Bon poked her playfully. 'You have a hideously pragmatic view of life. Where's your sense of romance?'

'I think I left it at Garrison Lodge. Besides, you're the poet, I'll leave romance up to you.'

Bon picked up the cigarillo and grinned. 'A very wise move,' she giggled. 'A very wise move . . .'

Helen closed the shutters of her little apartment on the Rue d'Eglise and sat down by her desk. Summer sunlight filtered through in broad white gold bands onto her elegant furniture. Below, from the street, she could hear the musical lilt of French voices and the hard bite of horns and engines from the main thoroughfare beyond. It struck her that she finally felt truly at ease.

Annie had settled in too, triumphant when she managed to arrive home from the market with what she'd set out to buy, struggling with pidgin French and wild gestures.

Bon had written to say she might be over for the last weeks of the summer, though of course, she pointed out, everybody who was anybody had headed down to the coast; no one stayed in Paris for the summer. Helen smiled, she no longer considered herself anybody, not that she ever really had; it was only Charles who worried about his status.

She'd heard from his solicitors; there would have to be divorce, of course, but he was anxious that it shouldn't show him or his family in a bad light. He suggested that in return for her co-operation he would be prepared to offer her a handsome settlement. She had already made up her mind that she would accept it. Helen had even kept her bargain with Max and written an edited account of her master plan and her weekend with Bon in return for his money.

'Mrs Garrison?'

Helen looked up thoughtfully from her desk.

'There's someone here to see you.'

Helen pulled a face. School had broken up a fortnight before. She wasn't expecting anyone. Before she could ask who it was, Annie vanished back into the shadows of the hallway.

'A very fine place you have here, lady.'

Helen looked up in astonishment. 'Jack Hartman?' she whispered incredulously.

The tall handsome Fen-man stepped into her sitting-room. 'Aye, I was passing by this way and thought I'd give you a call. I didn't think you'd mind.'

Helen gasped. 'But how?' she began. She was already on her feet, opening her arms to embrace him.

He grinned. 'Why is it you upper-class folk think the rest of us have no more sense than we're born with?

I bought meself a ticket and came across on the ferry the same as yourself. I was in France a while during the war, so it's not unfamiliar to me.' He pressed his lips to hers. Even now in the dusty heat of the Paris apartment he tasted and smelt of the fresh breeze of Norfolk.

She felt her whole body respond to him, drinking in his strength and heat. 'Did Nip bring you my note? I hoped you might write to the school.'

'Aye, he did, but what could I have said, lady, that you didn't already know?' he said softly, holding her tight.

'What about Anya, where is she?'

He laughed. 'She doesn't trust boats. She reckons, when she came across to England during the war, the tub they were in shipped water so fast it was all they could do to keep it afloat. No, she's back in Norfolk taking care of the cottage for me.'

Helen closed her eyes, imagining the little house out on the river and the dark beauty of the gypsy woman. She pressed herself to Jack. His hands lifted to tip her face towards him and she drank him in, letting him breathe life into her body. She hadn't realised how much she longed for his touch and the feel of his strong arms round her.

'How did you find my address? I wasn't sure if I wrote that you'd get the letters.'

Jack's fingers slid in amongst the lace of her soft summer blouse, searching out the pearl buttons. 'I had a message sent to me by someone called Bon Fielding, said she was a friend of yours? She said she was a poet and that you'd left the romance up to her.' He slid the thin fabric of her blouse back over her shoulder, pressing delicate kisses to her neck and throat. 'Now shall we stay here and make love on the floor amongst all this fine French furniture or will you show me to your bedroom?'

Helen shivered. 'I don't mind, but for the sake of propriety I think we'd better go to the bedroom.' She laughed. 'There's no fire for us to curl up in front of here.'

Jack slipped his fingers through hers. 'Best you lead the way then, lady.'

In Helen's bedroom, Jack undressed her slowly, teasing each garment off her hot glowing body. His lips sought out every inch of her skin, pressing wet kisses to her neck, her breasts, the soft plush rise of the belly. She lay back on the bed, relishing his attentions. He lifted her hips to pull down her knickers, smiling as he saw she was still shaved. His tongue flickered down over her navel, lapping at her salty skin before dipping to plant a kiss on the heavy lips of her sex.

'You haunt me still, lady,' he murmured, as his tongue teased them apart.

'I thought I'd never see you again,' she said, realising that she had given up all hope. When she'd left the Lodge she had thought, if she saw him again, it would be before she sailed for Calais. Even as she boarded the ferry she had looked desperately from the handrail, wondering if he might be there to see her off even though she had told Bon otherwise.

She stroked his dark shiny hair.

He glanced up at her, eyes bright, lips warm from her body. 'You should have known me better,' he whispered softly. He slipped his hands under her bottom and pulled her closer to his intimate kisses. She moaned, lifting her hips up to meet his mouth, spreading her legs to let him drink from her like an open cup. He moaned softly, fingers stroking and dipping inside her. She writhed, revelling in what he offered her. She could feel the heat rising like a forest fire in her stomach and moaned with delight. The flames roared higher, rolling through her until she was gasping for breath.

'I've missed you, so much,' she whispered between dry lips.

She fought the compulsion to surrender totally and pulled herself away from him. He looked startled but relaxed as her fingers moved to his shirt, practically tearing the buttons off. She ripped at his belt, suddenly needing him naked beside her. He didn't fight as she stripped him, playing her tongue over his broad chest and shoulders, drawing his tiny tight nipples into her mouth.

She sank lower, lapping at his belly, planting kisses in the thick dark hair around his phallus, finally closing her lips over its swollen slick head. The taste of his body and his masculine essence flooded her mouth. She moaned as she felt him pull her closer, sliding his hot body down over hers, closing his mouth over the lips of her quim.

It was as if every kiss and caress was repeated and echoed inside her own body. She whimpered and sucked him deeper, supporting the swollen bulk of his balls between her long fingers. She worked his silky foreskin back and forth, smoothly, strongly. Beneath her fingers she could sense his growing excitement. Between her legs the spiral of pleasure intensified as his tongue drove her harder and harder to the edge of heaven.

Suddenly she could taste the first salty prelude to his orgasm and renewed her efforts. She groaned, lapping at him, driving him mad with pleasure and sensation.

She felt the dam of her own ecstasy breaching and she was afraid that she wouldn't be able to hold back long enough to bring him with her. As the ripples spread out from the hard dark ridge of her clitoris she threw her hips forward, calling out with delight. She felt the throbbing sensation of his climax following hard on the heels of her own and suddenly there was only pleasure, only delight. Her body and his seemed to vaporise and vanish in the tidal wave of their mutual climax.

Slowly, slowly, they reappeared as flesh in Helen's mind, totally sated and satisfied. Jack moved lazily to lie beside her, his arms draped around her shoulders and belly. As they drifted towards the edge of sleep, Helen could hardly believe Jack was there with her.

She curled close, feeling safe and secure in his arms. He nuzzled sleepy kisses into her throat, wet lazy kisses of love and mutual desire. She wriggled blissfully, returning his affection with kisses of her own. He moaned and sucked her nipples between his lips, nibbling their peaks into hardness. His kisses were punctuated by soft words of love and pleasure. She opened her legs and gasped with delight as he rolled on top of her.

She felt his renewed hardness brushing the soft contours of her thighs and opened herself for his pleasure. For an instant he teased the very end of his cock between the sopping outer lips of her quim. It was almost too much to bear. Her body demanded him. She gasped as he slid home. Her sex closed around his shaft and held him tight as she wrapped her legs around his waist.

He looked down at her with dark wild eyes. 'I love you, Helen Garrison,' he whispered, 'and I'll never be free of you.'

Helen pressed her lips to his and pulled him deep inside her. 'I love you too, Jack Hartman,' she murmured. The soft ripples of pleasure that had lingered in her body suddenly glowed white hot and she thrust herself up onto him.

It was night when Helen woke again. She slipped out of bed and quietly dressed; her eyes resting on the dark Fen-man as he lay asleep amongst the tangle of white sheets. She went into the kitchen to find them some food, piling a tray high with fresh crusty bread and a bottle of wine.

Jack was awake when she came back into the bedroom and had lit the lamp.

'I missed you,' he purred.

'I thought you might be hungry,' she smiled and handed him a glass of wine. Sitting beside him in the intimate silence she let her fingers toy with the black hair on his chest.

He grinned sleepily at her. 'Will you show me the sights of Paris while I'm here?'

Helen nodded. 'Of course,' then she hesitated, realising what he'd said. 'Is there no way I can persuade you to stay here with me?' The words were out before she had chance to think.

Jack shook his head, 'People would not take kindly to the likes of you living with me. There would be no life for me here but you. Though, God knows, you alone are as much as one man should need.'

Helen nodded unhappily. 'I know. I don't know what made me say it.' She could feel the threat of tears. 'I just wish there was a way that we could be together.'

Jack opened his arms to her, drawing her back onto the bed. 'Not so sad, lady. I know where you live.'

Helen laughed unsteadily. 'And when you're by this way, you'll drop in?'

He nodded, holding her close to his chest. 'Aye, and as your friend Bon wrote me, there's always the New World.'

Helen pulled away sharply. 'Bon said that?'

'She said if I wanted you I could never expect to have you in England or Europe, but in Canada or Australia folk aren't so fussed about class or social standing. There's a great living to be made in such places for a man with a hunger in his belly to do well.'

Helen sat back on her heels. 'And you would consider going to a place like that with me. To begin afresh, together?'

He grinned, 'If you'll have me, lady.'

She nodded, 'Oh, I'd have you, Jack Hartman,' she whispered. 'I'd have you.'

Jack looked out of the bedroom window. He lifted his glass in salute to the stars glittering in the velvet canopy of the Paris sky. 'To the bright wild night,' he said with feeling.

'To freedom,' Helen said quietly, remembering their toast from the night in Jack's cottage.

Raising her glass, she downed the wine in one long fragrant swallow. The alcohol glowed in the pit of her stomach. Jack laid his glass on the tray and closed his lips on hers. She didn't hesitate as he pulled her down amongst the hot tangle of sheets. She shivered with expectation.

'And to the bird that sings,' he whispered throatily.

'And to the bird that sings,' Helen said, wrapping her arms around him.